The Trial

The Trial

Franz Kafka

Translated by IDRIS PARRY

W F HOWES LTD

This large print edition published in 2012 by
W F Howes Ltd
Unit 4, Rearsby Business Park, Gaddesby Lane,
Rearsby, Leicester LE7 4YH

1 3 5 7 9 10 8 6 4 2

First published as *Der Prozess*
in Germany in 1925

Translation copyright © Idris Parry, 1994

A CIP catalogue record for this book is available
from the British Library

ISBN 978 1 47121 654 1

Typeset by Palimpsest Book Production Limited,
Falkirk, Stirlingshire
Printed and bound in Great Britain
by MPG Books Ltd, Bodmin, Cornwall

MIX
Paper from
responsible sources
FSC
www.fsc.org   FSC® C018575

The translator acknowledges a debt of gratitude
to his friends Jo Desch, Nigel Howarth,
Ruedi Keller and Irmgard Krueger for
valuable advice.

CONTENTS

ARREST – CONVERSATION WITH FRAU GRUBACH – THEN FRÄULEIN BÜRSTNER

Somebody must have made a false accusation against Josef K., for he was arrested one morning without having done anything wrong. The cook employed by his landlady Frau Grubach who brought him his breakfast every morning at about eight o'clock did not come this time. That had never happened before. K. waited for a while and with his head on the pillow looked at the old lady living opposite who was observing him with a curiosity quite unusual for her, but then, feeling both annoyed and hungry, he rang the bell. Instantly there was a knock at the door and a man he had never before seen in the house came in. He was slim but solidly built, he wore a close-fitting black suit which was provided, in the manner of travelling outfits, with various pleats, pockets, buckles, buttons and a belt, and which consequently seemed eminently practical, though one could not be quite sure what its purpose was. 'Who are you?' asked K., starting to sit up in bed. But the man ignored the question, as if his appearance were to be accepted without query, and merely said: 'You rang?' 'Anna is supposed to be bringing me my breakfast,' said K., and then he tried to determine through silent observation and reflection who the man really was. The latter did not submit himself for long to this scrutiny but turned to the door and opened it a little to say to someone who must have been standing close behind the door: 'He wants Anna to bring him his breakfast.' This was followed by a short burst of laughter in the next room; from the sound it was hard to say if several persons might not be involved. Although the stranger could not have learned anything from this that he did not know before, yet he now said to K., as if making an announcement: 'It is impossible.' 'That's news to me,' said K., who leaped out of bed and quickly got into his trousers. 'I must see who these people in the next room are and what explanation Frau Grubach will give for this disturbance.' He immediately realized of course that he should not have said this and that by doing so he had to some extent recognized the right of the stranger to supervise his actions, but it did not seem important to him now. All the same, this is how the stranger took his words, for he said: 'Wouldn't you rather stay here?' 'I will neither stay here nor be talked to by you unless you tell me who you are.' 'I meant well,' said the stranger and he now opened the door without further objection. In the next room, which K. entered more slowly than he

He should have demanded to see their identity

2

intended, things looked at first glance almost exactly as they had on the previous evening. It was Frau Grubach's living-room; perhaps there was a little more space than usual in this room packed with furniture, rugs, china and photographs, but that was not immediately apparent, especially as the most striking change was the presence of a man who was sitting by the open window with a book, from which he now looked up. 'You should have stayed in your room! Didn't Franz tell you that?' 'Yes, but what do you want?' said K., and he looked from this new acquaintance to the one spoken of as Franz, who had remained in the doorway, and then back again. Through the open window the old woman was again visible; with true senile inquisitiveness she had moved to the corresponding window opposite so that she could continue to see everything. 'I want to see Frau Grubach –' said K., and he made an abrupt move-ment as if he were tearing himself free from the two men who were in fact standing some distance away from him, and made to leave the room. 'No,' said the man by the window; he threw the book on a little table and stood up. 'You are not allowed to go from here. You are after all under arrest.' 'So it would seem,' said K. 'And for what reason?' he then asked. 'It's not our job to tell you that. Go into your room and wait. The proceedings have now been started and you will learn everything in good time. I am exceeding my instructions by talking to you in such a friendly way. But I hope nobody can hear this except Franz, and he himself has been obliging to you in defiance of regulations. If you continue to have as much good luck as you've had in the choice of your warders you have reason to be confident.' K. wanted to sit down, but he now saw there was nowhere to sit in the whole room apart from the easy chair by the window. 'You will come to see how true that is,' said Franz, at the same time walking towards him with the other man. The latter in particular towered over K. and tapped him now and then on the shoulder. The two of them examined K.'s nightgown and said he would now have to wear a gown of much inferior quality, but they would take care of this gown as well as his other linen and would return everything to him if his case should turn out favourably. 'It's better to hand these things to us than to the depot,' they said, 'because there's a lot of thieving in the depot and, apart from that, things are sold after a specified time regardless of whether the relevant proceedings have been concluded or not. And how cases of this kind do drag on, especially as we've seen in recent times. Of course you would get the money eventually from the depot, but these proceeds are small enough in the first place because it's not the size of the offer which determines the sale but the size of the bribe, and secondly we know how such proceeds dwindle as they are passed from hand to hand over the years.' K. paid little attention to these words; the right which he still possessed to dispose of his things did not rank high in his estimation; to him it was much more important to understand his position clearly, but in the presence of these people he could not even think; the belly of the second warder – they could of course only be warders – bumped into him again and again in quite a friendly fashion, but when he looked up he saw that this fat body was out of keeping with the dry bony face, its prominent nose bent to one side, which was exchanging glances with the other warder over his head. What sort of people were they? What were they talking about? To which authority did they belong? After all, K. lived in a country which enjoyed law and order; there was universal peace; all the laws were upheld; so who dared pounce on him in his own home? He had always been inclined to take everything as easily as possible, to believe the worst only when the worst happened, not to worry about the future even when everything seemed threatening. But in this situation that did not seem right; one could of course regard the whole affair as a joke, a crude joke organized for some unknown reason by his colleagues at the bank, perhaps because today was his thirtieth birthday. This was of course possible, perhaps all he had to do was laugh in some way in the warders' faces and they would laugh with him, perhaps they were porters picked off the street, they looked rather like that – all the same, ever since he had first seen the warder Franz he had been utterly determined not to surrender the slightest advantage he might possess in relation to these people. K. saw a very slight danger that people might say later he could not take a joke but, even though it had not been usual for him to learn from experience, he now recalled certain incidents, not important in themselves, when, unlike his friends, he had deliberately set out to behave rashly without the slightest regard for possible consequences and had suffered as a result. This was not to happen again, not this time anyway; if this was just a bit of make-believe, he would go along with it.

He was still free. 'Do you mind!' he said and passed quickly between the warders to his room. 'He seems to be reasonable,' he heard one say behind him. In his room he immediately pulled out the drawers of his desk; everything was arranged in perfect order, but in his agitated state he could not instantly find the identity papers he was looking for. At last he found his bicycle licence and thought of taking this to the warders, but then the paper seemed too trivial and he looked further until he found his birth certificate. As he was going back into the next room the door opposite was just opening and Frau Grubach was about to come in. She was visible only for an instant, for as soon as she saw K. she became embarrassed, begged for forgiveness and disappeared, closing the door with extreme care. 'But do come in,' was all that K. could have said. Now he stood in the middle of the room with his papers, still looking at the door, which did not open again, until he was roused by a shout from the warders, who were sitting at the small table by the open window and, as K. now realized, were devouring his breakfast. 'Why didn't she come in?' he asked. 'She's not allowed to,' said the tall warder. 'You're under arrest, after all.' 'But how can I be under arrest? And above all in this way?' 'Now you're beginning again,' said the warder and he dipped his bread and butter in the honey jar. 'We don't answer such questions.' 'You'll have to answer them,' said K. 'Here are my identity papers; now show me yours, and especially the warrant for my arrest.' 'Dear God in heaven!' said the warder. 'Why can't you just accept your position, why do you seem determined to irritate us needlessly, we who probably stand closer to you now than any other of your fellow men?' 'That's how it is, do believe that,' said Franz; he did not raise to his mouth the coffee cup he held in his hand but looked at K. with a lingering glance which was probably meaningful but yet incomprehensible. In spite of himself, K. entered on an exchange of glances with Franz, but then slapped his papers and said: 'Here are my identity papers.' 'What have they got to do with us?' shouted the tall warder. 'You're behaving worse than a child. What do you want? Is it your idea to bring your damned great case to a quick conclusion by arguing with us, your warders, about identification and arrest warrant? We are junior officials who hardly know one end of an identity

7

document from another and have nothing more to do with your case than to stand guard over you for ten hours a day and be paid for it. That's all we are, but we are capable of seeing that the high authorities we serve would not order such an arrest without gathering exact information about the reasons for the arrest and about the person to be arrested. There's no room for mistake. Our authorities, as far as I know them, and I know only the lowest grades, do not go in search of guilt in the population but are, as it says in the law, drawn to guilt and must send us warders out. That is law. Where could there be a mistake in that?' 'This law is unknown to me,' said K. 'All the worse for you,' said the warder. 'It probably exists only in your heads,' said K., who wanted to worm his way somehow into the warders' minds, turn their thoughts to his advantage or entrench himself there. But the warder merely said in an indifferent manner: 'You'll soon come up against it.' Franz intervened and said: 'See, Willem, he admits he doesn't know the law and says at the same time he's innocent.' 'You're quite right, but you can't make him understand anything,' said the other. K. made no further answer; do I, he thought, have to let myself be even more confused by the twaddle of these lowest of instruments – they themselves admit that's all they are? Anyway, they are talking about things they don't understand at all. Their certainty is possible only because of their stupidity. A few words with someone on my own level will

8

make things incomparably clearer than the longest conversations with these two. He walked up and down a few times in the open space in the room; across the way he saw the old woman, who had dragged an even older man to the window and now held him tightly; K. had to make an end of this exhibition. 'Take me to your superior,' he said. 'When he tells us to, not before,' said the warder who had been addressed as Willem. 'And now I advise you,' he added, 'to go into your room, keep calm, and wait to see what will be decreed about you. We advise you not to disturb yourself with useless thoughts but to pull yourself together; great demands will be made on you. You haven't treated us in the way our considerate attitude might have deserved. You've forgotten that we, whatever we might be, are at this moment in relation to you at least free men, and that's no mean superiority. Nevertheless we are ready, if you have the money, to fetch you a light breakfast from the café opposite.'

Without making a reply to this offer, K. stood quietly for a moment. Perhaps if he were to open the door into the next room or even the door into the hall, these two would not dare get in his way, perhaps the simplest solution of the whole thing would be to take it to an extreme. But perhaps they might get hold of him all the same, and once he were thrown on the floor all the superiority he still preserved to a certain degree in relation to them would be lost. So he came down in favour of the solution which must come in the natural course of events and went back into his room without another word being uttered either by him or the warders.

He threw himself on his bed and took from the bedside table a fine apple he had put aside the previous evening for his breakfast. Now it was all the breakfast he had, and at any rate, as he ascertained from his first great bite, much better than the breakfast from the filthy night café which he might have got through the gracious favour of the warders. He felt well and confident. True, he was absent from his post in the bank this morning, but that could easily be excused because of the comparatively high position he held there. Should he tell them the real reason? He thought he might do so. If they did not believe him – which was understandable in this case – he could call Frau Grubach as witness, or even the two old people from over the way who were probably now moving to the opposite window. K. was surprised; at least, when he tried to follow the warders' train of thought, he was surprised they had forced him into his room and left him here alone with all the many possibilities he had of killing himself. But at the same time he asked himself, trying to see it from his own point of view, what reason he could have for doing such a thing. Because those two were sitting next door and had intercepted his breakfast? Killing himself would have been so senseless that even if he had wanted to he would not have been able to do it, because of its sense-lessness. If the intellectual limitations of the warders had not been so obvious, one might have assumed they too shared this conviction and there-fore saw no danger in leaving him on his own. They could watch if they liked as he went to a cupboard where he kept a bottle of fine schnapps and see how first of all he drank off a glass in place of breakfast and then a second to give himself courage, the second only as a precaution for the improbable event that it might be necessary.

Then a call from the next room startled him so much that his teeth struck against the glass. 'The supervisor wants you,' was the message. It was only the shout that startled him, this curt, clipped, military shout he would not have thought possible coming from the warder Franz. The command itself was very welcome. 'At last,' he shouted back and locked the wardrobe and hurried straight into the next room. There the two warders were standing and they drove him back into his room as if this were a matter of course. 'What are you thinking of?' they cried. 'You want to appear before the supervisor in your shirt? He'd have you thrashed, and us with you!' 'Let me be, for heaven's sake!' said K., who had already been pushed back as far as the wardrobe. 'If you pounce on me in my bed you can't expect to find me in my best suit.' 'That doesn't help,' said the warders who, when K. shouted, became quite calm, almost melancholy, and thus confused him or to some extent brought him to his senses. 'Ridiculous formalities!' he growled, but he had already taken a jacket from the chair and was holding it out with both hands as if spreading it for the warders' judgement. They shook their heads. 'It must be a black coat,' they said. K. threw the jacket on the floor and said – he himself did not know in what sense he meant this: 'After all, it's not the main hearing yet.' The warders smiled but kept to their 'It must be a black coat.' 'If I can hurry up the business in this way, I don't mind,' said K., and he opened the wardrobe, looked for some time among the collection of clothes, selected his best black suit, a two-piece that had caused quite a sensation among his acquaintances because of its cut, put another shirt on too, and began to dress with care. He secretly thought he had managed to expedite the whole affair because the warders had forgotten to make him take a bath. He watched them in case they might yet remember that, but of course it did not occur to them, although Willem did not forget to send Franz to the supervisor with the message that K. was getting dressed.

When he was fully dressed he had to walk in front of Willem through the empty room next door into the adjoining room whose double door was already open. This room, as K. well knew, had been taken recently by a Fräulein Bürstner, a typist, who went off to work very early, came back late, and with whom K. had exchanged little more than a passing greeting. Now the bedside table had been moved from the bed to the middle of the room to serve as the interrogator's desk, and the supervisor sat behind it. His legs were crossed, one arm was draped over the back of the chair. In the corner of the room stood three young persons looking at Fräulein Bürstner's photographs stuck on a board which hung on the wall. A white blouse was hanging on the latch of the open window. The two old people were again to be seen in the window across the way, but the group had increased in size, for behind them and towering over them was a man with an open-necked shirt who stroked and twirled his reddish goatee with his fingers.

'Josef K.?' queried the supervisor, perhaps only to draw K.'s distracted glances to himself. K. nodded. 'You must be very surprised by this morning's events?' the supervisor asked and at the same time used both hands to move the few objects on the bedside table, the candle with matches, a book and a pincushion, as if these were objects he required for his interrogation. 'Certainly,' said K., and he was overcome with pleasure at meeting a reasonable man at last and being able to discuss his case with him, 'certainly I am surprised, but I am by no means very surprised.' 'Not very surprised?' asked the supervisor and now placed the candle in the middle of the table and grouped the other objects around it. 'Perhaps you misunderstand me,' K. hastened to remark. 'I mean . . .' Here K. broke off and looked round for a chair. 'I can sit down?' he asked. 'It's not customary,' answered the supervisor. 'I mean,' said K. without further delay, 'I am as a matter of fact very surprised, but when you've spent thirty years in this world and had to fight your way through as I've had to, you become hardened to surprises and don't take them too seriously. Especially today's.' 'Why especially today's?' 'I'm not going to say I regard the whole thing as a joke; the arrangements that have been made seem too extensive for that. All the people in the boarding-house would have to be involved, and all of you too. That would take it beyond the limits of a joke. So I'm not going to say it's a joke.' 'Quite right,' said the supervisor, and he looked to see how many matches there were in the matchbox. 'But on the other hand,' K. went on, and he turned to them all and would have liked to include the three standing by the photographs, 'on the other hand, the matter can't be very important either. I deduce this from the fact that I'm accused of something but can't find the slightest guilt to justify an accusation. But that's a minor point. The main question is: who is accusing me? What authority is conducting these proceedings? Are you officials? Nobody's got a uniform unless' – here he turned to Franz – 'we can call what you are wearing a uniform, but it's more like a travelling outfit. I'd like to have these points cleared up, and I'm sure that after this clarification we'll be able to take leave of each other most amicably.' The supervisor slammed the matchbox down on the table. 'You are making a great mistake,' he said. 'These gentlemen here and I are of minor importance to your case, indeed we know almost nothing about it. We could be wearing the most correct uniforms and your business would be none the worse. I am absolutely unable to tell you that you stand accused, or rather I don't know if you are. You are under arrest, that's true, I don't know more than that. Perhaps the warders have said something more in gossip, but that's only their gossip. Even if I can't answer your questions I can, however, advise you to think less about us and about what may happen to you, and more about yourself. And don't make such a palaver about your feeling of innocence, it detracts from the not unfavourable impression you make otherwise. You should be more restrained in what you say too, nearly everything you said just now could have been inferred from your conduct even if you had said only a few words, and in any case it was nothing of great advantage to you.'

K. stared at the supervisor. Was he to get schoolboy maxims here from a person perhaps younger than himself? Was his openness to be punished with a reprimand? And was he to learn nothing about the reason for his arrest and who had ordered it? Thrown into a state of some agitation, he walked up and down without hindrance from the others, pushed his cuffs back, touched his chest, smoothed his hair down, went past the three gentlemen and said: 'But it's senseless,' whereupon these three turned towards him and looked at him in a sympathetic but earnest way, and finally he came to a stop by the supervisor's table again. 'Hasterer from the prosecutor's office is a good friend of mine,' he said. 'Can I phone him?' 'Of course,' said the supervisor, 'but I don't know what sense there's supposed to be in that, unless you have some private matter to discuss with him.' 'What sense?' cried K., more shaken than annoyed. 'But who are you? You ask for sense and you are putting on the most senseless exhibition yourself. Isn't it enough to melt a stone? First these gentlemen pounced on me and now they're sitting or standing around here expecting me to do tricks for you like a performing horse. What sense there might be in telephoning a lawyer when I'm supposed to be under arrest? All right, I won't telephone.' 'But do,' said the supervisor and he pointed to the hall, where the telephone was, 'but please do telephone.' 'No, I don't want to now,' said K. and went to the window. Across the way the group was still at the window and only now, because K. had come to the window, did their quiet contemplation seem a little disturbed. The old people tried to stand, but the man behind reassured them. 'There are more spectators over there,' shouted K. quite loudly to the supervisor and he pointed across with his finger. 'Away from there,' he then shouted at them. The three immediately fell back a few steps, the two old people even retreated behind the man, who shielded them with his broad body and, to judge by the movements of his mouth, was saying something which was incomprehensible at that distance. But they did not disappear completely, they seemed to be waiting for the moment when they could come to the window again without being observed. 'Impertinent, thoughtless people!' said K. as he turned back to the room. It was possible the supervisor agreed with him, or so K. thought when he gave him a sideways glance. But it was just as possible he had not even been listening, for he had pressed one hand firmly on the table and seemed to be comparing the lengths of his fingers. The two warders sat on a chest covered with an embroidered cloth and were rubbing their knees. The three young people had their hands on their hips and were looking around aimlessly. It was as quiet as in some abandoned office. 'Now, gentlemen,' cried K., who felt for a moment as if he were carrying them all on his shoulders, 'to judge from your expressions, this affair of mine must be at an end. In my opinion the best thing is not to brood any more about whether what you've done is justified or not justified but to bring the matter to a peaceful conclusion with a mutual handshake. If you share my opinion, then please . . .' and he stepped up to the supervisor's table and offered him his hand. The supervisor raised his eyes, chewed his lips, and looked at K.'s outstretched hand. K. still believed the supervisor would shake hands in agreement. But the latter stood up, took a hard round hat which lay on Fräulein Bürstner's bed and placed it carefully on his head with both hands, just as one does when trying on new hats. 'How simple everything seems to you,' he said to K. as he was doing this. 'We should bring the matter to a peaceful conclusion, is that your opinion? No, no, that really won't do. By which, on the other hand, I definitely don't mean to say you should despair. No, why should you? You're only under arrest, that's all. That's what I had to communicate to you, I've done that, and I've also seen how you've taken it. That's enough for today and we can take leave of each other; only for the time being of course. I suppose you'll want to go to the bank now?' 'To the bank?' asked K. 'I thought I was under arrest.' K. put this question with a certain defiance, for although his handshake had not been accepted he felt, especially since the supervisor had stood up, more and more detached from all these people. He was playing with them. What he had in mind, if they were to go away, was to run after them as far as the gate and offer to be arrested. So he said again: 'How can I go to the bank? I'm under arrest.' 'Ah yes,' said the supervisor, who was already by the door. 'You've misunderstood me. It's true you're under arrest, but that doesn't mean you can't follow your occupation. And you won't be hampered in your normal way of life.' 'Being arrested is not so bad,' said K., and he went up close to the supervisor. 'I never said it was,' said the latter. 'But then it seems it was not even very necessary to tell me about my arrest,' said K., who now went even closer. The others too had come nearer. All were now assembled in a confined space by the door. 'It was my duty,' said the supervisor. 'A stupid duty,' said K. unrelentingly. 'Maybe,' said the supervisor, 'but we don't want to waste our time talking like this. I had assumed you'd want to go to the bank. As you pay such close attention to every word I say, I will now add: I'm not forcing you to go to the bank, I had merely assumed you would want to go. And to make that easier for you and to make your arrival at the bank as unobtrusive as possible, I have retained these three gentlemen here, your colleagues, to be at your disposal.' 'What?' cried K. and looked at the three in amazement. These utterly insipid and colourless young men, whom he had noted mentally as merely a group by the photographs, were indeed officials from his bank; not colleagues, that was pitching it too high and revealed a gap in the supervisor's omniscience, but they really were subordinate officials from the bank. How could K. have overlooked this fact? He must have been absolutely absorbed in the supervisor and the warders not to recognize these three. The erect Rabensteiner with restless hands, fair-haired Kullych with his deep-set eyes, and Kaminer with the insufferable smile caused by chronic muscular spasm. 'Good morning,' said K. after a pause and held out his hand to the gentlemen, who were

exactly

19

bowing politely. 'I didn't recognize you at all. So now we'll go off to work, eh?' The three nodded with an eager laugh as if they had been waiting for this all the time, but when K. missed his hat, which had been left in his room, they all rushed out together to fetch it, and this revealed a certain embarrassment after all. K. stood where he was and watched them through the two open doors; the last of course was the apathetic Rabensteiner who had merely broken into an elegant trot. Kaminer gave him his hat, and K. had to make a point of telling himself, as he often had to in the bank, that Kaminer's smile was not intentional, indeed that he was quite incapable of smiling intentionally. In the hall the front door was then opened for the whole company by Frau Grubach, who did not give the impression of feeling very guilty, and K. looked down, as he often did, at the apron-string which made such a needlessly deep cut in her massive body. When they were outside, K. took his watch in his hand and resolved to call a cab so that there would be no unnecessary prolongation of the delay, which had already lasted half an hour. Kaminer ran to the corner to find a cab and the two others were evidently trying to take K.'s mind off things, when Kullych suddenly pointed to the house-door opposite, where the man with the pale goatee had just appeared; at first a little embarrassed at being seen at his full height, he then retreated to the wall and leaned on it. The old people were probably still on the stairs. K. was annoyed with Kullych for drawing attention to the man, whom he had already seen earlier and had in fact expected. 'Don't look over there,' he blurted, without thinking how extraordinary such a remark was when addressed to grown men. But no explanation was necessary, for the cab arrived just then and they took their seats and drove off. Then K. realized he had not noticed the departure of the supervisor and warders; the supervisor had hidden the three officials from him, and now the officials had done the same for the supervisor. This did not suggest he was very alert, and K. resolved to pay closer attention to such things. Yet he still turned involuntarily and leaned over the back of the cab to see if he could catch a glimpse of the supervisor and the warders. But he turned back again at once, without making any effort to look for anyone, and settled himself comfortably in the corner. In spite of appearances, he would have been glad of some words of encouragement at this time, but the gentlemen now seemed tired. Rabensteiner was looking out of the cab on the right, Kullych on the left, and only Kaminer was available with his grin, and common humanity forbade any joke about that.

That spring K. usually spent the evenings going for a short walk after work, either alone or with acquaintances, if this was still possible – he was in his office most days until nine o'clock – and then going to a beer hall where he was in the habit of sitting until eleven o'clock, mostly in the company of elderly gentlemen, at a table reserved for regulars. There were, however, exceptions to this arrangement, for example when the manager of the bank (who valued his capacity for work and trustworthiness very highly) invited him to go for a trip in his car or to dine at his villa. And once a week K. went to a girl called Elsa who worked all night until late morning in a wine tavern and during the day received her visitors only in bed.

But this evening – the day had passed quickly, what with intense work and many complimentary and friendly birthday greetings – K. decided to go straight home. He had thought about doing this during all the brief pauses in the day's work; without knowing exactly what he had in mind, it seemed to him as if, because of that morning's events, considerable disorder had been occasioned in Frau Grubach's whole house and his presence was necessary to restore order. But once this order was restored, then every trace of those events would be eliminated and everything would resume its old course. He noted specially that nothing was to be feared from the three officials; they had sunk back into the huge bureaucracy of the bank and no change could be seen in them. K. had called them into his office several times, individually and all three together, for no other purpose than to observe them; each time he had been able to dismiss them with satisfaction.

When he reached the house where he lived at

half-past nine that evening he met in the doorway a young lad who was standing there with his legs wide apart, smoking a pipe. 'Who are you?' K. asked, at once, bringing his face close to the lad's; it was not possible to see much in the gloom of the hall. 'I'm the caretaker's son, sir,' said the lad in reply, taking the pipe from his mouth and stepping to one side. 'The caretaker's son?' asked K., and he tapped on the floor impatiently with his stick. 'Do you want anything, sir? Shall I fetch my father?' 'No, no,' said K. with a note of forgiveness in his voice as if the lad had done something wrong but he forgave him. 'It's all right,' he then said, and he walked on, but before going up the stairs he turned round once again.

He could have gone straight to his room, but as he wanted to speak to Frau Grubach he knocked at her door without delay. She was holding an uncompleted stocking still on the needles and was sitting by a table on which there was a heap of old stockings. K. apologized in some confusion for coming so late, but Frau Grubach was most affable and would not hear of any apology: for him she was always available, he knew very well he was her best and most valued lodger. K. looked round the room; it had been restored exactly to its old condition, with the breakfast things which had been on the little table by the window that morning also cleared away. Women's hands do get a lot done without fuss, he thought; he would perhaps have smashed all the dishes on the spot, he certainly would not have been able to carry them out of the room. He looked at Frau Grubach with a certain gratitude. 'Why are you working so late?' he asked. Both were now seated at the table, and from time to time K. buried a hand in the stockings. 'There's a lot of work,' she said. 'During the day my time belongs to my lodgers. When I want to see to my own things, only the evenings are left to me.' 'I'm afraid I've caused you a lot of extra work today.' 'How is that?' she asked, becoming more attentive and letting her work rest in her lap. 'I mean the men who were here this morning.' 'Oh, that,' she said and reverted to her normal calm. 'That didn't give me any special work.' K. watched in silence as she took up the unfinished stocking again. 'She seems surprised that I mention it,' he thought. 'She seems to think it's not right for me to mention it. So it's all the more important that I do so. It's only to an old woman that I can mention it.' 'But surely it must have given you work,' he then said, 'but it won't happen again.' 'No, that can't happen again,' she said in agreement and smiled almost wistfully at K. 'Do you really mean that?' asked K. 'Yes,' she said quietly, 'but above all you mustn't take it too much to heart. What things happen in this world! As you are speaking so openly to me, Herr K., I can confess to you I listened a bit behind the door and the two warders told me something too. It's a matter that concerns your happiness, and that's really close to my heart, perhaps closer than it

24

should be, because I am after all only your land-lady. Well, so I heard a little, but I can't say it was anything particularly bad. No. You are indeed under arrest, but not like a thief is under arrest. When a man is arrested like a thief, then it's bad, but this arrest – it seems to me like something scholarly, forgive me if I'm saying something stupid, it seems to me like something scholarly which I don't understand, but which one doesn't have to understand either.'

'What you have said, Frau Grubach, is not stupid at all, at least I too share your opinion to some extent, but I judge the whole thing more strictly than you and I consider it to be not even scholarly but nothing at all. I was taken by surprise, that's all. If I had got up as soon as I woke, without letting myself be put off by Anna's absence, and had come to you without taking notice of anyone who might have got in my way, if for instance I had just for once had my breakfast in the kitchen, had got you to bring me my clothes from my room, in short, if I had acted in a sensible way, nothing further would have happened, everything would have been nipped in the bud. But one is so little prepared. In the bank for instance I am prepared for anything, it's impossible that anything like that could happen to me there; there I have my own assistant, the outside phone and the internal phone are on my desk and people, clients, officials are always coming and going; but also and of particular importance, when I'm there I'm always involved in work and therefore mentally alert; it would actually give me pleasure to be confronted with such a matter there. Now it's past and in fact I wasn't intending to speak of it, but I wanted to hear your judgement, the judgement of a sensible woman, and I'm very pleased that we are in agreement. Now you must give me your hand, an agreement like this must be sealed with a handshake.'

Will she give me her hand? The supervisor did not give me his hand, he thought; and he looked at the woman with a different, searching look. She stood up because he too was on his feet, she was a little diffident because not everything K. said had been comprehensible to her. But because of this diffidence she said something she did not intend and which was very much out of place: 'Don't take it so much to heart, Herr K.,' she said in a tearful voice and forgot of course about the handshake. 'I didn't know I was taking it to heart,' he said, suddenly feeling tired and realizing the worthlessness of this woman's approval.

At the door he asked: 'Is Fräulein Bürstner at home?' 'No,' said Frau Grubach, and as she gave this bare information she smiled with belated and sensible sympathy. 'She is at the theatre. Do you want something of her? Should I give her a message?' 'Oh, I only wanted to have a few words with her.' 'I'm afraid I don't know when she'll be back; when she's at the theatre she usually comes home late.' 'It doesn't matter,' said K. and was already turning his drooping head towards the door on the way out. 'I only wanted to ask her to forgive me for having made use of her room today.' 'That's not necessary, Herr K.; you are too considerate; the young lady of course knows nothing about it, she hasn't been home since early morning, everything has been put straight, see for yourself.' And she opened the door of Fräulein Bürstner's room. 'Thank you, I believe you,' said K., but all the same he went to the open door. The moonlight shone softly into the dark room. As far as one could see, everything was really in its place, even the blouse was no longer hanging from the window latch. The pillows on the bed seemed unusually high; they lay partly in moonlight. 'The young lady often comes home late,' said K., and he looked at Frau Grubach as if she were responsible for that. 'Just like all young people!' said Frau Grubach apologetically. 'Of course, of course,' said K., 'but it can go too far.' 'It can,' said Frau Grubach. 'How right you are, Herr K. Perhaps even in this case. I certainly don't want to say anything against Fräulein Bürstner. She is a good, dear girl, friendly, tidy, meticulous, hard-working. I value all that very much, but one thing is true: she should have more pride, be more reserved. This month I've already seen her twice in streets some way off, and each time with a different gentleman. I feel bad about it, I swear by God above I've told nobody else but you about it, Herr K., but nothing will stop me speaking to the young lady herself about it. In any case, it's not the only thing that makes me suspect her.' 'You are quite on the wrong track,' said K., in a rage and almost unable to hide it. 'Besides, you've obviously misunderstood what I said about the young lady. I didn't mean it like that. In fact, I warn you explicitly not to say anything to the young lady. You are completely mistaken, I know the young lady very well and nothing of what you say is true. But perhaps I am going too far; I won't stop you telling her what you like. Good night.' 'Herr K.,' said Frau Grubach imploringly, and she hurried after him as far as his door, which he had already opened, 'I don't want to talk to the young lady now, first I'll keep my eye on her a bit longer of course; you are the only one I've told about what I know. In the end it must be in every lodger's interest if I try to keep the boarding-house respectable, and that's all I'm trying to do.' 'Respectable!' shouted K. through the partly open door. 'If you want to keep the boarding-house respectable you'd better give me notice first.' Then he slammed the door and ignored a faint knocking.

But, as he did not feel at all sleepy, he decided to stay awake and take this opportunity to see when Fräulein Bürstner would come. Perhaps it would be possible to have a few words with her then, however ill-timed it might seem. As he lay by the window and strained his tired eyes he even thought for a moment of punishing Frau Grubach by persuading Fräulein Bürstner to join him in giving notice. But at once that seemed to him to be carrying things really too far and he even suspected himself of wanting to change his lodging because of that morning's events. Nothing would have been more senseless and above all more pointless and despicable.

When he had grown tired of staring out at the empty street he lay on the sofa, after opening the door to the hall a little so that he could see from his position on the sofa anyone who came into the house. Until about eleven o'clock he lay quietly on the sofa, smoking a cigar. But after that he could no longer bear to stay where he was and went a little way into the hall, as if he could hasten Fräulein Bürstner's arrival by doing this. He had no particular feelings about her, he could not even remember exactly what she looked like, but now he wanted to talk to her, and it annoyed him that by coming late she was introducing disturbance and disorder into the end of this day too. And it was her fault that he had had no supper this evening and had put off the visit to Elsa planned for today. He could still remedy both these omissions by going to the wine tavern where Elsa worked. He could do that later, after his talk with Fräulein Bürstner.

It was after half-past eleven when somebody could be heard on the stairs. K., deep in thought, was walking noisily up and down the hall as if this were his own room, and he now fled behind his door. Fräulein Bürstner had arrived. With a shiver she drew a silken shawl more closely round her thin shoulders as she locked the door. In a moment she would be going into her room, and K. would certainly not be allowed in there at this midnight hour; he would have to speak to her now, but unfortunately he had forgotten to switch the electric light on in his room, so his emergence from the dark room might look like an attack and at the least must give cause for alarm. Feeling helpless, and as no time was to be lost, he whispered through the partly opened door: 'Fräulein Bürstner.' It sounded like a plea, not like a challenge. 'Is there somebody there?' asked Fräulein Bürstner and looked round with a startled look. 'It's me,' said K. and he stepped forward. 'Ah, Herr K.' said Fräulein Bürstner with a smile. 'Good evening.' And she shook his hand. 'I wanted to talk to you. Will you permit me now?' 'Now?' asked Fräulein Bürstner. 'Does it have to be now? It's a little unusual, isn't it?' 'I've been waiting for you since nine.' 'Well, I was at the theatre. I didn't know you were waiting.' 'What I want to talk to you about happened only today.' 'All right, I've nothing against it really, except that I'm dead tired. So come to my room in a few minutes. In any case, we can't talk here, we'd wake everybody, wouldn't we? – and as far as I'm concerned that would be more of a nuisance to us than to them. Wait here till I put the light on in my room, then switch this light off.' K. did this but then waited until, from her room, Fräulein Bürstner quietly asked him once more to come in. 'Sit down,' she said and pointed to the ottoman, but she herself remained standing by the bedpost in spite of the weariness she had spoken of and did not even take off her little hat adorned with a profusion of flowers. 'So what did you want? I am really curious.' She crossed her legs slightly. 'You will perhaps say,' K. began 'that the matter is not so urgent that it had to be discussed now, but . . .' 'I never listen to preliminaries,' said Fräulein Bürstner. 'That makes my task easier,' K. said. 'This morning your room was thrown into some disorder, and it was in a way my fault. It was done by strangers, against my will, but, as I say, it was my fault. I wanted to ask you to forgive me for this.' 'My room?' asked Fräulein Bürstner and, instead of looking at the room, she looked at K. with an inquiring glance. 'It's true,' said K., and now they looked into each other's eyes for the first time. 'How it happened is not worth mentioning.' 'But that's the really interesting part,' said Fräulein Bürstner. 'No,' K. said. 'Now,' said Fräulein Bürstner, 'I don't want to pry into secrets. If you insist it's not interesting, I won't try to deny that. I grant with pleasure the forgiveness you ask for, especially as I can't find any trace of disorder.' With hands pressed flat and low on her hips she made a circuit of the room. She stopped by the board with the photographs. 'But look,' she cried, 'my photographs have been pushed around. But that's horrid. So somebody has been in my room without permission.' K. nodded and silently cursed the clerk Kaminer, who was never able to curb his dreary and idiotic

31

verve. 'It is strange,' said Fräulein Bürstner, 'that I have to forbid you something you should have forbidden yourself, that is, to enter my room in my absence.' 'But I have explained to you, Fräulein,' said K., and he too went up to the photographs, 'that it was not I who interfered with your photographs; but since you don't believe me I shall have to confess the investigating commission brought three bank employees here, and one of them, whom I shall sack from the bank at the first opportunity, probably handled the photographs.' 'Yes, there was an investigating commission here,' added K., since the Fräulein looked at him inquiringly. 'Because of you?' she asked. 'Yes,' K. replied. 'No,' cried the Fräulein with a laugh. 'But yes,' said K., 'do you believe then that I'm innocent?' 'Now, innocent . . .' said the Fräulein. 'Don't expect me to pronounce straight away a judgement which might perhaps have serious consequences; after all, I don't know you, but all the same a man must be a hardened criminal if he attracts the attention of an investigating commission. But as you're still at liberty – at least I guess from your calm behaviour that you haven't escaped from prison – you can't have committed a crime like that.' 'Yes,' said K., 'but the investigating commission may have seen that I am innocent, or at least not as guilty as was assumed.' 'Certainly, that may be,' said Fräulein Bürstner very attentively. 'Look,' said K., 'you don't have much experience in legal matters.' 'No, I haven't,' said Fräulein Bürstner, 'and I've often regretted it, because I'd like to know everything I can, and legal matters do interest me enormously. A law court has its own peculiar power of attraction, don't you think? But I'm sure to expand my knowledge in that direction because next month I'm joining the staff of a lawyer's office.' 'That's very good,' K. said. 'You'll then be able to help me a little with my case.' 'That might be possible,' said Fräulein Bürstner. 'Why not? I do like to make use of what I know.' 'But I mean it seriously,' said K., 'or at least half-seriously . . . as you mean it. To employ an advocate – my business is too trivial for that. But I could make good use of an adviser.' 'Yes, but if I'm to be an adviser I'd have to know what it's all about,' said Fräulein Bürstner. 'That's just the snag,' K. said. 'I don't know that myself.' 'Then you've just been playing a joke on me,' said Fräulein Bürstner with intense disappointment. 'It was totally unnecessary to choose this late hour for doing that.' And she walked away from the photographs, where they had stood so long together. 'But no, Fräulein,' said K., 'this is no joke. Why can't you believe me? I've told you everything I know. Indeed, more than I know, because it wasn't an investigating commission at all; I'm giving it that name because I don't know what else to call it. Nothing was investigated. I was only put under arrest, but by a commission.' Fräulein Bürstner sat on the ottoman and laughed again. 'What was it like?' she asked. 'Frightful,' said K., but he was not thinking of that now, he

33

was entirely taken up with the sight of Fräulein Bürstner, her face propped on one hand – her elbow rested on the cushion of the ottoman – while with the other hand she slowly stroked her hip. 'That's too vague,' said Fräulein Bürstner. 'What's too vague?' K. asked. Then he came to himself and asked: 'Shall I show you how it was?' He wanted to introduce some movement yet did not want to depart. 'I'm so tired,' said Fräulein Bürstner. 'You arrived so late,' K. said. 'Now we've got to the point where I get reproaches, and I deserve it, because I should not have let you come in. There was no need for it either, that's obvious now.' 'There was a need for it, you'll see now,' K. said. 'May I move the table from beside your bed to over here?' 'What are you thinking of?' said Fräulein Bürstner. 'Of course you shan't do that!' 'Then I can't show you what happened,' said K. in some agitation, as if this were causing him an immeasurable injury. 'Oh well, if you need it for your demonstration then move the table as you like,' said Fräulein Bürstner and after a while she added, in a fainter voice: 'I am so tired that I'm permitting more than I should.' K. placed the table in the middle of the room and sat down behind it. 'You must get a clear idea of the disposition of the people involved. I am the supervisor; there, on the chest, two warders are sitting; by the photographs stand three young men. I'll just mention by the way that a white blouse is hanging on the window latch. And now it begins. Oh, I've forgotten myself, the most important character; I'm standing here in front of the table. The supervisor is sitting very comfortably, his legs crossed, his arm hanging down here over the back of the chair, an absolute lout. So now it really begins. The supervisor shouts as if he has to wake me from my sleep, he really yells, and I'm afraid that if I'm to make this comprehensible to you I must yell too. It is by the way only my name that he yells like this.' Fräulein Bürstner, who was laughing while she was listening, put her finger to her lips to prevent K. from yelling, but it was too late. K. was too involved in the role he was playing and cried out slowly: 'Josef K.!' It was not as loud as he had threatened, but all the same loud enough so that the cry, after it had been suddenly expelled, seemed to spread only gradually through the room.

Then somebody knocked several times at the door of the next room, loudly, briskly, and with a regular rhythm. Fräulein Bürstner turned pale and put her hand to her heart. K. was particularly startled because for a moment he was quite unable to think of anything but that morning's events and of the girl to whom he was demonstrating them. No sooner had he come to his senses than he sprang to Fräulein Bürstner's side and took her hand. 'Don't be afraid,' he whispered, 'I'll see to everything. But who can it be? Here next door there's only the living-room, and nobody sleeps there.' 'Oh yes,' Fräulein Bürstner whispered in K.'s ear, 'since yesterday a nephew of Frau Grubach sleeps there, a captain. It just happens no other room is free. I'd forgotten about it. And you had to shout like that! I'm really upset.' 'You've no reason to be,' said K. and, as she now sank back on the cushion, he kissed her forehead. 'Go away,' she said, 'go away,' and she sat up quickly, 'but go, do go. What are you doing? He must be listening at the door. He can hear everything. How you torment me!' 'I won't go,' said K., 'until you've calmed down a bit. Come into this other corner of the room; he can't hear us there.' She allowed him to lead her there. 'You don't consider,' he said, 'that while this may indeed be a nuisance for you, it's by no means a danger. You know how Frau Grubach practically worships me and believes without question anything I say; she has the last word in this matter, especially as the captain is her nephew. And she's under an obligation to me too: she has borrowed a lot of money from me. I'll agree to any of your suggestions on how to explain our presence here together, as long as it's tolerably plausible, and I guarantee to persuade Frau Grubach to believe our explanation, not only ostensibly but actually and really to believe it. You don't have to consider me at all. If you want it spread around that I have assaulted you, that's what Frau Grubach will be told, and she'll believe it without losing her faith in me, she's so very attached to me.' Fräulein Bürstner looked down at the floor in silence, a little dejected. 'Why shouldn't Frau Grubach believe I've assaulted you?' K. added. He was looking at her hair with its parting, her reddish hair bunched out at the bottom and firmly held. He thought she would turn her gaze towards him, but without changing her position she said: 'Forgive me, I was scared because of the sudden knocking, not because of anything that might follow because the captain is there. It was so quiet after you shouted, then there was that knocking, that's why I was so frightened; and I was sitting by the door, the knocking was right by me. I am grateful for your suggestions, but I won't take them up. I can take responsibility for everything that happens in my room against no matter whom. I'm surprised you don't notice what an insult to me there is in your suggestions, together with your good intentions of course, which I certainly recognize. But now you must go, leave me to myself. That's more necessary now than it was before. The few minutes you asked for have grown into half an hour and more.' K. took her by the hand and then by the wrist. 'But you're not angry with me?' he said. She shook his hand off and answered: 'No, no, I'm never angry with anybody.' He again took her by the wrist; she allowed him to do so now and led him like this to the door. He was firmly resolved to go. But at the door he hesitated, as if he had not expected to find a door there, and Fräulein Bürstner used this moment to free herself, open the door, slip into the hall and from there to say softly to K.: 'But do come now, please. Look . . .' She pointed to the captain's door, under which a strip of light was visible. 'He has put his light on and is having fun at our expense.' 'I'm coming,' said K., who now dashed forward, seized her, and kissed her on the mouth and then all over her face like a thirsty animal who scours with his tongue the surface of a spring he has found at last. Finally he kissed her on the neck, on her throat, and lingered there with his lips. A sound from the captain's room made him look up. 'I'll go now,' he said. He wanted to call Fräulein Bürstner by her first name but did not know what it was. She nodded wearily and gave him her hand to kiss; she had already half turned away as if she knew nothing about it and went into her room with head bowed. Shortly afterwards K. was lying in his own bed. Very soon he was asleep, but before falling asleep he thought about his behaviour. He was satisfied with it, but surprised he was not even more satisfied. Because of the captain he was gravely concerned about Fräulein Bürstner.

FIRST EXAMINATION

K. had been notified by telephone that a brief examination into his case would be held the following Sunday. His attention was drawn to the fact that these examinations would take place regularly now, perhaps not every week but at frequent intervals. On the one hand, it would be in everybody's interest to bring the proceedings to a speedy conclusion, on the other hand the examinations must be thorough in every respect yet not last too long because of the strain involved. So they had chosen the expedient of these examinations following closely on each other but kept short. The choice of Sunday as the day for examinations had been made so that K. should not be interrupted in his professional work. It was assumed he would agree with this; should he ask for a different day, his wishes would be accommodated as far as possible. For example, it would be possible to hold the examinations at night, but in that event K. might not be sufficiently rested. At any rate, as long as K. had no objection, they would keep to Sunday. It went without saying that he would definitely have to attend; they hardly needed to draw his attention to that. He was given the number of the house at which he had to appear; it was a house in an outlying street in the suburbs, where K. had never been before.

When K. had received this message he replaced the receiver without making a reply; he had made up his mind immediately to go on Sunday, it was certainly necessary, the proceedings were getting under way and he must oppose them; this first examination must also be the last. He was still standing thoughtfully by the phone when he heard behind him the voice of the deputy manager who wanted to use the phone but found K. in his way. 'Bad news?' asked the deputy manager, not because he wanted to know but just to get K. away from the telephone. 'No, no,' said K. and he stepped to one side but did not go away. The deputy manager picked up the receiver and said, away from the mouthpiece as he waited for his connection: 'One request, Herr K. – would you do me the honour of joining us on my yacht next Sunday morning? It will be a large party and some of your friends are sure to be there. Among others, Hasterer from the prosecution service. Will you come? Do come!' K. struggled to pay attention to what the deputy manager was saying. It was not unimportant for him; this invitation from the deputy manager, with whom he had never got on very well, signified an effort at reconciliation on his part and showed how important K. had become in the bank and how valuable his friendship or at least his neutrality seemed to the bank's second highest official. The deputy manager was humbling himself by giving this invitation, even if it was only given as an aside while he was waiting for his connection. But K. had to provide a second humiliation, for he said: 'Many thanks, but unfortunately I'm not free on Sunday. I already have an engagement.' 'Pity,' said the deputy manager and turned to talk into the phone as his connection had just been made. It was not a short conversation, but in his confusion K. stayed there the whole time by the telephone. Only when the deputy manager rang off did he start and say, in an effort to excuse his pointless presence: 'I was told by telephone just now I was supposed to go somewhere, but they forgot to tell me what time.' 'Well, ask them again,' said the deputy manager. 'It's not so important,' said K. in spite of the fact that this made his first inadequate excuse even less convincing. The deputy manager talked about other things as he was going away; K. forced himself to give answers, but what he was really thinking was that it would be best to arrive on Sunday at nine o'clock in the morning as that was the time all law courts began work on weekdays.

The weather was overcast on Sunday. K. was very tired because he had stayed up late at some festivities among the regulars at the restaurant; he could have overslept. He dressed hastily, without having time to think over and coordinate the

41

various plans he had devised during the week, and rushed off, without breakfast, to the appointed suburb. Oddly, though he had little time to look around, he caught sight of the three employees involved in his case: Rabensteiner, Kullych and Kaminer. The first two were in a tram which crossed K.'s path, but Kaminer was sitting on a café terrace and leaned inquisitively over the parapet just as K. was passing. All three were probably staring after him, surprised to see their superior in such a hurry. A kind of defiance had prevented K. from summoning a vehicle; it was repugnant to him to ask for help, even the least outside help, in connection with this case of his, also he did not want to be obliged to anyone and so give them the slightest inkling; finally, he did not have the least wish to demean himself before the investigating commission by being too punctual. All the same, he hurried now to arrive as near as possible to nine o'clock even though he had not been summoned for any particular hour.

He had thought he would recognize the house from a distance by some sign, which he himself had not visualized exactly, or by some movement around the entrance. But Juliusstrasse, where it was supposed to be and at whose end K. stopped for a moment, consisted of almost identical houses along both sides, lofty grey tenements inhabited by poor people. Now, on Sunday morning, most of the windows were occupied; men in shirtsleeves leaned there smoking or held small children cautiously and tenderly at the window-ledges. Other windows were piled high with bedding, above which a woman's dishevelled head might be seen for a moment. People shouted to each other across the alley and one such shout produced a great burst of laughter just above K.'s head. At regular intervals along the street, below the level of the pavement, down a few steps, were tiny shops stocked with various foods. There women were going in and out or standing on the steps, chatting. A fruit-hawker, crying his wares to the windows above, might have knocked K. down with his handcart, so little attention was either of them paying to where he was going. At this moment a gramophone, worn out through long service in a better quarter of the town, began to grind out a mutilated melody.

K. penetrated further into the alley, slowly, as if he had time to spare or as if the examining magistrate could see him from some window and would therefore know he had arrived. It was a little after nine. The house was some way down and was rather unusually extensive, the main entrance being particularly high and wide. It was evidently intended for the passage of goods vehicles belonging to various warehouses, now closed, which were ranged round the large courtyard and bore names of firms, some of them familiar to K. from bank business. Examining these external details more closely than he usually would, he stayed for a while at the courtyard entrance. Nearby on a chest sat a barefooted man reading a newspaper. Two boys were rocking backwards and forwards on a handcart. An anaemic-looking young girl in a bedjacket stood by a pump and kept her eyes on K. as the water streamed into her can. In a corner of the courtyard a line on which the clothes were already hung out to dry was being strung between two windows. A man stood below and directed the work with occasional shouts.

K. turned to the stairs to go to the room where the examination would take place, then he stopped, for in addition to these stairs he saw in the courtyard three other flights of stairs and, apart from these, a little passage at the end of the courtyard seemed to lead to a second courtyard. He was annoyed that they had not given him more exact information about where the room was, they were really treating him with peculiar negligence or indifference; he intended to stress this fact vehemently and distinctly. In the end he went up the first stairs after all and turned over in his mind the remark made by the warder Willem to the effect that the law court is drawn to guilt – from which it must follow that the investigation chamber must be on the staircase K. had chosen at random.

On the way up he disturbed a lot of children playing on the stairs who glowered at him as he stepped through their ranks. 'If I come here again at any time,' he said to himself, 'I'll either have to bring sweets to win them over or a stick to beat them with.' Just before reaching the first floor he even had to wait a moment for a marble to stop rolling, two small boys with the artful faces of mature rogues holding him meanwhile by the trousers; if he had shaken them off he could have hurt them, and he feared their outcry.

The real search began on the first floor. As he could not after all ask for the investigating commission he invented a joiner called Lanz – the name occurred to him because this was the name of the captain, Frau Grubach's nephew – and his idea was to ask at all the apartments if a joiner called Lanz lived there, so that he could get an opportunity to look into the rooms. But this was possible anyway because nearly all the doors were open and children were running in and out. Most were small rooms with a single window, and cooking was going on in them as well. Many of the women had a baby on their arm and were working at the stove with their free hand. Adolescent girls apparently dressed only in aprons rushed about more actively than anybody. In all rooms the beds were still in use; sick people lay there, or others still asleep, or people stretched out fully dressed. Where an apartment door was shut, K. knocked and asked if a joiner named Lanz lived there. Most often the door was opened by a woman who listened to the question then turned to address someone just getting out of bed: 'The gentleman wants to know if a joiner named Lanz lives here.' 'A joiner named

Lanz?' asked the person from the bed. 'Yes,' said K. although it was obvious the investigating commission was not here, and so his business was finished. Many thought it must be very important for K. to find the joiner called Lanz, thought about it for some time, mentioned a joiner whose name, however, was not Lanz or had a name which remotely resembled Lanz, or they went to consult neighbours or took K. to a door some distance away where they thought such a man might be living as a sub-tenant or where there was someone who might be able to give better information than they could. In the end there was hardly any need for K. to ask his question: he was taken in this way through all the floors. He now regretted his plan, which had at first seemed so practical. Before reaching the fifth floor he made up his mind to give up the search, said goodbye to an amiable young workman who wanted to take him higher, and started downstairs. But then the futility of the whole exercise infuriated him; he went back again and knocked at the first door on the fifth floor. The first thing he saw in the little room was a large wall-clock which showed it was already ten. 'Does a joiner called Lanz live here?' he asked. 'Please come in,' said a young woman with lustrous black eyes who was busy washing children's garments in a tub, and she pointed with her wet hand to the open door of the adjoining room.

K. had the impression he was walking into a

great assembly. A crowd of the most varied people – nobody bothered about the one who now came in – packed a medium-sized room with a gallery running round just under the ceiling, this too filled with people who could stand only in a bent posture, their heads and backs pressed against the ceiling. K., for whom the atmosphere was too stuffy, stepped out again and said to the young woman, who must have misunderstood him: 'I asked about a joiner, a certain Lanz.' 'Yes,' said the woman, 'please go in.' K. would probably not have done as she said, had the woman not gone up to him, put her hand on the door-handle, and said: 'After you, I must shut this door. Nobody else may go in.' 'Very sensible,' said K., 'but it's already too full.' But he then went in all the same.

Between two men talking right by the door – one was making a gesture with both hands outstretched as if paying out money, the other looked him keenly in the eye – a hand reached out for K. It was a small boy with red cheeks. 'Come on, come on,' he said. K. let himself be led off by him. It became apparent that through the seething mass there was a narrow space, possibly a dividing line between two factions; this supposition was supported by the fact that in the nearest rows to right and left K. saw hardly a single face turned towards him but only the backs of people directing their words and gestures to people in their own faction. Most were dressed in black, in long and

47

ancient Sunday-best coats which hung on them loosely. These clothes baffled K.; but for them he would have taken this for a local political meeting.

At the far end of the hall, to which K. was taken, stood a very low and equally overcrowded platform. A small table was set across it, and behind this, near the edge of the platform, sat a short, stout, wheezing man, talking and laughing uproariously with another standing behind him who had one elbow propped on the back of the chair and had crossed his legs. Now and then he threw an arm into the air as if caricaturing somebody. The boy who brought K. had difficulty making himself heard. He had already gone up on tiptoe twice in an effort to pass on his message, without being noticed by the man above. Only when one of the people on the platform drew his attention to the boy did the man turn towards him and lean down to listen to his softly spoken report. Then he pulled out his watch and looked quickly at K.: 'You should have been here an hour and five minutes ago,' he said. K. was about to answer but had no time, for hardly had the man spoken than there was a general hum of disapproval from the right side of the hall. 'You should have been here an hour and five minutes ago,' the man now repeated in a raised voice, and now he also looked down quickly into the hall. At once the hum of disapproval grew stronger and, as the man said nothing more, it died down only slowly. It was much quieter in the hall now than when K. had come in. Only the people in the gallery were still talking. As far as could be seen in the semi-darkness up there, through the haze and dust, these seemed to be worse dressed than the people below. Some had brought cushions to put between their heads and the ceiling so as not to rub themselves sore.

K. had made up his mind to observe rather than to speak, so he put forward no defence of his alleged late arrival, and merely said: 'Even if I've come late, I'm here now.' A burst of applause followed, this too from the right half of the hall. 'These people are easy to win over,' thought K., who was disturbed only by the silence in the left half of the hall, which was directly behind him and from which only a few isolated handclaps were heard. He wondered what he could say to win them all over at the same time or, if that were not possible, to win the others over for the time being at least.

'Yes,' said the man, 'but I'm no longer obliged to examine you' – again the buzz, but this time its import was not clear, for the man continued, with a dismissive wave of his hand to the people – 'but today I'll make an exception and do it all the same. But such lateness must not happen again. And now step forward!' Someone jumped down from the platform to make room for K., who went up. He stood pressed against the table; the crush behind him was so great that he had to lean back against it if he was not to push the examining magistrate's table and even the man himself off the platform.

The examining magistrate paid no attention to this but sat comfortably enough in his chair and, after a final word to the man behind him, picked up a small notebook, the only object on his table. It was like a school exercise-book, old, misshapen through much use. 'Right,' said the examining magistrate, who was leafing through the book and now turned to K. with the air of making an assessment: 'You are an interior decorator?' 'No,' said K., 'I am senior administrator in a large bank.' This answer provoked such a hearty laugh from the right faction down below that K. had to laugh too. The people put their hands on their knees and shook as if they were having severe attacks of coughing. Even a few in the gallery laughed. The examining magistrate, who had become very angry and probably had no power over the people down below, tried to compensate for this by attacking the gallery; he jumped to his feet and threatened the people in the gallery, and his normally unobtrusive eyebrows swelled out until they were bushy, black, and huge over his eyes.

The left half of the hall was, however, still silent, the people there stood in rows with their faces turned towards the platform and listened to the words being exchanged up there as quietly as they listened to the noise of the other faction; they even tolerated contacts here and there between individual members from their ranks and members of the other faction. The people of the left faction, who incidentally were less numerous, might have been fundamentally just as unimportant as those of the right faction, but their calmness made them seem more important. When K. now began to speak, he was convinced he was saying what they were thinking.

'Your question, sir, as to whether I am an interior decorator – or rather, you didn't ask, you told me so outright – typifies the whole nature of these proceedings instituted against me. You may object that these are not proceedings at all. You are absolutely right, for they are only proceedings if I recognize them as such. But I do recognize them now, for the moment anyway, out of pity, so to speak. You have to regard them with pity if you're going to pay any attention to them at all. I'm not saying the proceedings are slapdash, but this is the expression I'd like to offer you for your private consideration.'

K. broke off and looked down into the body of the hall. What he had said was cutting, more cutting than he had intended, but it was true. It should have been greeted with some applause, but everyone was quiet, evidently waiting with keen anticipation for what was to come; perhaps in this silence there was brewing an outburst which would bring everything to an end. It was disturbing that the door at the end of the hall opened just at this moment to admit the young washerwoman who had probably finished her work and who, in spite of all her precautions, attracted several glances. Only the examining magistrate gave K. unqualified pleasure, for his words seemed to have made an immediate impact on him. Until now he had listened on his feet, for K.'s speech had taken him by surprise when he had risen to threaten the gallery. Now, while there was a pause, he resumed his seat slowly, as if he did not want this to be noticed. Probably in order to compose his features he picked up the notebook again.

'That doesn't help,' K. continued. 'Your little book, sir, confirms what I say.' Pleased at hearing only his own calm words in that strange assembly, K. even ventured to snatch the notebook without ceremony from the examining magistrate and hold it aloft in his fingertips as if to show his revulsion, dangling it by one of the middle pages so that the closely written pages, stained and yellow-edged, were hanging down on either side. 'These are the examining magistrate's records,' he said, and he let the book fall on the table. 'Please carry on reading it, sir; this account book doesn't worry me a bit, even though it's inaccessible to me since I can only touch it with two fingertips.' It could only be a sign of deep humiliation, or at least that is how it had to be construed, that the examining magistrate picked up the book where it had fallen on the table, tried to put it into some kind of order, and once more set about reading it.

The eyes of the people in the front row were fixed so eagerly on K. that he looked down at them for a little while. Without exception they were elderly men; some had white beards. Were these perhaps the crucial ones who could influence the whole assembly, whose members had not been stirred even by the humiliation of the examining magistrate out of the inertia into which they had sunk since K. had spoken?

'What has happened to me,' K. went on, more quietly than before, constantly scanning the faces in the front row; this gave his words an appearance of distraction. 'What has happened to me represents of course only one individual case, and as such it's not very important since I don't take it too seriously, but it's typical of the proceedings instituted against many people. I speak here for those, not for myself.'

He had raised his voice without being aware of it. Somewhere a man clapped with hands held high and shouted: 'Bravo! Why not? Bravo! And bravo again!' Some of the ones in the front row ran their hands through their beards, but none turned round in response to this shout. K. did not attach importance to it either, but was encouraged by it all the same; he no longer thought it necessary that all should applaud, it was enough if most of them began to think about the business and if only an occasional one were won over by persuasion.

'I'm not out for success as an orator,' said K., following up this reflection, 'and I don't suppose it's attainable for me either. The examining magistrate is probably a much better speaker; it's part of his job, after all. All I want is public discussion of a public outrage. Listen: I was arrested about ten days ago. I can laugh about the fact of the arrest itself, but that's not the point. I was pounced on in bed in the early morning; perhaps – and after what the examining magistrate has said, this possibility can't be excluded – perhaps the order had been given to arrest some interior decorator who is just as innocent as I, but they came for me. The room next to mine was taken over by two ill-mannered warders. If I'd been a dangerous bandit they could not have taken greater precautions. These warders were degenerate scum too; they talked my head off, they fished for bribes, they tried to take my clothes and underwear from me by false pretences, they asked me for money, supposedly to supply me with breakfast after they had shamelessly gobbled up my own breakfast before my very eyes. That wasn't enough. I was taken to a third room to face the supervisor. It was the room of a lady for whom I have much respect, and I had to look on as this room was to some extent, because of me and yet through no fault of mine, polluted by the presence of these warders and the supervisor. It wasn't easy to remain calm. But I managed it and, quite calmly, I asked the supervisor – if he were here he'd have to confirm this – why I had been arrested. And what was the answer of this supervisor whom I still see before me, sitting in the chair of the lady

I've mentioned, a picture of mindless arrogance? Gentlemen, in effect he gave me no answer; perhaps he really knew nothing, he had arrested me and that satisfied him. He had in fact done something else and introduced into that lady's room three minor employees of my bank who spent their time handling and disarranging photographs, the property of the lady. The presence of these employees had another purpose too; they, like my landlady and her maidservant, were to spread news of my arrest, damage my public reputation and in particular undermine my position at the bank. Now nothing of all this has been achieved in the slightest degree; even my landlady, a quite simple person – I'd like to mention her name here with due honour: she is called Frau Grubach – even Frau Grubach was intelligent enough to see that such an arrest has no greater meaning than an attack in the street by undisciplined young thugs. I repeat – I've suffered only a bit of trouble and passing annoyance from the whole thing, but couldn't it have had worse consequences?'

As K. broke off here and glanced at the silent examining magistrate he thought he saw him looking at someone in the crowd as if giving a signal. K. smiled and said: 'Here next to me the examining magistrate is just giving one of you a secret signal. So there are people among you who take their orders from up here. I don't know if the signal is supposed to produce hissing or applause and, by giving the game away before I have to, I deliberately renounce any possibility of finding out what the signal means. It's a matter of complete indifference to me, and I publicly authorize the examining magistrate to issue his orders to his paid assistants down there openly by word of mouth instead of through secret signals, by saying "Hiss now!" or, the next time, "Applaud now!"'

The examining magistrate shifted about in his chair with embarrassment or impatience. The man behind, with whom he had been in conversation earlier, bent down to him again, either to encourage him or to give some particular advice. Down below, people were conversing quietly but in a lively way. The two factions, who had previously seemed to have such differing opinions, were now mingling with each other; some people pointed with their fingers at K., others at the examining magistrate. The misty haze in the room was extremely tiresome; it even prevented him getting a clear view of those standing at a distance. It must have been a particular nuisance for the people in the gallery. They had to direct questions in a low voice to the participants in the assembly to discover what was going on, all the time shooting nervous side-glances at the examining magistrate. The answers were given just as quietly behind the shield of a raised hand.

'I've almost finished,' said K. and, since there was no bell, he struck the table with his fist and this startled the examining magistrate and his advisers out of their huddle for a moment. 'I can distance myself from the whole business, so I'm able to judge it calmly; and you, if you have any interest in this supposed court, will learn something to your advantage if you listen to me. I'll ask you to postpone until later any discussion among yourselves of what I have to say, because I haven't much time and I'll be going away soon.'

There was immediate silence, so completely did K. dominate the assembly. They did not all shout at once, as they had at the beginning, there was not even any more applause, but people seemed already won over, or well on the way to it.

'There is no doubt,' said K. very quietly, for he was pleased by the closely attentive attitude of the whole assembly; from this silence rose a buzz which was more exciting than the wildest applause. 'There is no doubt that behind all the utterances of this court, and therefore behind my arrest and today's examination, there stands a great organization. An organization which not only employs corrupt warders and fatuous supervisors and examining magistrates, of whom the best that can be said is that they are humble officials, but also supports a judiciary of the highest rank with its inevitable vast retinue of servants, secretaries, police officers and other assistants, perhaps even executioners – I don't shrink from the word. And the purpose of this great organization, gentlemen? To arrest innocent persons and start proceedings against them which are pointless and mostly, as in my case, inconclusive. When the whole organization is as pointless as this, how can gross corruption among the officials be avoided? That's impossible, not even the highest judge could manage that. That's why warders try to steal the very clothes arrested persons are wearing, that's why supervisors break into other people's houses, that's why innocent men, instead of getting a hearing, are humiliated in front of large gatherings. The warders told me about depots where the property of arrested persons is held. I would like to see these depots where the hard-earned assets of those arrested are allowed to rot, when they are not stolen by thieving depot officials.'

K. was interrupted by a shriek from the end of the hall. He shielded his eyes to see what it was, for the gloomy daylight made the haze dazzling white. It involved the washerwoman, recognized by K. as a likely source of disturbance as soon as she came in. Whether she was to blame now was not clear. K. could see only that a man had drawn her into a corner by the door and was pressing her against his body. But it was not she who was shrieking but the man; he had opened his mouth wide and was looking up at the ceiling. A small circle had formed round the pair, and the nearby people in the gallery seemed pleased that the gravity K. had introduced into the meeting had been interrupted in this way. K.'s first impulse was to run to the spot, and he thought everybody would want to have order restored and at least have the couple thrown out of the hall, but the front rows stayed put, nobody moved and nobody would let K. through. On the contrary, he was obstructed; old men held up their arms, and somebody's hand – he did not have time to turn round – seized him from behind by the collar. K. was not actually thinking of the couple now; he felt as if his freedom were being restricted, as if he were really being arrested, and he sprang recklessly down from the platform. Now he stood face to face with the crowd. Had he misjudged these people? Had he overestimated the effect of his speech? Had they hidden their true feelings while he was speaking and had they had enough of this dissimulation now that he had presented his conclusions? What faces these were around him! Small dark eyes flashed from side to side, cheeks sagged as they do in alcoholics; their long beards were stiff and sparse, and when they ran their hands through them they seemed to be growing claws, not combing beards. But under the beards – and this was K.'s real discovery – badges of various sizes and colours glittered on coat collars. Everybody had these badges, as far as one could see. All were connected, these apparent factions to right and left, and when he suddenly turned he saw the same badges on the collar of the examining magistrate, who was looking down calmly with his hands in his lap. 'Ah!' cried K., and he threw his arms up in the air – this sudden realization demanded space – 'You are all officials of course, I see now; you are the corrupt gang I was talking about, you've all squeezed in here as listeners and snoopers, you've pretended to form factions and one of these applauded just to test me; you were out to learn how to lead innocent people astray. Well, you haven't spent your time here in vain, I hope. Either you've been entertained at the idea that anyone could expect you to defend innocence or – get away or I'll hit you,' cried K. to a trembling old man who had come very close to him, 'or you've really learned something. And with that I wish you joy in your trade.' He quickly took his hat, which was lying near the edge of the table, and pushed his way to the exit amid general silence, at any rate the silence of utter surprise. But the examining magistrate seemed to have been even quicker than K., for he was waiting for him at the door. 'One moment,' he said. K. stopped but did nor look at the examining magistrate. He looked at the door, whose handle he already held. 'I only wanted to draw your attention to the fact' said the examining magistrate 'that today, although you may not be conscious of it yet, you have deprived yourself of the advantage which a hearing invariably confers on a person under arrest.' K. laughed into the door. 'You blackguards!' he shouted. 'I make you a present of all your hearings.' He opened the door and hurried down the stairs. Behind him rose the hum of an assembly which had come to life again and was probably about to discuss the events in the manner of a students' seminar.

IN THE EMPTY ASSEMBLY HALL –
THE STUDENT – THE OFFICES

During the following week K. waited from day to day for a fresh notification. He could not believe his refusal to attend hearings had been taken literally, and when the expected notification had not arrived by Saturday evening he assumed he was tacitly summoned to appear again in the same house and at the same time. So on Sunday he went there again, this time going straight upstairs and along the corridors. A few people who remembered him called out greetings from their doorways, but he had no need to inquire of anyone now and soon came to the right door. In reply to his knock the door was opened instantly, and without looking round at the familiar woman standing by the door he made straight for the next room. 'There's no session today,' said the woman. 'Why isn't there a session?' he asked, and was reluctant to believe it. But the woman convinced him by opening the door of the next room. It was indeed empty, and in its empty state it looked even more wretched than on the previous Sunday. On the table, which was in the same position on the platform, there were a few books. 'Can I look at the books?' asked K., not because he was particularly curious but only so as not to have had a completely wasted journey. 'No,' said the woman, and she closed the door again, 'that's not allowed. The books belong to the examining magistrate.' 'I see,' said K., and he nodded. 'The books must be law books and it's characteristic of this judicial system that a man is condemned not only when he's innocent but also in ignorance.' 'It's like that,' said the woman, who had not understood him properly. 'Right, so I'll be going now,' K. said. 'Can I give the examining magistrate a message?' asked the woman. 'You know him?' K. asked. 'Of course,' said the woman. 'My husband is a court usher.' Only now did K. notice that the room, in which there had been only a wash-tub the last time he was there, was now a fully furnished living-room. The woman saw his surprise and said: 'Yes, we live here rent-free, but we have to clear the furniture out on days when sessions are held. My husband's job has many disadvantages.' 'I'm not so much surprised about the room,' said K. as he looked at her disapprovingly, 'as at the fact that you are married.' 'Are you perhaps referring to what happened at the last session, when I interrupted your speech?' asked the woman. 'Of course,' said K., 'today that's all in the past, almost forgotten, but at the time it really infuriated me. And now you yourself say you are a married woman.' 'It was no disadvantage to you to have your speech cut short. People were passing very unfavourable judgements on you afterwards.' 'That may be,' said K., trying to turn the conversation, 'but that doesn't excuse you.' 'I am excused in the eyes of all who know me,' said the woman. 'The man who was embracing me then has been pursuing me for a long time. Not everybody may think I'm attractive, but I am for him. I have no protection; even my husband has become reconciled to it now; if he wants to keep his job he has to put up with it, for that man is a student and will probably reach a position of great power. He is always after me; he only went away just before you arrived.' 'It all hangs together,' K. said. 'It doesn't surprise me.' 'Do you want to improve things here?' asked the woman slowly, looking at K. searchingly as if she were saying something which held danger both for herself and for him. 'I gathered that from your speech, which pleased me personally very much. I admit I heard only part of it. I missed the beginning and during the last part I was on the floor with the student.' 'It's so disgusting here, isn't it?' she said after a pause, and she took K. by the hand. 'Do you think you'll manage to make an improvement?' K. smiled and turned his hand a little in her soft hands. 'Really,' he said, 'it's not my job to make an improvement here, as you put it, and if you were to say that to the examining magistrate, for instance, you would be ridiculed or punished. In fact, I would never have got mixed up voluntarily in these things, and

64

my sleep would never have been troubled by the need to make improvements in this judicial system. But because I was allegedly arrested – I am under arrest, in fact – I've been forced to intervene here, indeed in my own interest. But if I can be of any help to you while I'm doing this, I shall naturally be very pleased to be of service. Not only out of human compassion but because you can be of help to me too.' 'But how could I do that?' asked the woman. 'By showing me the books there on the table, for example.' 'But of course,' cried the woman, and she quickly pulled him along behind her. They were old, well-worn books; one cover had almost disintegrated in the middle, the sections hung together by threads. 'How dirty everything is here,' said K., shaking his head, and before he could reach for the books the woman wiped the dust off with her apron, superficially at least. K. opened the top book, to reveal an indecent picture. A man and a woman were sitting naked on a sofa; the artist's vulgar intention was clear enough, but his incompetence was so great that in fact all that could be seen was a man and a woman projecting their gross physique out of the picture, sitting rigidly upright and, because of false perspective, finding the greatest difficulty in turning towards each other. K. looked no further but merely opened the second book at the title page. It was a novel called *The Torments Grete Had to Suffer from Her Husband Hans*. 'So these are the law books studied here,' K. said. 'It's by people like this I'm supposed to be judged.' 'I'll help you,' said the woman. 'Do you want me to?' 'But could you really do that without putting yourself in danger? After all, you said just now your husband is very dependent on his superiors.' 'I want to help you all the same,' said the woman. 'Come, we must talk about it. Don't say any more about the danger to me, I'm only afraid of danger where I have it in mind to fear it. Come!' 'You have beautiful dark eyes,' she said when they had sat down and she was looking up into K.'s face. 'I'm told I have beautiful eyes too, but yours are much more beautiful. I noticed them, by the way, as soon as you walked in here for the first time. That's why I came into this assembly room later. I never do that usually and in a sense it's forbidden to me.' 'So that's how it is,' thought K., 'she is offering herself to me, she is depraved like everybody here. She has had enough of the law officers, which is understandable, so she welcomes any stranger she fancies with a compliment to his eyes.' And K. stood up without a word, as if he had uttered his thoughts out loud and so explained his behaviour to the woman. 'I don't believe you can help me,' he said. 'To be able to help me properly you'd have to have contacts with high officers. But you probably know only the minor employees who mill round here in droves. I'm sure you know these very well and could achieve a lot with them, I don't doubt that, but the most tremendous achievement with them would have absolutely no effect on the final outcome of my case. And in this way you would have lost some friends. I don't want that. Carry on with the relationship you've enjoyed so far with these people; it seems to me you really need that. I say this not without regret for, to return your compliment in some form, you too appeal to me, especially when you look at me in that sad way, as you're doing now: there's really no reason for that. You belong to the group of people I must fight against, and you are quite at home with them. You are even in love with the student or, if you don't love him, you do at least prefer him to your husband. It was easy to tell that from what you said.' 'No,' she cried and from her sitting position she seized K.'s hand, which he did not withdraw quickly enough, 'you can't go away now, you can't go away with a false opinion of me. Could you really go away now? Am I really so worthless that you don't even want to do me the favour of staying for a little while?' 'You misunderstand me,' said K. and he sat down. 'If you really want me to stay, I'll stay with pleasure. I have time to spare. I came here expecting there would be a hearing today. What I said earlier was only meant as a request not to undertake anything for me in connection with my case. But that should not offend you when you consider I don't care about the outcome of my case, and a conviction will only make me laugh. That's assuming there ever will be a definite conclusion to the proceedings – which I very much doubt. My belief is that the case has already been dropped because of laziness or negligence or perhaps even fear on the part of the officials, or will be dropped quite soon. Of course it's also possible they'll pretend to pursue the case further in the hope of getting a bigger bribe. That's a waste of time, I can tell you now, because I never pay bribes to anyone. All the same, you could do me a favour by telling the examining magistrate or anyone else who likes to spread important news that I'll never be persuaded to pay a bribe, not even by the tricks with which these gentlemen are probably so well supplied. Their efforts would be quite in vain, you can tell them that candidly. But of course they may perhaps have already noticed this themselves, and even if this isn't the case, I don't care so very much whether they find it out now. It would spare these gentlemen some work and of course save me unpleasantness, which I would, however, willingly bear if I knew that at the same time it would be a lash for their backs. And I'll take good care that's what it will be. Do you really know the examining magistrate?' 'Of course,' said the woman. 'He was the first one I thought of when I offered you my help. I didn't know he is only a minor official, but as you say so it must probably be true. All the same I think the report he sends up to higher authorities must have some influence. And he writes so many reports. You say the officials are lazy; certainly not all of them are, and especially this examining magistrate isn't; he writes a lot.

Last Sunday, for instance, the session went on until evening. Everybody went away, but the examining magistrate remained in the hall. I had to fetch him a lamp. I had only a small kitchen lamp, but he was satisfied with that and immediately began to write. In the meantime my husband had arrived; he happened to be off duty that Sunday. We brought the furniture in, put the room straight again, then neighbours came and we talked by the light of a candle; in short, we forgot all about the examining magistrate and we went to bed. In the night, it must have been far into the night, I suddenly wake up; the examining magistrate is standing by our bed, shielding the lamp with his hand so that no light falls on my husband – a needless precaution because my husband sleeps so soundly that not even the light would have woken him. I was so startled I could have screamed, but the examining magistrate was very kind, urged me to be careful, whispered to me that he had been writing until now, was returning the lamp to me, and that he would never forget the picture I made lying asleep. I'm telling you all this just to let you know the examining magistrate does in fact write many reports, especially about you, for your examination was certainly one of the main events of Sunday's session. Such lengthy reports can't after all be completely without significance. And in addition to that you can also see from this incident how the examining magistrate fancies me and it's just now in these early days (he must have just noticed me) that I can have the greatest influence over him. Yesterday he sent me a present of silk stockings through the student, who works with him and in whom he has great confidence, ostensibly because I keep the assembly chamber clean and tidy, but that's only a pretext; this work is my duty, after all, and my husband gets paid for it. They are lovely stockings, look . . .' She stretched out her legs, pulled her skirt up as far as her knees, and looked at the stockings. 'They are lovely stockings, but really too exquisite and not right for me.'

She suddenly broke off, put her hand on K.'s hand as if to reassure him, and whispered: 'Quiet, Bertold is watching us!' K. slowly raised his eyes. A young man was standing at the door of the assembly chamber; he was small, his legs were not quite straight, and he had attempted to give himself dignity by wearing a short, sparse, reddish beard, through which he was constantly running his fingers. K. looked at him with interest; this was of course the first student of the unknown jurisprudence he had encountered man to man, so to speak, a person who some day would probably reach high official position. But the student did not seem to bother his head about K., he just beckoned the woman with a finger withdrawn for an instant from his beard, and then went to the window. The woman leaned over K. and whispered: 'Don't be angry with me, I beg of you, and don't think badly of me. I must go to him now, this horrible man, just look at his bandy legs. But I'll come back straight away and then I'll go with you wherever you like, if you'll take me with you. You can do whatever you like with me. I'll be glad to get away from here for as long as possible, preferably for ever.' She caressed K.'s hand again, jumped up, and ran to the window. K. could not help making a grab for her hand in the empty air. The woman really tempted him; in spite of giving the matter much thought, he could not find any valid reason why he should not yield to this temptation. He was able to dismiss without difficulty the fleeting objection that the woman might be laying a trap for him on behalf of the court. How could she trap him? Was he not still sufficiently at liberty to smash the whole court with one blow, at least as it concerned him? Could he not have this slight confidence in himself? And her offer of help sounded genuine and was perhaps not without its value. And there was perhaps no better revenge he could take on the examining magistrate and his crew than to take this woman from them and keep her for himself. Then it could happen some time that, after working laboriously far into the night on lying reports about K., the examining magistrate would find the woman's bed empty. And empty because she belonged to K., because this woman by the window, this voluptuous, supple, warm body in coarse thick clothes, belonged only to him.

After disposing of his doubts about the woman

like this, K. began to feel that the whispered conversation by the window was going on too long. He knocked on the platform with his knuckles, then with his fist. The student glanced briefly at K. over the woman's shoulder but took no further notice, indeed moved closer to the woman and put his arms round her. She bent her head down low, as if she were listening to him attentively, and as she leaned down he gave her a loud kiss on the neck without any perceptible pause in what he was saying. K. saw in this a confirmation of the tyranny which, according to the complaints of the woman, the student exercised over her. He stood up and walked about the room, glancing sideways at the student and considering how to get rid of him with the least possible delay, so it was not unwelcome to him when the student, obviously annoyed by K.'s perambulation, now turning into a steady tramp, remarked: 'If you are impatient, you can go. You could have gone before this, nobody would have missed you. Yes, you should have gone in fact as soon as I came in, and in fact as quickly as possible.' Extreme rage might lie behind this remark but in it was also expressed the arrogance of a future law officer addressing a defendant he scorned. K. came to a stop near him and said with a smile: 'I am impatient, that's true, but this impatience can most easily be cured by your departure. But if you've come here to study – I've heard you are a student – then I'll willingly make room for you by going away with this woman.

Incidentally, you'll have to study a lot more before you can become a judge. I admit I don't know all the facts about your judicial system yet, but I assume it's not just a matter of making the objectionable speeches at which you are already so outrageously competent.' 'He shouldn't have been let free to run around like this,' said the student as if wanting to give the woman some explanation for K.'s insulting words. 'It was a mistake. I said so to the examining magistrate. At the very least he should have been confined to his room between hearings. Sometimes it's hard to understand the examining magistrate.' 'Idle talk,' said K., and he held out his hand to the woman: 'Come on.' 'I see,' said the student, 'no, no, you're not going to get her.' And, with a strength one would not have thought possible, coming from him, he lifted her on his arm and ran crouching to the door, looking up at her tenderly. In doing this he betrayed a certain fear of K., but all the same he ventured to provoke K. further by caressing and squeezing the woman's arm with his free hand. K. ran alongside him for a few steps, ready to seize him and, if necessary, to strangle him, when the woman said: 'It can't be helped. The examining magistrate has sent for me, so I can't go with you. This little horror . . .' As she said this she passed her hand over the student's face: 'This little horror won't let me.' 'And you don't want to be rescued?' shouted K., putting his hand on the shoulder of the student, who snapped at it with his teeth. 'No,' cried the woman, and she pushed K. away with both hands, 'no, no, not that. What are you thinking of? That would be the ruination of me. Let him be, oh please let him be. He's only obeying the orders of the examining magistrate and carrying me to him.' 'Then he can run, and I don't want to see you any more,' said K., furious with disappointment, and he gave the student a push in the back so that he stumbled for a moment but then sprang even higher with his burden out of relief at not having fallen. K. followed them slowly. He realized this was the first indubitable defeat he had suffered at the hands of these people. It was of course no reason at all for despondency; he had been defeated only because he had set out to do battle. If he stayed at home and led his normal life he was infinitely superior to any of these people and could clear them out of his way with a kick. And he pictured to himself the most ridiculous scene possible – if, for example, this pathetic student, this puffed-up child, this deformed wearer of a beard, were to kneel by Elsa's bed and beg for mercy with hands clasped in prayer. This idea pleased K. so much that he made up his mind to take the student with him sometime to see Elsa, if the opportunity arose.

K. hurried to the door out of curiosity; he wanted to see where the woman was carried to; the student was unlikely to carry her through the streets, for example, on his arm. The journey turned out to be much shorter. Just opposite the door of the apartment a narrow wooden staircase led presumably to the attic; there was a turning in it, so its destination was not visible. The student was carrying the woman up these stairs, very slowly now, and groaning, for he was weakened by the running he had done. The woman waved her hand to K. down below and tried to show by shrugging her shoulders that she was an innocent party in the abduction, but there did not seem to be much regret in this gesture. K. looked at her blankly as if she were a stranger; he did not want to show he was disappointed or that he could easily get over the disappointment.

The two had already disappeared. But K. still stood in the doorway. He had to assume the woman had not only deceived him but had also lied to him when she said she was being carried to the examining magistrate. The examining magistrate would not be sitting up in the attic, waiting. The wooden staircase explained nothing, however long one looked at it. Then K. noticed a small card by the entrance to the stairs; he went over to it and read, in a childish and unpractised script: 'Entrance to the Court Offices'. So the court offices were here in the attics of this block of flats? This was not an arrangement to inspire much respect, and it was comforting for a defendant to reflect how short of cash this court must be if its offices were located where the tenants, themselves the poorest of the poor, threw their useless junk. Of course, it was not outside the bounds of possibility that there was plenty of money available but that it was embezzled by the officials before it could be used for judicial purposes. Judging by what K. had experienced so far, this must even be very probable, but then such corruption in the court must be very debasing for a defendant yet fundamentally more reassuring than poverty in the court might be. Now K. could understand why at the first hearing they had been ashamed to summon him to appear in the attics and preferred to pester him in his apartment. But what a position K. found himself in, compared with the judge who had to sit in an attic while he himself had a spacious room at the bank with an ante-room and could look down on the busy life of the square through a huge plate-glass window. It was true he had no subsidiary earnings from bribes or misappropriations, nor could he have a woman carried to his room on a servant's arm. But K. was willing to forgo these, at least in this life.

K. was still standing by the card when a man came up the stairs, looked through the open door into the living-room, from which one could also see into the assembly hall, and finally asked K. if he had not seen a woman here a short time ago. 'You are the court usher, aren't you?' K. asked. 'Yes,' said the man. 'Ah yes, you are the defendant K., now I recognize you. You are welcome.' And he offered his hand to K., who had not expected this. 'But there's no session down for today,' said the court usher as K. remained silent. 'I know,' said K., and he examined the court usher's civilian jacket which displayed, as sole indication of official rank, two gilt buttons along with several ordinary ones, gilt buttons which seemed to have been detached from an old military greatcoat. 'I spoke to your wife a short time ago. She is no longer here. The student has carried her off to the examining magistrate.' 'You see,' said the usher, 'she is always being carried away from me. Today is after all Sunday and I have no official duties, but just to get me away from here they sent me on a quite unnecessary errand. And in fact I'm not sent too far, so I live in hope that if I really hurry I can still get back here in time. So I run as hard as I can, and at the office to which I'm sent I shout my message through the partly opened door so breathlessly that they'll hardly be able to understand it, then I run back again, but the student has hurried even more than I. He had of course a shorter way to come, he only had to run downstairs. If I were not so dependent on them I would have squashed that student against this wall long ago. Here, next to this notice. I dream about that all the time. Here, a little above the floor, he is pinned to the wall, arms stretched out, bandy legs in a circle, and streaks of blood all round. But so far that's only a dream.' 'There's no other way?' asked K. with a smile. 'I don't know of one,' said the usher, 'and now it's getting even worse. Until now he carried her off only for himself, now he carries her to the examining magistrate too, something I've expected for a long time.' 'But has your

77

wife no share of blame in this?' asked K., who had to control his feelings while putting this question, since he also felt very jealous. 'But of course she has,' said the usher. 'She bears the greatest share of blame. She is infatuated with him. As for him, he runs after every woman. In this building alone he has been thrown out of five apartments he has sneaked into. My wife happens to be the most beautiful woman in the whole building, and of course I'm just the one who can't defend what is mine.' 'If that's how things are, then there's nothing to be done,' K. said. 'But why not?' asked the usher. 'The student is a coward, and all that's necessary is to give him such a hiding when he tries to lay hands on my wife that he'll never dare to again. But I can't do it, and others won't do me the favour because they're all afraid of his power. Only a man like you could do it.' 'Me? Why me?' asked K. in astonishment. 'You are after all a defendant,' said the usher. 'Yes,' said K., 'but this gives me all the more reason to fear that, even if he perhaps can't influence the outcome of my case, yet he can probably exert some influence on the preliminary examination.' 'Yes, of course,' said the usher, as if K.'s view were just as correct as his own. 'But as a rule no hopeless proceedings are instituted here.' 'I don't share your opinion,' said K., 'but that won't prevent me taking the student in hand when the opportunity arises.' 'I should be most grateful to you,' said the usher rather formally; he did not seem to believe his highest wish would be gratified. 'Perhaps,' said K., 'others among your officials too, perhaps even all of them, deserve the same treatment.' 'Yes, yes,' said the usher as if they were talking about something self-evident. Then he gave K. a look which was more trusting than any he had given him so far in spite of his friendly attitude, and added: 'There's always a rebellion going on.' But the conversation seemed to have become a bit uncomfortable for him, and he broke it off by saying: 'Now I have to report to the offices. Do you want to come with me?' 'I have no business there,' K. said. 'You could look at the offices. Nobody will bother about you.' 'Are they worth seeing?' asked K., hesitating but also very keen to go with him. 'Well,' said the usher, 'I thought you'd be interested.' 'Right,' said K., 'I'll come with you,' and he ran up the stairs faster than the usher.

As he went in he almost fell, because behind the door was one more step. 'They don't show much consideration for the public,' he said. 'They show no consideration at all,' said the usher, 'just look at this waiting-room.' It was a long passageway with crudely made doors leading to various compartments of the attic. Although there was no direct source of daylight the place was not entirely dark, for some of the compartments had on the corridor side instead of solid wooden walls wooden grilles which reached up to the ceiling and through which some light penetrated and through which also some officials could be seen writing at desks or standing by the grille and watching people in the corridor through the gaps. Probably because it was Sunday, there were few people in the corridor. These made a very modest impression. They sat at almost regular intervals along two rows of wooden benches against the two sides of the corridor. All were poorly dressed, though to judge from their faces and bearing, the cut of their beards and other scarcely definable details, most belonged to the upper classes. As there were no hooks for hanging clothes they had, probably following each other's example, placed their hats under the bench. When those nearest the door caught sight of K. and the usher they stood up in salutation; as the next ones saw that, they too felt they should salute, so that everybody got to their feet as the two went past. Not one of them stood completely erect; their backs were bowed, their knees bent – they stood like beggars in the street. K. waited for the usher, who was walking a little behind him, and said: 'How humbled these people must be.' 'Yes,' said the usher. 'They are defendants, all the people you see here are defendants.' 'Really?' K. said. 'Then they are colleagues of mine.' And he turned to the nearest of them, a tall, slim man whose hair was almost totally grey. 'What are you waiting for?' asked K. politely. But this unexpected question confused the man, and this was all the more embarrassing because he was obviously a man of the world who in other circumstances would be completely in command of himself and would not have surrendered easily the superiority he had gained over so many people. But here he could not even answer such a simple question and looked at the others as if it was their duty to help him and as if no answer could be expected from him if this help was not forthcoming. Then the usher stepped up and said, to reassure and encourage the man: 'The gentleman here is only asking what you are waiting for. So give him an answer.' The usher's voice, probably known to him, had a better effect. 'I am waiting . . .' he began and then stopped. Obviously he had chosen these opening words in order to give a precise answer to the question, but now could not find what was to follow. Some of the waiting people had come nearer and were standing round the group; the usher said to them: 'Back, get back, keep the corridor clear.' They retreated a little but not as far as where they had been sitting before. In the meantime the man who had been questioned had collected his thoughts and was even smiling slightly as he answered: 'I submitted some depositions of evidence respecting my case a month ago and I'm waiting for the outcome.' 'You seem to be going to a lot of trouble, aren't you?' K. said. 'Yes,' said the man, 'it's my case, after all.' 'Not everyone thinks like you,' said K. 'I for example am also a defendant, but it's as true as I'm standing here that I have neither submitted a deposition nor undertaken anything else of that kind. Do you think it's really necessary?' 'I don't know exactly,' said the man, completely uncertain again; he evidently thought K. was having a joke with him, so he would have preferred to repeat his previous answer just as it was, for fear of making some fresh mistake, but, reacting to K.'s impatient look, he said only: 'As far as I'm concerned, I've put in depositions of evidence.' 'You probably don't believe I'm a defendant?' K. asked. 'Oh yes, of course,' said the man and he stepped a little to one side, but in his answer there was no belief, only anxiety. 'So you don't believe me?' asked K., and, unconsciously provoked to it by the man's humble demeanour, he seized him by the arm as if to compel him to believe. But he did not want to hurt him and had gripped him only gently, yet in spite of that the man shrieked as if K. had taken hold of him not with two fingers but with glowing hot pincers. In the end this ridiculous shrieking made K. lose patience with him. If the man did not believe him when he said he was a defendant, all the better; perhaps he even thought he was a judge. As he was going off he grasped him even more firmly, pushed him back on to the bench, and carried on walking. 'Most defendants are so sensitive,' said the usher. Behind them all those who were waiting had now gathered round the man, who had stopped shrieking, and seemed to be questioning him closely about the incident. K. was now met by a guard, recognizable as such mainly by his sabre, whose scabbard, to judge by its colour, was made of aluminium. K. was astonished to see this and even stretched his hand towards it. The guard, who had come because of the shrieking, asked what had happened. The usher tried to reassure him in a few words, but the guard said he must look into it himself, saluted, and walked on with very hurried but very short steps, probably the result of gout.

K. did not trouble himself for long about this man and the people in the corridor, especially as, about halfway down the corridor, he saw it was possible to turn off to the right through a doorless opening. He asked the usher if this was the right way; the usher nodded, and K. turned in there. He found it tiresome to be walking always a step or two in front of the usher; it might seem, at least in this place, as if he was being escorted under arrest. So he waited now and then to let the usher come up, but the man immediately fell back again. Finally K. said, just to bring an end to his discomfort: 'I've now seen what it looks like here; I'll go now.' 'You haven't seen everything yet,' said the usher with the utmost innocence. 'I don't want to see everything,' said K., who in any case felt really tired, 'I'd like to go, how do we get to the way out?' 'You haven't lost your bearings already?' asked the usher in surprise. 'You go along here as far as the corner and then to the right along the corridor straight to the door.' 'Come with me,' said K., 'show me the way. I'll make a mistake, there are so many ways here.' 'There's only one way,' said the usher, getting a bit reproachful. 'I can't go back with you again. I have to deliver my message and I've already lost a lot of time with you.' 'Come with me,' said K. again, this time more sharply as if he had caught the usher out in an untruth. 'Don't shout like that,' whispered the usher. 'There are offices everywhere here. If you don't want to go back alone, then come a little way with me or wait here till I've delivered my message, then I'll be glad to go back with you.' 'No, no,' said K., 'I won't wait, and you must come with me now.' K. had not yet looked round the area in which he was standing; only when one of the surrounding wooden doors was opened did he look in that direction. A girl who must have been drawn to the spot by the sound of K.'s loud voice came in and asked: 'What can I do for you, sir?' In the distance behind her a man was approaching through the gloom. K. looked at the usher. This man had said no one would bother about K., and now two persons had appeared; it would not take much more for the whole body of officials to become aware of him and demand an explanation for his presence. The only comprehensible and acceptable explanation was that he was a defendant trying to find out the date of the next hearing, but he did not want to offer this explanation, particularly as it was not in accordance with the truth, for he had come only out of curiosity or (and this was even more impossible as an explanation) from a desire to ascertain whether this judicial system was just as loathsome on the inside as it appeared from the outside. And it did seem he was right in this assumption; he did not want to penetrate any further, he was constricted enough by what he had already seen, and just now he was in no fit state to cope with a senior official who might bob up from behind any door. He wanted to go, and in the company of the usher, or alone if that had to be.

But by standing there saying nothing he must be very noticeable, and indeed the girl and the usher were staring at him as if at any moment he would undergo some great transformation which they were determined not to miss. And in the doorway stood the man K. had previously noticed in the distance; he was holding the top of the low door and rocking on his toes like an impatient spectator. But it was the girl who first noticed that K.'s behaviour was due to a slight indisposition. She brought him a chair and asked: 'Won't you sit down?' K. sat down at once and propped his elbows on the arms of the chair to steady himself. 'You're a bit dizzy, aren't you?' she asked him. Her face was now close to his; it had the severe expression seen in many women when young and most beautiful. 'Don't worry about it,' she said. 'That's nothing out of the ordinary here, nearly everybody suffers an attack like this on their first visit. You are here for the first time? All right then, so it's nothing out of the ordinary. The sun strikes down on the roof-beams here and the hot timber makes the air so close and heavy. For that reason, this place is not very suitable for office premises, whatever great advantages it might have otherwise. As for the air . . . on days when large numbers of clients attend, and that's nearly every day, it's hardly breathable. When you consider too that a lot of washing is hung out here to dry – you can't really forbid the tenants to do this – then you can't be surprised if you feel a bit unwell. But one eventually gets used to the air. When you come for the second or third time you'll hardly notice the heavy atmosphere. Do you feel better now?' K. made no answer; it was too distressing to him to be put at the mercy of these people because of his sudden weakness. Also, now that he had learned the reasons for his indisposition, he did not feel better but even a little worse. The girl noticed this at once and, to give K. some relief, she took a hooked pole from against the wall and used it to push open a small skylight situated just above K. which opened out into the air. But so much soot fell in that the girl had to close the skylight again without delay and then wipe the soot off K.'s hands with her handkerchief, for K. was too exhausted to do this himself. He would have liked to sit there quietly until he had recovered enough strength to walk away, and that would happen all the sooner the less they fussed about him. But on top of this the girl now said: 'You can't stay here, we are obstructing traffic here.' K. inquired with his eyes what traffic he was obstructing. 'If you like, I'll take you to the sick-room. Please help me,' she said to the man in the doorway, and he came at once. But K. did not want to go to the sick-room, he wanted to avoid just that, being taken further, for the further he went the worse it would become. So he said, 'I can walk now,' and he stood up shakily, weakened by sitting so comfortably. But he could not stand upright. 'I can't manage it after all,' he said, shaking his head, and he sat down again with a sigh. He remembered about the usher, who could lead him out easily in spite of everything, but he seemed to have gone long ago. K. looked between the girl and man standing in front of him but could not find the usher.

'I think,' said the man, who was elegantly dressed and especially conspicuous for a grey waistcoat ending in two fashionably cut points, 'the gentleman's indisposition is due to the atmosphere in here, so it would be best, and also what he would prefer, if we don't take him to the sick-room but right out of the offices.' 'That's it,' cried K., and out of sheer joy he almost broke into the man's words, 'I'll be better at once, I'm sure. I'm not really so weak; a little support under the arms is all I need. I won't give you much trouble, it's not a long way after all, just take me as far as the door, then I'll sit on the stairs for a bit and I'll be all right in no time, I never have attacks like this, it surprises even me. I am an official too, after all, and accustomed to the air in offices, but here conditions are just too awful, you say so yourselves. So will you please be kind enough to take me part of the way, you see I feel giddy and I'm sure to be unsteady if I get up by myself.' And he raised his shoulders to make it easier for the couple to take him under the arms.

The man did not respond to this request but calmly kept his hands in his trouser pockets and laughed out loud. 'See,' he said to the girl, 'I've hit on the truth. It's only here the gentleman feels unwell, not in other places.' The girl smiled too but tapped the man gently on the arm with her finger-tips as if, by joking about K., he had gone too far. 'But what are you thinking?' said the man, still laughing. 'I'll take the gentleman out, really I will.' 'Then it will be all right,' said the girl, inclining her pretty head for a moment. 'Don't pay too much attention to his laughter,' said the girl to K., who was again staring sadly into space and seemed to require no explanation. 'This gentleman . . . but may I introduce you?' The gentleman gave his permission with a wave of the hand. 'This gentleman is our information officer. He gives waiting clients all the information they need, and as our judicial system is not very well known among the public a great deal of information is asked for. He has an answer for every question. You can test him if you ever feel like doing so. But that's not his only distinc-tion, his second distinction lies in his elegant clothes. We, that is to say the officials, decided some time ago that our information officer, who is always dealing with clients and is indeed the first to see them, should be dressed elegantly to make a suitable first impression. The rest of us, as you can see from me, unfortunately wear very shabby and old-fashioned clothes. There's not much sense in spending on clothes, since we are in these offices nearly all the time, we even sleep here as well. But, as I said, we made up our minds at one time that smart clothes were necessary for the information officer. But as we couldn't get them from our administration, which in this respect is rather peculiar, we made a collection – the clients contributed too – and bought him this fine suit and others as well. Everything was done so that he could make a good impression, but he spoils it all by laughing and he frightens people.' 'That's how it is,' said the gentleman derisively, 'but, my dear girl, I don't understand why you are telling the gentleman all our intimate secrets or rather forcing them on him, for he just doesn't want to hear them. Look at him sitting there, obviously absorbed in his own affairs.' K. did not even feel like contradicting him. The girl's intention might be good, she perhaps wanted to take his mind off things or give him an opportunity to pull himself together, but her method was wrong. 'I had to explain to him why you were laughing,' said the girl. 'It was insulting, you know.' 'I think he would forgive even worse insults if I were to take him out.' K. said nothing, he did not even look up, he tolerated the fact that these two were arguing about him as if he were an inanimate object, he even preferred this.

But suddenly he felt the information officer's hand under one arm, the girl's hand under the other. 'All right then, up, you weakling,' said the information officer. 'I thank you both very much,' said K., pleasantly surprised, and he got up slowly, himself moving the strangers' hands to the places where he was most in need of support. 'It looks,' said the girl quietly in K.'s ear as they approached the corridor, 'as if it's a matter of great importance to me to show the information officer in a good light, but I have to tell you the truth. He is not hard-hearted. It is no part of his duties to help sick clients off the premises, but he does it, as you can see. Perhaps none of us is hard-hearted, perhaps we would all like to help, but as court officials we can easily seem hard-hearted and unwilling to help anyone. That's something that worries me.' 'Wouldn't you like to sit here for a while?' asked the information officer; they had reached the corridor and were directly opposite the defendant K. had spoken to earlier. K. was almost ashamed to be seen by him. Previously he had been standing up so straight before him, now two people had to support him, the information officer was balancing his hat on outstretched fingers, his hair was disarranged and hanging down his sweating forehead. But the defendant seemed to notice nothing of this; he stood humbly by the information officer, who looked past him, and tried only to excuse his presence. 'I know,' he said, 'the reply to my submissions can't be given today. But I've come all the same. I thought I could wait here, it's Sunday, I have of course time to spare, and here I'm in nobody's way.' 'You don't have to be so apologetic about that,' said the information officer. 'Your solicitude is in fact very praiseworthy. It's true you're taking up room here unnecessarily, but as long as I'm not inconvenienced I shall not hinder you in any way from following closely the course of your business. After seeing people who neglect their duty scandalously, one learns to have patience with people like you. Do sit down.' 'He certainly knows how to talk to clients,' whispered the girl. K. nodded, then gave a start when the information officer asked him again: 'Wouldn't you like to sit down here?' 'No,' said K., 'I don't want a rest.' He had said this as firmly as possible, but in fact it would have done him good to sit down; he felt as if he were seasick. He thought he was on a ship plunging through heavy seas. It seemed to him as if water were surging against the wooden walls, a roar coming from the depths of the corridor like water flooding, over, the corridor rocking sideways and the waiting clients falling and rising on either side. All the more incomprehensible therefore was the composure of the girl and man who were escorting him. He was entirely at their mercy; if they let him go he would fall like a plank. From their little eyes they shot quick glances all round; K., was aware of their regular steps without being able to match them, for he was almost being carried from step to step. At last he noticed they were talking to him, but he did not understand what they were saying, he could hear only the noise which filled everything, with a constant high-pitched note like a siren seeming to sound through it. 'Louder,' he whispered with his head drooping, and he felt ashamed because he knew they had spoken loudly enough, even if he had not understood what they said. At last a current of fresh air came to meet him, as if the wall in front had been broken through, and he heard someone say: 'First he wants to go, then you can tell him a hundred times this is the way out and he doesn't move.' K. noticed he was by the outside door, which the girl had opened. He felt as if all his strength had suddenly returned; to get a foretaste of his liberty he quickly stepped down to the stairs and from there took leave of his companions, who were leaning down to him. 'Many thanks,' he said repeatedly, shook hands with them again and again, and only stopped when he thought he could see that they, accustomed as they were to the office atmosphere, could not endure the relatively fresh air coming from the staircase. They were hardly able to answer, and the girl would perhaps have collapsed if K. had not quickly closed the door. K. then stood still for a moment, tidied his hair with the aid of a pocket mirror, picked up his hat from the next step – the information officer must have thrown it there – and then ran down the stairs so blithely and with such lengthy jumps that he was almost worried by the sudden transformation. His usually sound constitution had never given him such surprises before. Was his body planning perhaps to start a revolution, to give him a new way of life, since he had borne the old one so effortlessly? He did not entirely reject the idea of consulting a doctor at the next opportunity; but at any rate he proposed – in this he could he his own adviser – to make better use of all Sunday mornings in future.

B.'S FRIEND

In the next few days K. found it impossible to exchange even a few words with Fräulein Bürstner. He tried to contact her in several different ways, but she always managed to avoid him. He came straight home from the office, sat on the sofa in his room without putting the light on, and concentrated on watching the hall. If the maid went past and closed the door of what seemed an empty room, he got up after a while and opened it again. In the morning he got up an hour earlier than usual in the hope of catching Fräulein Bürstner by herself before she went to the office. But none of these efforts succeeded. Then he wrote her a letter addressed to her both at the office and at her apartment in which he tried once again to justify his behaviour, offered any satisfaction she might require, promised never to overstep any bounds she might set, and asked only to be given an opportunity to speak to her sometime, especially as he could make no arrangement with Frau Grubach before consulting her first, and finally he informed her that on the following Sunday he would wait in his room all day for a sign from her that there was a possibility his request might be granted or at least for her to tell him why she could not grant his request even though he had after all promised to defer to her wishes in everything. The letters were not returned, but there was no answer either. On Sunday, however, there was a sign whose meaning was clear enough. Quite early in the morning K. noticed through the keyhole an unusual amount of activity in the hall, and this was soon explained. A teacher of French, a German girl named Montag, a feeble pale girl who limped slightly and had up to now occupied a room on her own, was moving into Fräulein Bürstner's room. Hour after hour she could be seen shuffling through the hall. There was always some item of linen or a tray-cloth or a book which had been forgotten and now had to be fetched specially and transported to its new home.

When Frau Grubach brought K. his breakfast – since the time she had so angered K. she had not delegated the least bit of service to the maid – K. could not resist speaking to her for the first time in five days. 'Why is there so much noise in the hall today?' he asked as he poured his coffee. 'Couldn't that be stopped? Does there have to be cleaning on a Sunday of all days?' Although K. did not look up at Frau Grubach, he noticed all the same that she breathed a sigh of relief. She took even these stern questions to be forgiveness or the beginning of forgiveness. 'There's no cleaning going on, Herr K.,' she said. 'It's only Fräulein Montag moving into Fräulein Bürstner's room, carrying her things there.' She said no more but waited to see how K. took it and whether he would allow her to say anything further. But K. kept her in suspense, he stirred his coffee thoughtfully with the spoon and was silent. Then he looked up at her and said: 'Have you given up that suspicion you had about Fräulein Bürstner?' 'Herr K.,' cried Frau Grubach, who had been waiting for just this question and now stretched out her clasped hands to him, 'you recently took my chance remark so seriously. I never had the remotest intention of offending you or anyone. You've known me long enough, Herr K., to be sure of that. You have no idea how I've suffered in these last few days! I, to slander my own lodgers! And you, Herr K., believed it! And said I should give you notice! Give you notice!' The final exclamation was stifled in tears; she raised her apron to her face and sobbed aloud.

'But don't cry, Frau Grubach,' said K. as he looked out of the window. He was thinking only of Fräulein Bürstner and that she had taken a stranger into her room. 'But don't cry,' he said again as he turned back to the room and Frau Grubach continued to cry. 'I didn't mean it so seriously either. We just misunderstood each other. That can happen even with old friends sometimes.' Frau Grubach moved the apron from her eyes to see whether K. was really reconciled. 'But yes, that's how it was,' said K. and, as he had concluded from Frau Grubach's behaviour that the captain had not said anything, he ventured to add: 'Do you really think I could fall out with you because of a girl I hardly know?' 'That's just it of course, Herr K.,' said Frau Grubach; it was her misfortune that as soon as she felt in any way relaxed she immediately said something tactless. 'I kept asking myself: why does Herr K. take such an interest in Fräulein Bürstner? Why does he quarrel with me because of her, although he knows an angry word from him is enough to rob me of my sleep? What I said about the Fräulein was only what I've seen with my own eyes.' K. made no reply to this; he would have driven her out of the room, had he spoken, and he did not want that. He contented himself with drinking his coffee and letting Frau Grubach feel she was unwelcome. Outside, the dragging steps of Fräulein Montag could be heard as she crossed the hall. 'Do you hear it?' asked K., waving his hand towards the door. 'Yes,' said Frau Grubach, and she sighed, 'I wanted to help her and get the maid to help her, but she's stubborn, she wants to move everything herself. I'm amazed at Fräulein Bürstner. I often regret having Fräulein Montag as a lodger, but Fräulein Bürstner is actually letting her share the room with her.' 'Don't let that worry you,' said K., crushing the residue of sugar in his cup. 'Does it mean a loss for you?' 'No,' said Frau Grubach. 'In itself it's quite welcome; it means I have a room free and can put my nephew the captain there. I've been afraid for some time he might have disturbed you when I've had to accommodate him in the living-room next door these last few days. He's not very considerate.' 'What an idea!' K. said, and he stood up. 'There's no question of that. You seem to think I'm hypersensitive just because I can't stand listening to Fräulein Montag traipsing about – she's going back again now.' Frau Grubach felt quite helpless. 'Herr K., should I tell her to postpone the rest of her move? If that's what you'd like, I'll do it at once.' 'But she has to move her things to Fräulein Bürstner's!' K. said. 'Yes,' said Frau Grubach, not quite understanding what K. meant. 'Well then,' said K., 'she has to carry them there.' Frau Grubach merely nodded. This dumb helplessness, which on the surface looked just like defiance, irritated K. even more. He began to pace up and down the room between window and door, thus depriving Frau Grubach of the opportunity of going away, as she would otherwise probably have done.

K. had just reached the door again when there was a knock. It was the maid with the message that Fräulein Montag would like to have a few words with Herr K. and that she therefore invited him to come to the dining-room where she was waiting for him. K. listened to the maid thoughtfully, then he turned to dart an almost scornful look at the astounded Frau Grubach. This look seemed to say that K. had anticipated Fräulein

Montag's invitation and that it was perfectly in keeping with the torment he had had to endure from Frau Grubach's lodgers this Sunday morning. He sent the maid back with the reply that he was coming at once, then went to the wardrobe to change his jacket, and his only response to Frau Grubach, who was quietly grumbling about this tiresome person, was to ask her to clear the breakfast things away. 'But you've hardly touched anything,' said Frau Grubach. 'Oh, do clear them away,' cried K., who felt that Fräulein Montag was somehow present in all these things and made them offensive.

As he passed through the hall he looked at the closed door of Fräulein Bürstner's room. He was not invited there, however, but to the dining-room, whose door he jerked open without knocking.

It was a very long but narrow room with a single window. There was just enough space to have two cupboards positioned obliquely in the corners by the door, while the rest of the space was taken up almost entirely by the long dining-table which stretched from the door right up to the large window, making this almost inaccessible. The table had already been laid, and for a large number of people, as nearly all the lodgers had their midday meal here on Sunday.

As K. walked in, Fräulein Montag came from the window and along the side of the table towards him. They greeted each other in silence. Then Fräulein Montag, who was holding her head uncommonly erect as usual, said: 'I'm not sure if you know me.' K. narrowed his eyes and looked at her. 'Yes, I do,' he said. 'You've been living here at Frau Grubach's for some time.' 'But I don't think you take much interest in what goes on in this house,' said Fräulein Montag. 'No,' K. said. 'Won't you sit down?' said Fräulein Montag. In silence they drew out two chairs at the extreme end of the table and sat down opposite each other. But Fräulein Montag immediately stood up again, for she had left her handbag on the window-sill and went to fetch it, dragging her way along the whole length of the room. When she returned, swinging the handbag gently, she said: 'I've been asked by my friend to have a few words with you. She wanted to come herself, but she's feeling rather unwell today. She asks you to excuse her and to listen instead to what I have to say on her behalf. In any case, she couldn't have said anything more than I shall say to you. On the contrary, I think I can say even more to you, since I am, comparatively speaking, neutral. Don't you think so too?' 'What is there to say!' answered K., who was tired of seeing Fräulein Montag staring at his lips all the time. She was trying by this means to assume control of whatever he might say. 'Evidently Fräulein Bürstner will not consent to the discussion I asked for.' 'That's true,' said Fräulein Montag, 'or rather, that's not how it is at all. You put it very bluntly. After all, consent is not generally required for discussions, nor does the opposite happen. But it can happen that discussions are not thought necessary, and that's how it is here. After what you said, I can of course speak openly. You have asked my friend in writing or by word of mouth to have a talk with you. But my friend knows – at least this is what I must assume – what this talk would be about and is therefore convinced, for reasons unknown to me, that it would serve no purpose to anybody if the talk were to take place. Incidentally, she told me about this only yesterday, and only very briefly, and said too that in any case you couldn't be attaching much importance to the talk because you thought of it only by chance, and you yourself would, even without particular explanation, come to recognize the senselessness of the whole thing, if not now then very soon. I replied that this might be true, but I felt it would be better, if the matter were to be made absolutely clear, that you should be given an explicit answer. I offered to do this, and after some hesitation my friend agreed. But I hope I've acted in your interest too, for even the smallest uncertainty in the most trifling matter is always distressing, and when this uncertainty can be easily removed, as it can in this case, it is better it should be done without delay.' 'I thank you,' K. said at once; he stood up slowly, looked at Fräulein Montag, then across the table, then out of the window – the house opposite was bathed in sunshine – and went to the door. Fräulein Montag followed him for a few steps as if she did not quite trust him. But by the door both had to step back, for it opened and Captain Lanz came in. K. was seeing him at close hand for the first time. He was a tall man of about forty with a chubby sunburnt face. He bowed slightly, to include K., then went up to Fräulein Montag and respectfully kissed her hand. He was very elegant in his movements. His courtesy to Fräulein Montag was in stark contrast to the treatment K. had afforded her. In spite of this she did not seem angry with K., for she even wanted to introduce him to the captain, or so K. believed. But K. did not wish to be introduced, he was in no mood to be polite either to the captain or to Fräulein Montag; by indulging in hand-kissing they had become in his eyes accomplices trying to keep him away from Fräulein Bürstner under the guise of perfectly innocent altruism. And K. believed he not only saw through this, he also saw that Fräulein Montag had chosen an effective if double-edged weapon. She was exaggerating the meaning of the relationship between himself and Fräulein Bürstner; above all she was exaggerating the importance of the requested interview, and at the same time she was trying to twist everything to make it appear it was K. who was doing the exaggerating. She was going to be disappointed; K. had no intention of exaggerating, he knew Fräulein Bürstner was a mere typist who could not resist him for long. When this went through his mind he deliberately ignored what he had heard from Frau Grubach about Fräulein Bürstner. He was thinking all this as he was leaving the room with hardly a gesture of farewell. He was making straight for his room, but Fräulein Montag's faint laugh from the dining-room behind him gave him the idea he could give them both a surprise, the captain as well as Fräulein Montag. He looked about him and listened in case an interruption was likely from one of the surrounding rooms. Everything was quiet, apart from the voices coming from the dining-room and Frau Grubach saying something in the passage leading to the kitchen. The moment seemed opportune. K. went to Fräulein Bürstner's door and knocked gently. As there was no reaction he knocked again, but still no answer. Was she asleep? Or was she really unwell? Or was she not answering because she guessed it must be K. who was knocking so gently? K. assumed she was not answering and knocked louder, and in the end, since his knocking had no effect, he opened the door cautiously and not without feeling that he was doing something both wrong and futile. There was nobody in the room. It hardly looked like the room as K. remembered it. Two beds were now ranged against the wall, three chairs near the door were heaped with clothes and linen, a wardrobe stood open. Fräulein Bürstner had probably gone out while Fräulein Montag was making her speeches to K. in the dining-room. K. was not really upset; he hardly expected to contact Fräulein Bürstner easily now; he had made this attempt for almost no other reason than to defy Fräulein Montag. But as he was closing the door behind him, it was all the more disconcerting to see Fräulein Montag and the captain talking together at the open door of the dining-room. Perhaps they had been standing there ever since K. had opened the door. They did not seem to be watching K., they conversed quietly, their eyes following K.'s movements only with the abstracted gaze people have when they look around during conversations. But these glances weighed heavily on K.; he hurried along close to the wall to get to his room.

THE WHIPPER

On one of the next evenings, as K. was passing along the corridor which separated his office from the main staircase – today he was almost the last to leave, only two employees in despatch were still at work by the light of a single bulb – he heard sighs from behind a door which he had always assumed concealed a lumber-room, though he had never seen the room himself. He stopped in amazement and listened again to make sure he was not mistaken. It was quiet for a while, then again there were sighs. At first he thought of fetching one of the clerks – it might be useful to have a witness – but then he was seized by such burning curiosity that he positively tore the door open. It was, as he had correctly guessed, a lumber-room. Useless old printed forms and empty earthenware inkpots were strewn beyond the threshold. But in the room itself stood three men, stooping under the low ceiling. A candle on a shelf gave them light. 'What are you doing here?' K. asked, his words tumbling out in his excitement, but not speaking loudly. The one who clearly dominated the others and first caught the eye was

105

wearing a kind of leather outfit which left his neck down to the chest and both his arms bare. He made no answer. But the two others cried: 'Sir, we are to be flogged because you complained about us to the examining magistrate.' Only now did K. see it was the warders Franz and Willem and that the third man held in his hand a cane to flog them with. 'Why,' said K. and he stared at them, 'I made no complaint, I only said what happened in my rooms. And your conduct was not blameless.' 'Sir,' said Willem, while Franz was obviously trying to shield himself behind him from the third man, 'if you knew how poorly we are paid you would judge us more favourably. I have a family to support, and Franz here was planning to get married. A man tries to make money as best he can; it can't be done just by working, even at the most strenuous job. Your fine linen tempted me; of course warders are forbidden to do what we did, it was wrong, but it's traditional that linen belongs to the warders, it has always been like that, you can believe me. It's understandable too; what importance can such things have for anyone unfortunate enough to be arrested? But if he then mentions it publicly, punishment is sure to follow.' 'I had no knowledge of what you are saying now, nor have I asked in any way for you to be punished. I was concerned about the principle.' 'Franz,' Willem turned to the other warder, 'didn't I tell you the gentleman never asked for us to be punished? Now you've heard him say he didn't even know we would have to be punished.' 'Don't let yourself be influenced by such talk,' said the third man to K., 'the punishment is as just as it is inevitable.' 'Don't listen to him,' said Willem, breaking off only to lift his hand quickly to his mouth after getting a slash of the cane across it, 'we are only being punished because you reported us. Otherwise nothing would have happened to us, even if they had found out what we had done. Can that be called justice? We two, but particularly I myself, we had proved our worth as warders over many years. You yourself would have to admit that, judged from the point of view of the authorities, we guarded you well. We had every prospect of advancement and would surely soon have become whippers like this man, who had the good fortune never to have a complaint made against him, for such a complaint comes up only very rarely. And now, sir, everything is lost, our careers are ended, we'll have to do much more menial work than that of warders and in addition we'll have this dreadfully painful whipping.' 'Can this cane really be so painful?' asked K., and he examined the cane which the whipper was swinging in front of him. 'We'll have to strip quite naked,' said Willem. 'I see,' said K., and he looked more closely at the whipper. He was tanned like a sailor and had a fierce glowing face. 'Is there no possibility these two can be spared this whipping?' he asked him.

'No,' said the whipper and he shook his head and smiled. 'Strip!' he commanded the warders. And to K. he said: 'You must not believe everything they say. They're so scared of the whipping they've already gone a bit weak in the head. What this one here, for example' – he pointed at Willem – 'said about his possible career is downright ridiculous. See how fat he is; the first strokes of the cane will be quite lost in his fat. Do you know how he got so fat? He has a habit of eating the breakfast of everyone he arrests. Didn't he eat your breakfast too? See, I told you. But a man with a belly like that can never become a whipper, that's quite out of the question.' 'But there are whippers like me,' declared Willem, who was just unfastening his trouser belt. 'No!' said the whipper, and he gave him such a cut on the neck with his cane that he cowered back. 'You are not to listen, just get undressed.' 'I'd pay you well if you let them go,' said K., and without looking at the whipper – such transactions are best conducted with averted eyes on both sides – he took out his wallet. 'I suppose you want to report me too,' said the whipper, 'and get me whipped as well. No, no!' 'But be reasonable,' K. said. 'If I had wanted to have these two punished, I wouldn't be trying to buy them off now. I could just close this door, not bother to see or hear anything further, and go home. But I'm not doing that. On the contrary, I'm serious about wanting to let them go free. If I'd thought they might be punished or even could be punished, I

108

would never have mentioned their names. As it happens, I don't think they are guilty; it's the organization which is guilty, the senior officers who are guilty.' 'That's how it is,' cried the warders, who immediately got a cut across their backs, now bare. 'If you had a senior judge here under your cane,' said K., and as he spoke he pressed down the cane which was just being raised again, 'I wouldn't try to stop you letting go. On the contrary, I would pay you to make a good job of it.' 'What you say sounds credible,' said the whipper, 'but I won't be bribed. I am appointed to whip, so I whip.' The warder Franz, who until now had kept in the background, perhaps hoping K.'s intervention might have a favourable result, now came to the door dressed only in his trousers, fell to his knees, hung on to K.'s arm and whispered: 'If you can't get him to spare both of us, at least try to get him to let me off. Willem is older than I and less sensitive in every respect, and he had a minor whipping some years ago too, but I've never been disgraced, and I acted as I did only because of Willem, who is my teacher for better or worse. Down below in front of the bank my poor sweetheart is waiting to hear the outcome. I am so miserably ashamed.' He used K.'s jacket to dry the copious tears on his face. 'I'm not waiting any longer,' said the whipper. He raised the cane with both hands and went to work on Franz while Willem cowered in a corner and watched secretly without daring to turn his head. The scream

109

uttered by Franz rose up in one unchanging note; it did not seem to come from a man but from a tortured instrument. The whole corridor rang with it, and it must surely be audible throughout the whole building. 'Don't scream!' shouted K., who could not contain himself, and as he was looking anxiously in the direction from which the clerks must come he bumped against Franz, not roughly but roughly enough to throw the semi-conscious man over until he was convulsively scouring the floor with his hands. But he did not escape the blows, the cane reached him on the floor too, and as he writhed under it, the tip swung rhythmically up and down. And already a clerk was appearing in the distance, and a few steps behind him a second. K. had quickly slammed the door shut, gone over to a nearby window overlooking the courtyard and opened it. The screaming had stopped completely. To prevent the clerks coming too near he called out: 'It's me.' 'Good evening, sir,' they called back. 'Has anything happened?' 'No, no,' answered K., 'it was only a dog howling in the courtyard.' As the clerks still did not move he added: 'You can go back to work.' To avoid having to get into a conversation with the clerks he leaned out of the window. When, after a while, he looked down the corridor again, they had gone. But K. now stayed by the window; he did not dare go into the lumber-room, and he did not want to go home either. The courtyard into which he was looking down was small and square, there were offices all round, all the windows already dark apart from a gleam of moonlight in the top ones. K. made a strenuous effort to pierce the darkness in one corner of the courtyard where some hand-carts had been jumbled together. It distressed him that he had not been able to stop the whipping, but it was not his fault he had failed: if Franz had not screamed – of course it must have been very painful, but in a decisive moment a man must control himself – if Franz had not screamed, K. would, at least in all probability, have found another way to persuade the whipper. If all the lower officials were riff-raff, why should the whipper, who held the most inhuman office, prove an exception? K. had noticed how his eyes lit up when he saw the banknote. Obviously he had gone on with the whipping just to increase the bribe a bit. And K. would not have been stingy, he was really anxious to have the warders let off. Having begun his battle against the corruption of this judicial system, it was natural he should intervene from this quarter too. But as soon as Franz began to scream, everything was of course at an end, K. could not allow the clerks and possibly all kinds of other people to come and surprise him in his dealings with the crew in the lumber-room. Nobody could expect K. to make this sacrifice. If he had thought of doing that, it would almost have been simpler to take his own clothes off and offer himself to the whipper as substitute for the warders. In any case, the whipper would certainly not have accepted this replacement, because by doing so he would be guilty of a severe violation of duty, without any advantage, and probably a double violation, for as long as K. was the subject of court proceedings his person must be inviolable to all employees of the court. Of course, special regulations might also be in force here. In any event, K. had not been able to do anything but slam the door shut, although this by no means removed all the dangers threatening him. That he had bumped into Franz was regrettable and could only be excused by his agitation.

In the distance he heard the footsteps of the clerks; so as not to attract their attention he closed the window and walked towards the main staircase. At the door of the lumber-room he stopped for a moment and listened. Everything was quiet. The man could have beaten the warders to death: they were entirely at his mercy. K. had already put his hand out to grasp the knob but then withdrew it. He could help nobody now, and the clerks would soon be there, but he vowed to bring the matter out into the open and, as far as lay in his power, bring down appropriate punishment on the really guilty persons, the senior officials, not one of whom had yet ventured to face him. As he went down the flight of steps outside the bank he looked carefully at all the passers-by, but even in the furthest distance there was no sign of a girl who might be waiting for someone. Franz's assertion that his sweetheart was waiting for him was now exposed as a lie, pardonable of course, whose sole purpose was to arouse greater sympathy.

And on the next day too K. could not get the warders out of his mind. He could not concentrate on his work and, in order to complete it, he had to stay in the office a little longer than on the previous day. As he passed the lumber-room on his way home, he opened the door as if by habit. What he saw, instead of the darkness he expected, completely robbed him of his composure. Everything was unchanged, just as he had found it on opening the door the previous evening. The printed forms and inkpots just over the threshold, the whipper with his cane, the warders still fully dressed, the candle on the shelf, and the warders began to wail and cried out: 'Sir!' K. instantly slammed the door and even beat it with his fists, as if it could be made more secure that way. Almost in tears, he ran to the clerks who were working quietly at the copying machine and now stopped in astonishment. 'It's about time that lumber-room was cleared out!' he cried. 'We're being smothered in filth.' The clerks were willing to do it the next day; K. nodded – now, so late in the evening, he could not compel them to tackle the job, as he had originally thought of doing. He sat for a moment so as to have the clerks near him for a while, riffled through some papers, hoping to give the impression he was checking them, and then, because he realized the clerks would not venture to depart when he did, he went home tired out and with his mind blank.

THE UNCLE – LENI

O ne afternoon – K. happened to be very busy just before the post despatch – his uncle Karl, a small landowner from the country, pushed his way into the room between two clerks bringing papers for signature. K. was less alarmed at seeing him than he had been by the thought that he would come. It was inevitable that his uncle would come; K. had been sure of it for about a month now. Even as long ago as that he had pictured him, a little bent, the crushed panama hat in his left hand, the right stretched out to him from far off and thrust across the desk with reckless haste as he upset everything in his path. His uncle was always in a hurry, for he was pursued by the unfortunate idea that on each visit to the capital – which never lasted longer than one day – he must get through all the business he had planned, and also not lose any opportunity for a chance conversation or transaction or amusement that might present itself. In this he had to be assisted in every possible way by K., who was particularly indebted to his uncle, as the latter had been his guardian; in addition, K. had to put him up for the night.

As soon as they had greeted each other – he had no time to sit down in the armchair K. offered him – he asked K. if they could talk in strict privacy. 'It is necessary,' he said, swallowing painfully, 'it is necessary for my peace of mind.' K. immediately sent the clerks out of the room with orders not to admit anyone. 'What's this I've heard, Josef?' cried his uncle when they were alone. He sat down on the desk and, to make himself more comfortable, stuffed a batch of papers under him without looking at them. K. said nothing; he knew what was to come but, suddenly released from the tension of hard work as he was, he surrendered to a pleasant feeling of weariness and looked out of the window at the opposite side of the street; from where he sat only a small triangular section could be seen, a stretch of blank house-wall between two shop windows. 'You look out of the window!' shouted his uncle, flinging his arms up. 'For heaven's sake, Josef, answer me. Is it true? Can it be true?' 'My dear uncle,' said K., shaking off his mood of abstraction, 'I don't know what you're talking about.' 'Josef,' said his uncle in a tone of reproof, 'you've always spoken the truth, as far as I'm aware. Am I to interpret your last words as a bad omen?' 'I can guess what you're talking about,' said K. obediently. 'You've probably heard about the proceedings against me.' 'That's it,' said his uncle, nodding slowly. 'I've heard about the proceedings against you.' 'From whom then?' K. asked. 'Erna told me in a letter,' said the uncle. 'She hardly sees you. You don't have much to do with her, I'm sorry to hear, but all the same she heard about it. I got her letter today, so of course I came immediately. For no other reason, but that seems enough of a reason. I can read you the part of the letter that concerns you.' He took the letter out of his wallet. 'Here it is. She writes: "I have not seen Josef for a long time. I was at the bank last week, but Josef was so busy I wasn't allowed in. I waited nearly an hour but then had to go home because I had a piano lesson. I would have liked to talk to him – perhaps there will be an opportunity soon. For my name-day he sent me a big box of chocolates, it was very kind and thoughtful. I forgot to tell you about it the last time I wrote, I've remembered about it only now that you ask. In the boarding-house chocolates disappear in a flash, you know; you've hardly realized you've had a present of chocolates before they've all gone. But I wanted to tell you something else about Josef. As I said, I wasn't allowed in to see him at the bank, and this was because he was discussing business with a gentleman. After I had been waiting quietly for some time I asked a clerk if the transaction would last much longer. He said that might well be, for it concerned legal proceedings being taken against the senior administrator. I asked what sort of proceedings these were and whether he was not making a mistake, but he said

117

he wasn't making a mistake, it concerned proceedings and in fact grave proceedings, more than that he did not know. He himself would like to help the senior administrator, for he was a very fair and upright man, but he did not know how to go about it and could only hope that influential gentlemen would take up his cause. This would certainly happen too, and everything would come to a satisfactory conclusion, but he could sense from the senior administrator's mood that just now things were not going well. Of course I didn't attribute too much importance to what he said and tried to reassure this naïve clerk and told him not to talk to other people about it. I think it's all just idle talk. All the same, perhaps it would be a good thing if you, dearest Father, could look into it on your next visit. It will be easy for you to find out more about it and, if it's really necessary, to intervene through your wide circle of influential friends. But if it should not be necessary (and this is of course most probable) it will at least give your daughter an early opportunity to embrace you, and this would give her such pleasure." A good child,' said the uncle when he had finished reading, and he wiped some tears from his eyes. K. nodded. Because of the distractions of recent days he had completely forgotten about Erna, he had even forgotten her birthday, and the story about the chocolates had evidently been invented just to put him in a good light with his uncle and aunt. It was very touching, and the theatre tickets he now resolved to send her regularly were certainly not sufficient reward, but he did not feel in the mood for visits to her boarding-house and conversations with a little seventeen-year-old schoolgirl. 'And what do you say now?' asked the uncle, who had forgotten all his hurry and excitement while reading the letter and now seemed to be reading it over once again. 'Yes, uncle,' said K., 'it is true.' 'True?' cried his uncle. 'What's true? How can it be true? What sort of proceedings? Surely not criminal proceedings?' 'Criminal proceedings,' K. answered. 'And you're calmly sitting here with criminal proceedings hanging over you?' shouted the uncle, his voice getting louder all the time. 'The calmer I am, the better it will be for the outcome,' said K. wearily. 'Don't be alarmed.' 'That doesn't reassure me,' cried the uncle. 'Josef, dear Josef, think of yourself, of your relations, of our good name. Until now you've been an honour to us, you can't now bring shame on us. Your attitude . . .' he looked at K. with his head sharply tilted, '. . . doesn't please me. No innocent man who still has energy left behaves like this. But tell me quickly what it's all about, so that I can help you. It's to do with the bank, of course?' 'No,' K. said, and he stood up. 'But you are talking too loudly, dear uncle. My clerk is probably listening at the door. I don't like that. We'd better go somewhere else. I shall then answer all your questions to the best of my ability. I know very well I owe the family an explanation.' 'True,' cried the uncle, 'very true. But hurry, Josef, hurry.' 'I only have to give a few instructions,' said K., and he phoned for his deputy, who entered some moments later. In his agitation the uncle gestured to indicate it was K. who had sent for him, though there was no doubt about this. Standing in front of his desk, K. took up various documents and explained to the young man, who was listening in an aloof but attentive manner, what still had to be dealt with today during his absence. His uncle's presence was unsettling because he was standing there with an expression of alarm on his face and biting his lips nervously; not indeed listening, but the fact that he looked as if he were listening was unsettling enough. And then he started walking up and down the room and would stop now and then by a window or in front of a picture and break out with various exclamations such as 'It's utterly incomprehensible to me' or 'Now just tell me what will become of this'. The young man behaved as if he noticed nothing; he listened calmly to K.'s instructions until he had finished, made a few notes, and departed after bowing to K. and to the uncle, who happened to have his back turned towards him and was looking out of the window and crumpling the curtains with his outstretched hands. The door had hardly closed before the uncle cried out: 'At last that jumping jack has gone; now we can go too. At last!' There was unfortunately no way of getting the uncle to suspend his questions about the case in the entrance hall, where some officials and messengers were standing around and where the deputy manager was just crossing the floor. 'Well, Josef,' his uncle began, acknowledging with the faintest of gestures the bows of the people standing around, 'now tell me honestly what sort of proceedings these are.' K. made some inconsequential remarks and laughed a little too; only when they got to the steps did he explain to his uncle that he had not wanted to speak openly in front of those people. 'Quite right,' said the uncle, 'but now talk.' With head inclined and puffing jerkily on a cigar, he listened. 'The first thing is, uncle,' said K., 'this is not a case being tried before the usual kind of court.' 'That's bad,' said the uncle. 'How do you mean?' K. said, and he looked at his uncle. 'That it's bad, that's what I mean,' the uncle repeated. They were standing on the flight of steps leading down to the street; as the porter seemed to be listening, K. took his uncle down and they were swallowed up in the busy traffic. The uncle, who had slipped his arm through K.'s, no longer asked so urgently about the proceedings, they even walked for a while in silence. 'But how did it happen?' the uncle asked finally, stopping so abruptly that the people walking behind him dodged to one side in alarm. 'Such things don't happen all at once, they're brewing for a long time, there must have been indications; why didn't you write to me? You know I'll do anything for you. To some extent I am still your guardian, and until today I was proud of that fact.

Of course I'll still help you even now, but now that the proceedings are under way it is very difficult. The best thing at any rate would be for you to take a short leave of absence and come to us in the country. You've lost a little weight too, I notice it now. In the country you will regain your strength. That will be a good thing because you'll certainly have to face a lot of pressure. But apart from that you'll be distanced to some extent from the court. Here they have all sorts of powerful legal instruments they will of necessity use against you, even automatically; in the country they would first have to appoint agents or try to get at you by letter, by telegraph, by telephone. That naturally weakens the effect; it doesn't set you free but lets you breathe.' 'They could forbid me to go,' said K., who felt somewhat attracted by his uncle's line of thought. 'I don't think they'll do that,' said his uncle thoughtfully. 'They wouldn't lose much authority by your departure.' 'I thought,' K. said, and he took his uncle by the arm to prevent him stopping, 'you would attribute even less significance to the whole matter than I, and now you yourself are taking it so seriously.' 'Josef,' cried the uncle and tried to free his arm so that he could come to a stop, but K. would not let him, 'you are a changed man. You always had such tremendous intelligence, and are you going to lose it now? Do you want to lose your case? Do you know what that means? That means you will simply be eliminated. And that all your relatives will be dragged down with you or at least deeply humiliated. Josef, pull yourself together. Your indifference is driving me out of my mind. When I look at you I can almost believe the old saying "To stand accused is to stand to lose".' 'My dear uncle,' said K., 'your excitement is pointless, and it would make no sense in me either. Cases are not won by excitement, do give me credit for my practical experience, just as I have always respected yours and still do, even when it surprises me. Because you say the family would be detrimentally affected by the case – which I for my part don't understand at all, but that's by the way – I'll gladly follow your advice in all things. Only I don't think a spell in the country would be advantageous in the way you mean it, for it would imply flight and feelings of guilt. And in addition, here I am more open to persecution, but I can also pay more attention to the case myself.' 'You are right,' said the uncle, speaking as if they were now at last coming closer in their opinions. 'I made the suggestion only because it seemed to me that if you stayed here the business would be jeopardized by your indifference and I thought it better I should act on your behalf. But if you're going to apply all your energy to the case yourself, then that of course is much better.' 'So we are agreed on that,' K. said. 'And do you have any suggestion about what I should do next?' 'I'll have to give the matter more thought, of course,' said the uncle. 'You must remember I've been living in the country now for almost twenty years without a break, and that weakens one's capacity for this kind of business. Various important connections with distinguished people perhaps more knowledgeable in this field have slackened over the years. In the country I am a bit isolated, you know that. It's only when things like this occur that one becomes conscious of it. To some extent your business came upon me unexpectedly, even if I did have a remarkable premonition of something of this sort after Erna's letter and was almost certain of it today when I saw you. But that's unimportant, the main thing now is not to lose time.' Even while talking he had stood on tiptoe to hail a taxi and now dragged K. into it, at the same time shouting an address to the driver. 'We are now going to see the advocate Huld,' he said. 'He was a colleague of mine at school. You've probably heard of him? No? But that's amazing. He has a considerable reputation as a defence lawyer and for his work on behalf of poor litigants. But I have a special regard for him as a human being.' 'I'll go along with anything you decide,' said K., although the hurried and pressing way his uncle was handling the affair made him uneasy. As a defendant it was not very gratifying to be taken to see a poor man's lawyer. 'I didn't know,' he said, 'that one could have the help of an advocate in a case like this.' 'But of course,' said his uncle, 'that goes without saying. And now tell me everything that has happened up to now, so that

I know all the details.' K. immediately began his relation of events without hiding anything; his absolute frankness was the only protest he could make against his uncle's assertion that the case was a great disgrace. He mentioned Fräulein Bürstner's name only once, in passing, but that did not qualify his frankness, for Fräulein Bürstner had no connection with the case. As he was relating the events he looked out of the window and noticed they were coming to the suburb where the court offices were located; he brought this to the attention of his uncle, who did not, however, find the coincidence particularly significant. The taxi stopped in front of a darkened house. The uncle pressed the bell at the first door on the ground floor. While they were waiting he bared his big teeth in a smile and whispered: 'Eight o'clock, an unusual time for clients to call. But Huld won't mind, as it's me.' In a peep-hole in the door two large dark eyes appeared, looked at the two visitors for a moment, and disappeared. But the door did not open. The uncle and K. confirmed to each other that they had seen two eyes. 'A new maid afraid of strangers,' said the uncle, and he knocked again. The eyes appeared once more, and now they almost seemed melancholy, but that may have been an illusion caused by the naked gas jet which hissed noisily above their heads but threw little light. 'Open up!' cried the uncle, and he gave the door a blow with his fist. 'We are friends of the advocate.' 'Herr Huld is ill,' came a whisper from behind them. In a doorway at the far end of the short passage stood a man in a dressing-gown who was giving them this information in an extremely quiet voice. The uncle, already enraged at being kept waiting so long, spun round and cried: 'Ill? You say he's ill?' And he went towards the man almost threateningly, as if the man himself were the illness. 'The door is open,' said the man, who pointed to the advocate's door, gathered his dressing-gown around him, and disappeared. The door really had been opened; a young girl in a long white apron – K. recognized the dark, slightly bulbous eyes – was standing in the hall with a candle in her hand. 'Open it quicker next time,' said the uncle by way of greeting as the girl made a slight curtsy. 'Come on, Josef,' he said to K., who was squeezing slowly past the girl. 'Herr Huld is ill,' said the girl as the uncle was without hesitation hurrying towards a door. K. was still looking with interest at the girl, who had turned to lock the apartment door again. She had a round face like a doll's; not only were her pale cheeks and chin rounded but also her temples and the margins of her forehead. 'Josef!' cried the uncle again, and he asked the girl: 'It's the heart trouble?' 'I think so,' said the girl. She had found time to precede them and open the room door. In a corner of the room to which the candlelight had not yet penetrated a face with a long beard rose up in bed. 'Leni, who's there?' asked the advocate, too dazzled by the candle to recognize his visitors. 'It's your old friend Albert,' said the uncle. 'Ah, Albert,' said the advocate, falling back against the pillows as if there were no need for pretence before these visitors. 'Are things really so bad?' asked the uncle, and he sat down on the edge of the bed. 'I don't believe it. It's a touch of your heart trouble and will pass like all the earlier attacks.' 'Possibly,' said the advocate softly, 'but it's worse than it has ever been before. I'm breathless, I don't sleep at all, and I'm losing strength every day.' 'I see,' said the uncle, and he fixed the panama hat firmly on his knee with his big hand. 'That's bad news. But are you getting the right treatment? And it's so dreary here, so dark. It's a long time since I was here last. It seemed a lot more cheerful then. And your little maid here doesn't seem very jolly, or she is hiding it.' The girl was still by the door, holding the candle. As far as one could see from her veiled glance, she was looking at K. rather than at the uncle, even when the latter now spoke of her. K. was leaning on a chair he had placed near the girl. 'When somebody is as ill as I am,' said the advocate, 'it's necessary to have peace and quiet. It's not dreary to me.' After a short pause he added: 'And Leni looks after me well. She's a good girl.' But the uncle was not convinced by this; he was visibly prejudiced against the nurse and though he made no answer to the patient he followed the nurse with a stern look as she now went to the bed, put the candle down on the bedside table, leaned over the patient and whispered to him as she rearranged the pillows. He almost forgot every consideration for the sick man, walked backwards and forwards behind the nurse, and it would not have surprised K. if he had seized her by the skirt from behind and dragged her away from the bed. K. himself was content to be a silent observer; as far as he was concerned, the advocate's illness was not entirely unwelcome, for he had not been able to counter the enthusiasm his uncle had developed for his case, and he was happy to see this enthusiasm diverted without any prompting from him. Then the uncle said, perhaps only to annoy the nurse: 'Fräulein, please leave us alone for a while. I want to discuss a personal matter with my friend.' The nurse, who had stretched far over the sick man and was smoothing the sheet by the wall, merely turned her head and said very calmly, in striking contrast to the enraged stutter and rush of words from the uncle: 'You can see how ill my master is. He can't discuss any matters.' She had probably echoed the uncle's words without thinking, but even a detached observer might have taken it as mockery; the uncle of course jumped as if he had been stung. 'You damned woman,' he said, almost incomprehensible in the first spluttering of anger. K. took fright even though he had expected something like this, and he ran to his uncle with the firm intention of clapping both hands over his mouth. But fortunately the sick man rose up behind the girl; the uncle made a sullen grimace as if he were swallowing something horrible and then said, more calmly: 'We haven't taken leave of our senses yet. If what I'm asking were not possible, I would not ask for it. Please go now.' The nurse was standing erect by the bed and had turned to face the uncle; K. thought he could see that with one hand she was caressing the hand of the advocate. 'You can say anything in front of Leni,' said the advocate as if making an urgent request. 'I'm not the one concerned,' said the uncle, 'it's not my secret.' And he turned away as if he did not wish to enter into further negotiations but was allowing a little time for consideration. 'So whom does it concern?' asked the advocate in a fading voice and he lay back again. 'My nephew,' said the uncle. 'I've brought him with me.' And he made the introduction: 'Josef K., senior administrator.' 'Oh,' said the sick man in a more lively way, extending his hand to K., 'forgive me, I didn't even notice you. Go, Leni,' he said to the nurse, who made no further objection, and he gave her his hand as if they were taking leave before a long absence. 'So you haven't come,' he said at last to the uncle, who had come nearer now that he had been placated, 'to see me because I'm ill, you've come on business.' It was as if the very idea of a sick visit had stupefied the advocate up to now; he looked much stronger now, stayed propped up on one elbow, which must have been rather a strain, and persistently tugged at a strand of hair in the middle of his beard. 'You look much better already,' said the uncle, 'now that witch has gone.' He stopped and whispered: 'I bet she's listening,' and sprang to the door. But there was nobody at the door. The uncle returned, not disappointed, for the fact that she was not listening seemed to him even more offensive, but certainly annoyed. 'You are misjudging her,' said the advocate without offering any further defence of the nurse; perhaps he wanted to suggest by this that she had no need of defence. But he went on, in a much more sympathetic tone: 'As far as your nephew's business is concerned, I would count myself lucky if my strength proved equal to this extremely difficult task, but I'm very much afraid it will not be sufficient, though at any rate I shall leave no avenue unexplored. If my efforts are not enough you could of course call in somebody else. To be honest with you, I find the matter so interesting that I can't bring myself to give up this chance to participate. If it's too much for my heart, then at least it could hardly find a more worthy occasion on which to give up completely.' K. could not understand a word of this speech. He looked to his uncle for an explanation, but the uncle, with the candle in his hand, was sitting on the bedside table from which a medicine bottle had already rolled down to the carpet and was nodding at everything the advocate said, agreeing with everything and looking now and again at K. as if inviting similar agreement from him. Had his uncle perhaps briefed the advocate earlier about the case? But that was impossible; everything that had gone before ruled this out. So he said: 'I don't understand . . .' 'Yes, perhaps it is I who have misunderstood you?' asked the advocate, just as astonished and embarrassed as K. was. 'I was perhaps too hasty. What did you want to talk to me about? I thought it was in connection with your case?' 'Of course,' said the uncle, who then asked K.: 'What do you want to do?' 'Yes, but how do you know about me and my case?' K. asked. 'Ah, I see,' said the advocate with a smile. 'I am an advocate, after all, I move in legal circles, people talk about various cases, and the more striking ones are remembered, particularly when they concern the nephew of an old friend. But there's nothing remarkable in that.' 'What do you want to do?' asked the uncle again. 'You are so restless!' 'You move in these legal circles?' asked K. 'Yes,' said the advocate. 'You're asking questions like a child,' said the uncle. 'With whom should I associate if not with men in my profession?' added the advocate. It sounded so irrefutable that K. did not answer. 'But you work at the court in the Palace of Justice, not at the one in the attics,' was what he wanted to say but could not bring himself actually to say it. 'You must take into account,' continued the advocate in the tone of one making in passing a superfluous explanation of self-evident fact, 'you must take into account that through all these contacts I get great advantages for my clients, in fact in many respects – but one shouldn't mention this too often. Of course I've been a bit handicapped because of my illness, but all the same I do have visits from good friends connected with the court and get to know quite a lot. Get to know more perhaps than some who are in the best of health and spend all day at the court. For instance, I am at this moment enjoying a visit from a dear friend.' And he pointed to a dark corner of the room. 'Where is he?' asked K. almost rudely in the first shock of surprise. He looked round uncertainly. The light from the tiny candle fell far short of the opposite wall. And something really began to stir there in the corner. By the light of the candle which the uncle was now holding on high an elderly gentleman became visible, sitting there at a small table. He could not have been breathing, to be unnoticed for so long. Now he stood up ceremoniously, obviously not at all pleased that attention had been drawn to him. It was as if he wanted to fend off with his hands, which he moved like abbreviated wings, all introductions and greet-ings, as if he had no wish to disturb the others in any way by his presence, and asked only to be returned to the darkness where his presence might be forgotten. But that could not be granted him now. 'You took us by surprise, you see,' said the advocate by way of explanation, encouraging the gentleman with a gesture to come nearer, and this he did, slowly and looking around hesitantly, yet with a certain dignity. 'The director of the court offices . . . Ah, yes, forgive me, I haven't introduced you . . . This is my friend Albert K., his nephew Josef K., this is the director of the court offices. The director is kindly paying me a visit. The value of such a visit can only be truly appreciated by those who know the law and are aware how inundated with work the director is. Well, he came all the same, we were having a quiet conversation, as far as my weakness allowed; we had not actually forbidden Leni to admit visitors because we did not expect any, but we thought we would be left to ourselves; then you came hammering at the door, Albert, and the director moved into the corner with his chair and table, and now it seems possible we have a topic of common concern to discuss – that is, if we are to discuss – that is, if we are all agreed – so it might be profitable for us to move close together again. Herr Director . . .' he said, bowing his head and smiling obsequiously and pointing to a chair by the bed. 'Unfortunately I can only stay a few minutes longer,' said the director amiably, and he stretched out comfortably in the armchair and looked at his watch. 'Business calls. But I don't want to miss the opportunity to get to know a friend of my friend.' He inclined his head slightly to the uncle, who seemed most gratified to have made this new acquaintance but was prevented by his temperament from giving expression to feelings of obligation and greeted the director's words with loud self-conscious laughter. A horrible sight! K. was able to observe it all quietly, for nobody paid attention to him. Now that he had been drawn forward, the director dominated the conversation, as he was obviously used to doing. The advocate, whose initial weakness had perhaps been merely a device to deter the new visitors, listened attentively with his hand to his ear, while the uncle as candleholder – he was balancing the candle on his leg, the advocate glancing at him now and again apprehensively – was soon free of embarrassment and merely delighted by the director's words and the gentle undulation of hands with which he accompanied them. K., who was leaning on a bedpost, was completely ignored by the director, perhaps intentionally, and he served the old gentleman only as a listener. In any case, he hardly knew what the conversation was about and was thinking either about the nurse and the harsh treatment she had received from his uncle or about whether he had not seen the director somewhere before, perhaps indeed in the assembly at his first examination. Even if he were perhaps mistaken, the director could have fitted admirably into that front row of participants at the sitting, the elderly men with their sparse beards.

Then a noise from the hall like a crash of china made them all listen. 'I'll go and see what has happened,' said K., and he walked out slowly as if giving the others a chance to call him back. Hardly had he entered the hall and was trying to get his bearings in the darkness than the hand with which he was still holding the door was touched by a small hand, much smaller than K.'s, and the door was gently closed. It was the nurse, who had waited there. 'Nothing's happened,' she whispered. 'I threw a plate against the wall just to bring you out.' In his embarrassment K. said: 'I was thinking of you too.' 'All the better,' said the nurse. 'Come on.' After a step or two they came to a door made of frosted glass which the nurse opened for him. 'Do go in,' she said. It was evidently the advocate's office. As far as one could see in the moonlight, which was now illuminating only a small rectangular patch of floor by each of the two tall windows, it was fitted out with ponderous old furniture. 'Over here,' said the nurse, and she pointed to an old settle with a carved wooden back. K. was still looking round the room after he had sat down; it was a large, lofty room; the clients of this legal-aid lawyer must feel quite lost in it. K. imagined he could see their timid steps as they approached the enormous desk. But then he forgot all about this, he had eyes only for the nurse, who was sitting really close to him, almost pressing him against the arm of the settle. 'I thought,' she said, 'you would come out to me without my having to call you. Strange. When you came in you stared at me all the time, then you let me wait. By the way, call me Leni,' she added quickly without a pause as if no instant of this conversation was to be wasted. 'Gladly,' said K., 'but as far as the strangeness is concerned, Leni, that's easily explained. First, I had to listen to the

135

old men chattering and couldn't just go off without giving a reason, and secondly I'm not bold, shy rather, and you, Leni, didn't look as if you could be won just at one stroke.' 'It's not that,' said Leni, putting her arm over the side of the settle and looking at K., 'but you didn't like me and probably don't like me even now.' 'Liking would not be saying much,' said K. evasively. 'Oh!' she said and seemed to gain a certain ascendancy because of K.'s remark and this brief exclamation. So K. kept quiet for a while. Now that he had got used to the darkness in the room he could distinguish various details in the furnishings. He was especially struck by a large picture which hung to the right of the door. He leaned forward to see it better. It showed a man in the robes of a judge. He was sitting on a high throne-like chair whose gilding stood out prominently in the picture. The unusual thing about it was that this judge was not sitting in tranquil dignity but was pressing his left arm hard against the back and side of the chair and had his right arm completely free and just held the other arm of the chair with this hand as if his intention was to spring up at the next moment with a violent and perhaps outraged gesture to utter something decisive or even pronounce judgement. The defendant had to be imagined at the foot of the steps, whose upper ones, covered in yellow carpet, were visible in the picture. 'Perhaps that is my judge,' said K., and he pointed his finger at the picture. 'I know him,' said Leni, and she too looked up at the picture. 'He often comes here. This picture was painted when he was young, but he could never have looked like that, he's really a tiny little man. In spite of that he had himself stretched out in the picture, because he's madly vain like everybody here. But I'm vain too and miserable because you don't like me.' The only reply K. made to this last remark was to put his arm round Leni and draw her towards him; she quietly put her head on his shoulder. But with reference to the rest of what she had told him he said: 'What is his rank?' 'He is an examining magistrate,' she said, taking the hand K. had put round her and playing with his fingers. 'Again only an examining magistrate,' said K. in disappointment, 'the top officials keep out of sight. But he's sitting in a judge's chair.' 'That's just make-believe,' said Leni, bending her face over K.'s hand, 'actually he's sitting on a kitchen chair with an old horse-blanket thrown over it.' And she added slowly: 'But do you have to be thinking about your case all the time?' 'No, not at all,' K. said. 'I probably give too little thought to it.' 'That's not the mistake you're making,' said Leni. 'You are too obstinate, that's what I've heard.' 'Who told you that?' K. asked. He felt her body against his chest and looked down on her thick, firmly shaped dark hair. 'I would give too much away if I told you that,' answered Leni. 'Please don't ask for names but get rid of your failings. You can't defend yourself against this

137

court; you have to acknowledge your guilt. Acknowledge your guilt at the first opportunity. Only then are you given the possibility of escape, only then. But even that isn't possible unless you get outside help, but you mustn't worry about this help: I'll give you that myself.' 'You know a lot about this court and the deceptions that go with it,' K. said, and because she was pressing too heavily against him he lifted her on to his knee. 'It's nice like this,' she said; and she made herself comfortable on his knee, smoothing her skirt down and putting her blouse straight. Then she clasped both hands round his neck, leaned back, and looked at him for a long time. 'And if I don't acknowledge my guilt, then you can't help me?' asked K. speculatively. I seem to recruit female helpers, he thought with some surprise, first Fräulein Bürstner, then the court usher's wife, now this little nurse who seems to have an inexplicable desire for me. She's sitting here on my knee as if it's the only place for her! 'No,' answered Leni and she shook her head slowly, 'then I can't help you. But you don't really want my help. It's of no importance to you. You're stubborn, you won't be persuaded.' After a while she asked: 'Have you a girlfriend?' 'No,' K. said. 'But you must have,' she said. 'Yes, I have actually,' K. said. 'Just think – I've denied her existence and I even carry her photo with me.' At her request he showed her Elsa's photo, and curled on his knee she studied the picture. It was a snapshot of Elsa taken as she was spinning at the end of a dance she liked to perform at the wine tavern, her skirt still billowing up in folds flung out by the pirouette, her hands on her hips and head held rigidly aloft as she looked sideways, laughing. From the picture it was impossible to tell whom she was laughing at. 'She is tightly laced,' said Leni, and she pointed to the place where she thought this could be seen. 'I don't like her. She is clumsy and coarse. But perhaps she's gentle and kind with you. Big strong girls like that often can't be anything but gentle and kind. But could she sacrifice herself for you?' 'No,' said K., 'she is neither gentle and kind nor could she sacrifice herself for me. But so far I've not asked her for either one or the other. In fact, I've not even looked at the picture as closely as you have.' 'You're not really very attached to her,' said Leni, 'she's not really your girlfriend.' 'But she is,' K. said, 'I don't take back what I said.' 'Even if she's your girlfriend now,' said Leni, 'you wouldn't miss her very much if you lost her or changed her for somebody else, me for instance.' 'Certainly,' said K. with a smile, 'that's conceivable, but she has one great advantage over you – she knows nothing about my case and even if she knew something about it she wouldn't give it a thought. She wouldn't try to persuade me to be submissive.' 'That's not an advantage,' said Leni. 'If she has no other advantages than that, I won't lose heart. Has she any physical defect?' 'A physical defect?' K. asked. 'Yes,' said Leni. 'You see,

I have a little one – look.' She stretched the middle and ring fingers of her right hand apart and revealed a connecting membrane of skin reaching nearly to the topmost joints of the stubby fingers. In the darkness K., did not immediately realize what she was trying to show him, so she moved his hand there to feel it. 'What a freak of nature!' said K., and he added, when he had examined the whole hand: 'What a pretty claw!' Leni looked on with a kind of pride as K. kept opening and closing the two fingers in amazement until finally he gave them a fleeting kiss and let them go. 'Oh!' she cried at once. 'You've kissed me!' With her mouth open she quickly scrambled up until she was kneeling in his lap. K. looked at her almost with consternation; now that she was so near him she gave off a bitter, provocative smell like pepper; she took his head in her hands, bent over him, and bit and kissed his neck, bit into his hair even. 'You've changed her for me!' she cried from time to time. 'You see, you've changed her for me now!' Then her knee slipped, with a stifled cry she fell almost down to the carpet, K. put his arms round her to stop her fall and was pulled down to her. 'Now you belong to me,' she said.

'This is the house-key. Come when you like,' were her parting words, and a badly aimed kiss touched his back as he went away. When he walked out of the front door a light rain was falling; he thought of going to the middle of the street to catch a last glimpse perhaps of Leni at the window when his uncle rushed out of a waiting taxi he had not noticed because of his distraction, seized him by the arms and pushed him against the house door as if he would like to nail him to it. 'Boy!' he cried. 'How could you do it? You've done terrible injury to your cause, which was going well. You sneak off with a filthy little creature who is obviously the advocate's mistress, and you stay away for hours. You don't even make an excuse, you hide nothing, no, you're quite open, you run to her and you stay with her. And in the meantime there we are sitting together, your uncle who is doing his best for you, the advocate who must be won over to your side, and above all the director, this important man who has virtual control of your case at its present stage. We are going to discuss how you can best be helped; I have to handle the advocate carefully, he must handle the director with equal tact, and you after all had every reason to support me at least. Instead of that, you stay away. In the end it can't be hidden any more. Now these are polite and civilized men, they say nothing about it, they spare me, but in the end even they can't ignore it and, as they can't talk about the matter, they fall silent. We sat there minute after minute without a word, listening to see if you would come at last. All in vain. Finally the director gets up to go; he has stayed much longer than he originally intended, he is visibly sorry for me but unable to help me, he shows indescribable kindness by waiting at the door for some time, then he goes. I of course was relieved when he went, for I could hardly breathe. All this had an even stronger effect on the invalid advocate; the good man was speechless when I took leave of him. You've probably contributed to his total collapse and thus hastened the death of a man on whom you're dependent. And I, your uncle, am left by you to wait in the rain for hours. Just feel – I am wet through.'

ADVOCATE – MANUFACTURER – PAINTER

One winter morning – outside the snow was falling in dreary light – K. sat in his office feeling utterly tired in spite of the early hour. To shield himself, from junior officials at least, he had given his clerk an order not to admit any of them as he was busy with an important piece of work. But instead of working he shuffled about in his chair, slowly pushed some objects around on his desk, and then, without being conscious of it, left his arm outstretched on the desk-top and sat motionless with his head bowed.

Thoughts about his case never left him now. Several times he had considered whether it would not be advisable to prepare a written document in his defence and lodge it with the court. His idea was to present a short account of his life and, in the case of each relatively important event, explain the reasons for his action, say whether he now thought that course of action should be condemned or approved, and give his reasons for this judgement. Such a written defence document had undoubted advantages over plain defence by an advocate who was himself not faultless. K. did not of course know what the advocate was doing; it could not be much, he had not asked to see K. for a month, and even from the earlier interviews K. had not had the impression that this man could do much for him. For one thing, he had scarcely questioned him at all. And there was so much to ask. Asking questions was the main thing. K. had the feeling he himself could ask all the pertinent questions. But the advocate just talked, instead of asking questions, or sat opposite him in silence, leaning forward across the desk a little, probably because of his weak hearing, or pulled at a strand of hair in his beard and looked down at the carpet, perhaps at the very spot where K. had been lying with Leni. Now and again he gave K. empty admonitions, the sort one gives to children. And speeches as useless as they were boring, for which K. resolved to pay nothing at the final reckoning. When the advocate thought he had humbled him enough, he usually began to give him a little encouragement. Many such cases, he said then, had been won by him either wholly or in part, cases which in reality were perhaps not as difficult as this one but in externals seemed even more hopeless. He had a list of these cases here in this drawer – at this he tapped one or other drawer in his desk – unfortunately he could not show these documents, official secrets were involved.

Nevertheless, K. would now benefit from the vast experience he had gained from all these cases. He had of course set to work at once and the first plea was almost ready. This was highly important because the first impression made by the defence often determined the whole course of the case. Unfortunately – and he must draw K.'s attention to this – the first pleas filed with the court were sometimes not read at all. They were simply added to the other documents with an indication that for the time being interrogation and observation of the defendant were more important than written material. It was also said, if the petitioner became insistent, that before the final decision when all the material had been assembled, all documents, including this first plea, would of course be reviewed in their context. But unfortunately even this was not entirely correct; the first plea was usually mislaid or completely lost, and even if kept in being until the end of the proceedings it was – so the advocate had heard, admittedly only through rumour – hardly ever read. All this was regrettable but not entirely without justification; K. should not ignore the fact that proceedings were not held in public; they could, if the court deemed it necessary, be held in public, but the law did not stipulate this. As a consequence, the written records of the court and in particular the document recording the accusation were not available to the accused and his defending counsel, so it was not known in general or at least not exactly what the first plea had to be directed against, so really it could only be fortuitous if it contained anything of significance for the case. Truly pertinent and convincing pleas could only be prepared later when through questioning of the accused the separate charges against him and their basis emerged more clearly or could be guessed at. In these circumstances the defence was naturally in an unfavourable and difficult position. But that too was intentional. The defence was in fact not really sanctioned by the law but merely tolerated, and even whether toleration could be read into the relevant clause of the law was a matter of dispute. So, strictly speaking, there were no advocates recognized as such by the court; all those who appeared before this court as advocates were basically only back-street lawyers. The effect of this on the whole profession was very degrading, and if K. happened to be visiting the court offices some time he should take a look at the advocates' room to see for himself. He would probably be shocked at the sight of the people there. The cramped low chamber allotted to them was enough to show the contempt felt for these people by the court. The only source of light was a small skylight so high up that if anyone wanted to look out – smoke from a nearby chimney would go up his nostrils and blacken his face – he would first have to find a colleague willing to take him on his back. In the floor of this chamber – to mention only one further example of these conditions – there was a big hole that had been there for more than a year, not so big that a man could fall down into it but big enough for his leg to sink right through. The advocates' room was on the second floor of the attics, so if one of them sank through, his leg would hang down into the lower attic and in fact into the very corridor where the clients were waiting. It was no exaggeration when the advocates described such conditions as scandalous. Complaints to the administration would not have the slightest chance of success, but the advocates were strictly forbidden to institute any changes in the room at their own expense. But even this treatment of the advocates had a rational basis. The aim was to eliminate all defence, the accused man must be left to his own devices. Basically not a bad principle, but nothing would be more mistaken than to infer from this that advocates for the defence were not necessary at this court. On the contrary, at no other court were they so necessary as here. For the proceedings were in general kept secret not only from the public but from the defendant too. Of course, only as far as this was possible, but it was possible to a considerable degree. The accused too had no access to the documents in the case and it was very difficult to draw conclusions from the hearings themselves about the documents on which they were based, and especially so for the defendant, diffident after all, and distracted by all sorts of worries. This is where defence counsel would intervene. As a rule defence counsel were not permitted to be present during hearings, so after each hearing they had to question the accused about the hearing, right at the courtroom door if possible, and extract from his often very jumbled reports whatever might be useful for the defence. But this was not the most important thing, since not much could be learned by this means, though of course in this as in other matters a capable man would learn more than others. But nevertheless the most important thing was the advocate's personal connections, this was where the main value of defence counsel lay. Now K. would have learned from personal experience that the lower echelons of the judicial system were not exactly perfect and included employees who neglected their duties and took bribes, so that to some degree cracks appeared in the stern structure of the court. This was where the majority of advocates forced their way in, this was where the bribing and sounding out was done, indeed there were even, in earlier times, cases where documents had been stolen. It could not be denied that for a while some surprisingly favourable results could be obtained for the accused in this way, and these petty advocates strutted around and attracted new clients, but for further progress in the case this signified nothing or at least nothing beneficial. True value was to be found only in respectable personal connections, and indeed with higher officials – by which was meant only higher officials of the lower grade. Only by this means could the progress of the case be influenced, even if imperceptibly at first, then more clearly later. Of course only few advocates could achieve this, and this is where K. had made a fortunate choice. Perhaps no more than one or two other advocates could lay claim to connections like Dr Huld's. These did not concern themselves about the lot in the advocates' room and indeed had nothing to do with them. Their connection with the court officers was all the closer because of this. It was not even always necessary for Dr Huld to attend court and wait in the ante-rooms of the examining magistrates in case these might appear, and then, depending on the mood of these gentlemen, achieve some illusory success or not even that. No, K. himself had of course seen how officials, and among them really high ones, came of their own volition, willingly gave information which was unambiguous or at least easily interpreted, discussed the next stage in the proceedings, indeed even in some individual cases allowed themselves to be won over and gladly accepted the outsider's opinion. Of course it was not advisable to place too much trust in them in this respect; however definitely they might express a new opinion more favourable to the defence, they could go straight back to their chambers and the next day hand down a court decision containing an exactly contrary opinion which was perhaps more severe on the accused than their original intention, the one they said they had utterly abandoned. There was naturally no defence against that, for what they said in private was said only in private and could not be inferred in public even if defence counsel were not constrained to retain the favour of these gentlemen for other reasons too. On the other hand it was also true that it was not only from philanthropic motives or feelings of personal friendship that these gentlemen established connections with defence counsel, of course only with highly qualified counsel; they were to a certain extent dependent on them. It was just here one could see the disadvantage inherent in a judicial organization which at its very beginnings created the secret court. Contact between officials and the public at large was non-existent; they were well equipped to handle common cases of average difficulty, a case of this kind ran its course almost of its own volition and required only a nudge here and there; faced with very simple cases however, or especially difficult ones, they were often at a loss; because they were immersed in the law day and night without a break they did not have the right feeling for human relationships, and in cases of that kind this was a severe deprivation. Then they came to the advocate for advice, and behind them would come the clerk carrying the documents which were normally so secret. At this very window you could have seen gentlemen, among them some you would least have expected to see, gazing miserably down into the alley while the advocate was studying the documents at his desk in order to offer them learned advice. It was also possible to see from these occasions how very seriously these gentlemen regarded their work and how they fell into the depths of despair when they encountered obstacles they could not overcome because of their temperament. Their position was by no means easy; one should not be unjust to them and think their position was easy. The hierarchical structure of the court was endless and beyond the comprehension even of the initiated. Court proceedings were in general kept secret from the minor officials, so they could hardly ever follow later developments in the matters they were dealing with; legal business simply appeared in their orbit and they did not know where it had come from, then it passed on, and they were not told where it was going. So the lessons to be learned from a study of the separate stages in the proceedings and from the final verdict and reasons for it were lost to these officials. They were allowed to concern themselves only with that part of the case demarcated for them by the law and knew less about later developments than defence counsel, who as a rule kept in touch with the accused until almost the conclusion of the case. So in this respect too they could learn much that was valuable from defence counsel. In view of all this, was K. still surprised at the irritability of officials, often expressed – everybody had come across instances of this – as insulting behaviour towards clients? All officials were irritable, even when they seemed to be calm. Of course, junior advocates suffered a lot because of this. For example, the following story was told – and it had the ring of truth: An elderly official, a benevolent quiet gentleman, had spent a day and a night without a break studying a difficult legal matter which had been made particularly complicated by the pleadings of advocates – these officials were really conscientious, more so than anyone else. Well, towards morning, after twenty-four hours of probably not very productive work, he went to the entrance door, stationed himself there in ambush, and threw downstairs every advocate who tried to come in. The advocates gathered below on the half-landing and discussed what they should do. On the one hand, they had no real right to be admitted, so could hardly undertake anything in law against the official. But on the other hand, each day not spent in court was a day lost to them, so it was important for them to get in. Finally they agreed they would try to tire the old gentleman out. One advocate after another was sent running up the stairs and, after a great show of what was really passive resistance, he let himself be thrown down again, to be caught by his colleagues. This lasted for about an hour, then the old gentleman, already exhausted by his night's work, got really tired and went back to his chambers. Those down below could not believe it at first and sent out a scout to look behind the door and see if the place was really empty. Only then did they go in, and they probably did not even dare to complain. For the advocates – and even the most junior could see to some extent what conditions were like – had absolutely no wish to introduce or push through improvements, while – and this was very revealing – nearly every defendant, even when quite artless, began to think about suggestions for improvement as soon as he was caught up in a case, and often wasted time and energy which could have been used more profitably in other ways. The only right thing to do was to come to terms with circumstances as they were. Even if it were possible to rectify certain details – but that was just a senseless delusion – the best one could hope for would be to achieve something for the benefit of future cases, but that would be at the expense of doing oneself immeasurable harm through attracting the particular attention of a bureaucracy which was always vengeful. Just never attract attention! One had to keep quiet, even when this went against the grain! And try to see that this great legal organism was always in a state of equilibrium, so to speak, and that anyone who independently made an alteration in his own area would be cutting the ground from under his feet and could come crashing down, while the great organism itself compensated for the slight disturbance by easily producing a replacement at another point – everything was after all connected – and remained unchanged, assuming it did not become (and this was probable) even more secretive, even more observant, even more severe, even more malevolent. One should leave the work to the advocate instead of meddling with it. Reproaches did not serve much purpose, especially when the full significance of the reasons for them could not be made clear, yet it had to be said that K. had damaged his cause badly through his behaviour towards the director. This influential man could almost be struck off the list of those who might be approached for help on K.'s behalf. He had deliberately ignored even fleeting references to the case. In many respects the officials were of course like children. Often they could be so offended by trivial things – K.'s behaviour unfortunately did not fall into this category – that they stopped talking even to good friends, turned away when they met and opposed them in every possible way. But then, surprisingly and without any obvious reason, they condescended to laugh at some little joke one had ventured to make only because everything seemed so hopeless, and they were reconciled. It was at the same time both difficult and easy to conduct business with them; there were hardly any ground rules. Sometimes one simply felt astonished that an average lifetime was long enough for the acquisition of the amount of knowledge one needed to work here with any degree of success. Of course there were depressing periods, such as everyone experienced, when one could believe nothing had been achieved, when it seemed that only those cases destined from the beginning to reach a favourable outcome had turned out well, which they would have done in any event, while all the others had been lost in spite of dancing attendance on them all the time, in spite of all effort and all the little apparent successes which gave such pleasure. Then of course nothing seemed certain any more and, if definitely asked, one would not even dare deny that some cases moving along in an entirely satisfactory way had been led off in a false direction by the advocate's intervention. Even that could be a reason for self-confidence, but it was the only one left. Advocates were especially prone to such moods – they were moods, nothing more – when a case they had taken some distance to their own satisfaction was suddenly removed from them. That must be the worst that could happen to an advocate. The case was never removed by the accused, that never happened; once an accused man had briefed a particular advocate he had to stay with him whatever happened. How could he manage by himself once he had asked for help? So that did not happen, but it did sometimes happen that the case took a direction in which the advocate was not permitted to accompany it. The case and the accused and everything were simply removed from the advocate; then the most intimate connections with officials were no help, for they themselves knew nothing. The case had entered a stage where help was no longer permitted, where it was being dealt with by inaccessible courts, where even the accused could no longer be contacted by the advocate. Then one day you could come home and find on your desk all the various pleas prepared by you for this case with such intense application and with the highest hopes; they had been returned because they could not be carried over into the new stage of the proceedings; they were worthless scraps of paper. That did not mean the case was lost, not at all, at least there was no firm basis for this assumption, it was merely that one knew nothing more about the case and would learn nothing more about it. Now such occurrences were fortunately exceptions, and even if K.'s case were such an occurrence it was at the moment very far from being at such a stage. So there were many opportunities here for the advocate to go to work and K. could be sure they would be exploited. As he had mentioned, the plea had not yet been filed, there was no hurry about that, much more important were the introductory discussions with authoritative officials, and these had already taken place. With varying success, it had to be frankly admitted. It was much better for the time being not to mention details which might have a bad effect on K. by making him either too hopeful or too depressed, but this much could be said – that some individuals had spoken out favourably and showed great willingness to help, while others had spoken less favourably but had by no means refused their assistance. The result was therefore very gratifying on the whole, but no particular conclusions should be

156

drawn from this as all preliminaries began in a similar way and it was only later developments which revealed the value of these preliminaries. At any rate, nothing had been lost yet, and if they still succeeded in winning over the director in spite of everything, then the whole affair was, as the surgeons put it, a clean wound, and future developments could be awaited with confidence.

The advocate had an inexhaustible supply of speeches like this. They were repeated at every visit. Always progress was being made, but the nature of this progress could never be communicated. Work was constantly going on with the first plea, but it was not finished, and this turned out at the next visit to have been very advantageous because this recent period would have been a very unfavourable time to file it, something nobody could have foreseen. If K., quite stupefied by the speeches, sometimes remarked that, even taking into consideration all the difficulties, things were making very slow progress, he was told progress was by no means slow, but even more progress could have been made if K. had turned to the advocate in good time. Unfortunately, however, he had neglected to do this, and this neglect would bring other disadvantages too, apart from time lost.

The only pleasant interruption at these visits was Leni, who always contrived to bring the advocate his tea when K. was there. Then she stood behind

K., apparently just looking on as the advocate bent down low over his cup with a kind of craving and poured out the tea and drank, but she was secretly letting K. take hold of her hand. There was complete silence. The advocate was drinking, K. was squeezing Leni's hand, and Leni sometimes ventured to stroke K.'s hair gently. 'You are still here?' asked the advocate when he had finished. 'I wanted to take the tea things away,' said Leni, there was a final squeezing of hands, the advocate wiped his mouth and with renewed strength he began to go on and on at K. again.

Was it consolation or despair the advocate was aiming for? K. did not know, but he soon became convinced his defence was not in good hands. Everything the advocate said might be true, even though it was transparent that he was trying as far as possible to place himself in the foreground and probably had never conducted such an important case as K.'s seemed to be in his opinion. But there was something suspect about these personal connections with officials he was constantly mentioning. Was it true they were being exploited exclusively for K.'s benefit? The advocate never forgot to remark that only minor officials were concerned, officials in a very dependent position, for whose promotion certain developments in court cases could be important. Were they perhaps using the advocate to achieve such developments, which were of course always to the disadvantage of the defendant? Perhaps they did not do that in every case, that was not probable surely, there must be cases in which they conceded advantages to the advocate for his services, since it must be in their interest to keep his reputation unblemished. If this was really how things were, how would they act in K.'s case, which, as the advocate explained, was a very difficult and therefore important case and had aroused great interest in court from its beginning? There was not much doubt about what they would do. Indications could already be seen in the fact that the first plea had still not been filed although the case had been going on for months and that the whole thing, according to the advocate, was in its early stages; this was calculated to lull the defendant and keep him in a helpless condition, suddenly to be surprised by the verdict or at the least by a declaration that an unfavourable report from the first examination had been forwarded to the higher authorities.

It was absolutely necessary for K. himself to intervene. This conviction seemed indisputable, especially when he was very tired, as he was this winter morning, with thoughts racing wildly through his head. He no longer felt the contempt he had previously had for the case. If he had been alone in the world he could easily have disregarded the case, even though it was certain the case would not then have come into existence. But now his uncle had taken him to this advocate, and family considerations played a part; his position was no longer entirely independent of the course of the case, he himself had carelessly mentioned the case in the presence of acquaintances with a certain inexplicable satisfaction, others had heard about it by unknown means, his relationship with Fräulein Bürstner seemed to fluctuate in parallel with the case – in short, he hardly had the choice now whether to accept or reject the case, he was in the middle of it and must fend for himself. If he was tired, that was unfortunate.

But for the time being there was no cause for excessive concern. He had shown his ability to work his way up in the bank in a comparatively short time to his senior position and in this position to retain the regard felt for him by all; now he had only to transfer to the case some part of the abilities which had made that possible for him, and there was no doubt that all would turn out well. Above all, if anything was to be achieved, it was necessary to reject from the start any thought of possible guilt. There was no guilt. The case was nothing but a large business deal of the kind he had so often concluded to the bank's advantage, a business deal in which there lurked, as one normally found, various dangers which just had to be warded off. To this end one should not play about with thoughts of any guilt but should concentrate as far as possible on considerations which worked to one's own advantage. Seen from this point of view, it was inevitable that he would have to take the case out of the hands of the advocate very soon, preferably this very evening. According to what the advocate had said, this was outrageous and probably very insulting, but K. could not tolerate the fact that his own efforts in the case encountered obstacles which were perhaps caused by his own advocate. But if the advocate were once shaken off, then the plea would have to be filed immediately and action taken every day if possible to see that it was taken into account. To this end it would not be enough for K. to sit in the corridor like the others with his hat under the bench. He himself or the women or other agents must pester the officials day after day and force them to sit down at their desk and study K.'s plea instead of gazing through the grille at the people in the corridor. These efforts must not be relaxed, everything must be organized and supervised, the court would for once come up against a defendant who knew how to safeguard his rights.

But although K. was confident he could carry all this out, the difficulty of drawing up the plea was overwhelming. Earlier on, about a week previously, it was only with a feeling of shame that he had thought he might sometime have to draft such a plea himself, but the thought that this could also be difficult had not crossed his mind. He recalled how one morning when he happened to be overwhelmed with work he had suddenly pushed everything to one side and taken up his writing-pad to sketch out some general ideas for such a plea, to be perhaps put at the disposal of his heavy-handed advocate, and how at that very moment the door of the manager's office had opened and the deputy manager had walked in, laughing heartily. It had been an uncomfortable moment for K., although the deputy manager had not been laughing about the plea, of which he knew nothing, but at a Stock Exchange joke he had just heard, a joke which required for its understanding a drawing which the deputy manager, taking the pencil from K.'s hand and leaning over his desk, now executed on the writing-pad intended for the plea.

Today K. was no longer conscious of shame; the plea must be drafted. If he found no time for it at the office, as was very probable, he must do it at home during the nights. If the nights were not sufficient he must take some leave. But not stop halfway – that was not only the most senseless course in business matters but always and in everything. Admittedly the plea meant an almost constant burden of work. Without having a particularly apprehensive nature one could easily come to believe that it was impossible ever to get the plea ready. Not because of laziness or cunning (only the advocate could be hampered by these) but because in ignorance of the actual accusation and even of any further charges arising from it one had to recall the most trivial actions and events of one's life, present them and review them from every angle. And furthermore, how depressing such a task was. It was perhaps a suitably puerile occupation to help a pensioner while away the long days. But now, just when he was having to concentrate all his thoughts on his work, when each hour passed with astonishing speed as he was making his way up, already posing a threat to the deputy manager; when, as a young man, he wanted to get all the enjoyment he could out of the brief evenings and nights; it was now he would have to start drafting this plea. Again his thoughts were ending in lamentation. Almost involuntarily, just to make an end to this, he felt with his finger for the button of the bell which rang in the outer office. As he pressed it he looked up at the clock. It was eleven o'clock, he had wasted two hours dreaming, a long and valuable period of time, and of course he was feeling even more jaded than before. All the same, the time had not been completely lost; he had taken decisions which could prove valuable. The clerk brought, in addition to the post, two visiting-cards from gentlemen who had been waiting to see K. for some time. These happened to be very important clients of the bank who should on no account have been kept waiting. Why did they come at such an inconvenient time and why, the gentlemen might be asking on the other side of the closed door, did the diligent K. devote the best business hours to his own private affairs? Weary from what had gone before and wearily

163

expecting what was to come, K. stood up to receive the first of them.

He was a short, cheerful man, a manufacturer K. knew well. He apologized for disturbing K. in important work, and K. for his part apologized for keeping the manufacturer waiting so long. But he spoke this apology in such a mechanical way, almost stressing the wrong words, that the manufacturer would have noticed, had he not been totally absorbed in his business interests. Instead, he rapidly produced lists and calculations from every pocket, spread these out in front of K. and explained various items, corrected a small arithmetical error he noticed even during this cursory review, reminded K. of a similar transaction he had concluded with him approximately a year before, mentioned in passing that this time another bank was making great sacrifices to secure the business, and then stopped talking in order to get K.'s opinion. And at the beginning K. had indeed followed the manufacturer's words closely, the thought of this important business engrossed him, but unfortunately this did not last; soon he stopped listening and then for a while responded to the manufacturer's louder utterances just by nodding his head, but in the end he even stopped doing that and confined himself to looking at the bald head bent over the papers and asking himself when the manufacturer would eventually realize that all his words were useless. When he now stopped talking, K. really thought at first this was to give him an opportunity to confess he was not in a fit state to listen. So it was with regret that he noticed from the expectant look of the manufacturer, obviously alert to answer all objections, that the business discussion would have to be continued. So he inclined his head as if in response to a command and began to go up and down the papers slowly with his pencil, stopping here and there to stare at a figure. The manufacturer suspected there might be objections, perhaps the figures were not explicit enough, perhaps they were not the decisive factor; at any rate the manufacturer covered the papers with his hand, moved quite close to K., and started again on a general presentation of the deal. 'It is difficult,' said K., pursing his lips, and because the papers, the only tangible element, were now concealed he sank back limply against the arm of his chair. He could only look up feebly as the door of the manager's office opened and the deputy manager appeared there indistinctly as if behind a veil. K. gave this no further thought but only observed the immediate consequence, which was a great relief to him. For the manufacturer immediately leaped out of his chair and hurried over to the deputy manager; K., however, would have liked him to be ten times more nimble, as he was afraid the deputy manager might disappear again. He need not have worried; the gentlemen met, shook hands and moved together towards K.'s desk. The manufacturer complained he had found little interest for the deal in this office, and he pointed to K. who, under the eyes of the deputy manager, was bending over the papers again. As the two then leaned against his desk and the manufacturer went about trying to win over the deputy manager, it seemed to K. that over his head two men whose size he greatly exaggerated were striking a deal about him. Slowly he tried to discover by turning his eyes up cautiously what was happening up there; he picked up one of the papers from his desk without looking, placed it on the palm of his hand and gradually raised it to the level of the two men as he himself got to his feet. He had no definite thought in mind as he was doing this but acted only because he felt this was how he must conduct himself once he had completed the great plea which was to relieve him completely of anxiety. The deputy manager, who was participating most attentively in the conversation, only glanced casually at the paper and made no attempt to read what was on it, for what was important to K. was unimportant to him, then took it from K.'s hand and said: 'Thank you, I know all about it now,' and put it back on the desk. K. gave him an angry sideways look. But the deputy manager did not notice this, or if he did he was merely amused by it; he laughed out loud several times, once reduced the manufacturer to evident chagrin through a quick-witted retort and immediately rescued him from it by raising some objection himself, finally inviting him to come to his office where they could pursue the matter to a conclusion. 'It's a very important matter,' he said to the manufacturer, 'I am fully aware of that. And my colleague' – even as he was saying this he was speaking only to the manufacturer – 'will surely be pleased if we take it over from him. This matter requires calm consideration. But he seems to be overburdened with work today, and some people have been waiting for hours in the outer office to see him.' K. just had sufficient composure to turn away from the deputy manager and direct his affable but rigid smile exclusively at the manufacturer; apart from this he did not intervene but leaned forward a little with both hands on the desk like a respectful clerk and looked on as the two gentlemen, still talking, took the papers from the desk and disappeared into the management offices. The manufacturer turned round again in the door with the observation that he was not yet saying goodbye but would of course inform Herr K. about the outcome of the discussion, and also there was something else he wanted to say to him.

At last K. was alone. He had no intention of admitting any other client to see him and was vaguely conscious how pleasant it was that the people outside thought he was still occupied with the manufacturer and for this reason nobody, not even his clerk, could come in. He went over to the window and sat down on the sill, steadying himself with one hand on the window-latch, and looked into the courtyard. Snow was still falling, the sky was still dark.

He sat like this for a long time, not knowing what was really worrying him; now and again he looked over his shoulder in slight trepidation at the door to the outer office, where he thought he had heard a noise. But when nobody came he calmed down, went to the wash-basin, washed in cold water and returned with a clearer head to his place at the window. His decision to take his defence into his own hands now appeared to him more momentous than he had originally assumed. As long as the defence was the responsibility of the advocate, he himself had in fact been little affected by the case; he had been able to observe it from a distance and had not been directly accessible to it; he had been able to see whenever he liked how his affairs stood, but he had also been able to draw his head back whenever he liked. But now, if he was to conduct his own defence, he must at least for the time being be utterly exposed to the court; later of course the result would be his complete and final acquittal, but to attain this he must in the interim put himself in far greater danger than he had up to now. If he had ever thought of doubting this, his meeting today with the deputy manager and the manufacturer would have been more than enough to convince him of the contrary. How could he have sat there, completely bemused by the mere resolve to take on his own defence? But what would happen later?

What days lay ahead of him! Would he find the way through all this to a successful conclusion? Did not a vigilant defence – and any other kind was pointless – did not a vigilant defence mean at the same time that he had to cut himself off from everything else as far as possible? Could he endure that? And how would he manage to do this in the bank? It was not only a matter of the plea, for which one spell of leave would probably be enough – though a request for leave just now would be a risky business – it was after all a matter of a whole legal case whose duration could not be foreseen. What an obstacle had suddenly been thrown into the path of K.'s professional career!

And he was expected to work for the bank at this time? He looked at his desk. Was he supposed to admit clients now and do business with them? While his case was rolling on, while up in the attics the officers of the court were studying the documents in the case, was he supposed to be applying himself to bank business? Did it not look like a torture sanctioned by the court as part and parcel of the proceedings? And was it likely that the people in the bank would take into consideration his special circumstances when assessing his work? Nobody, never. Of course his case was not an absolute secret, though it was not yet clear who knew about it, and how many. He could hope the rumour had not yet reached the deputy manager, otherwise it would already have been obvious that he was making full use of this against K. with no regard for human feelings or loyalty to a colleague. And the manager? He was certainly well disposed towards K. and probably, as soon as he heard of the case, would be inclined to make things easier for K., as far as he could, but it was likely he would not be able to do this because, as the counterbalance formed by K. began to grow lighter, he was falling more and more under the influence of the deputy manager, who was also taking advantage of the manager's ill-health to augment his own power. So what had K. to hope for? Perhaps all this brooding was weakening his powers of resistance, but it was vital not to deceive himself and to see everything as distinctly as was possible at this time.

Without any particular reason, just to avoid returning to his desk for a while, he opened the window. It was hard to open; he had to use both hands to turn the latch. Then a mixture of fog and smoke poured through the wide-open window into the room and filled it with a faint smell of burning. Some snowflakes were blown in too. 'A ghastly autumn,' said the manufacturer behind K., having come unnoticed into the room from his interview with the deputy manager. K. nodded and looked uneasily at the manufacturer's briefcase, from which he would doubtless be taking the papers out to inform K. about the result of his consultation with the deputy manager. But the manufacturer noticed K.'s glance and tapped his bag and said, without opening it: 'You want to know how things have turned out. Fairly well. The deal is almost in my pocket. A charming fellow, your deputy manager, but not without his perils.' He laughed, shook K.'s hand, and tried to make him laugh too. But to K. it seemed suspicious that the manufacturer did not want to show him the papers and he found nothing to laugh at in the manufacturer's remark. 'Herr K.,' said the manufacturer, 'the weather must be getting you down. You look so depressed today.' 'Yes,' K. said and he put his hand to his forehead, 'a headache, family worries.' 'Yes, true,' said the manufacturer, a brisk man who could never listen quietly to anyone, 'everyone has his cross to bear.' Without thinking, K. had taken a step towards the door as if to show the manufacturer out, but the latter said: 'Herr K., I have something else to tell you. I very much fear that I'm perhaps giving you extra work today, but I've been to see you twice lately and I forgot about it each time. But if I put it off any longer it will probably lose its point completely. That would be a pity because basically what I have to say is not without its value.' Before K. had time to answer, the manufacturer came up close to him, tapped him gently on the chest with his knuckle, and said: 'You are involved in a case, aren't you?' K. stepped back and instantly cried: 'The deputy manager told you that.' 'Oh no,' said the manufacturer, 'how should the deputy know?' 'And you?' asked K., who was already more in control of himself. 'I hear things here and there concerning the court,' said the manufacturer. 'What I have to say to you is connected with this.' 'So many people have connections with the court!' said K. with his head bowed, and he led the manufacturer to his desk. They sat down again as they had earlier and the manufacturer said: 'Unfortunately I can't tell you very much. But in such things one should not neglect even the most trivial aspects. But apart from that I'm eager to help you in any way I can. Up to now we've always been good friends in business, haven't we? Well then.' K. wanted to apologize for his behaviour at today's interview, but the manufacturer would not let him interrupt. He tucked his briefcase under his arm to show he was in a hurry and said: 'I heard about your case from a certain Titorelli. He's a painter. I don't know what his real name is. He has been coming to my office from time to time over the years, bringing small pictures for which I give him – he's almost a beggar – a kind of donation. They're quite nice pictures, by the way, moorland scenes and things like that. These transactions went off quite smoothly – we'd had enough practice. But then the visits were repeated a bit too often; I reproached him and we began to talk; it interested me to know how he could make a living from painting alone, and I was surprised to hear that his main source of income was portrait painting. He worked for the court, he said. For what court, I asked. And then he told me about this court. You in particular can imagine how amazed I was at what he told me. Since that time I've been hearing something new about the court every time he comes, so I'm gradually getting some insight into the thing. Mind you, Titorelli is very talkative and I often have to shut him up, not only because he certainly tells lies sometimes, but also because a businessman like myself who's almost crushed under the burden of his own business worries hasn't really the time to bother about other things. But that's by the way. Perhaps – so I thought – perhaps Titorelli can help you in some small way; he knows a lot of judges and even if he himself may not have much influence he can probably give you hints about how to get in touch with various influential people. And even if these hints may not be crucial in themselves, yet I think it might be very significant for you to have them. After all, you're as good as an advocate. I always say: Herr K. is as good as an advocate. Oh, I have no anxiety about your case. But do you want to go to see Titorelli? On my recommendation he is sure to do all he possibly can. I really think you ought to go. Of course not today – sometime, when it suits you. Just because it's me that's given you this advice – I must repeat this – you're not in the least obliged to go to see Titorelli. No, if you think you can do without Titorelli it's certainly better to leave him out of it. Perhaps you already have a detailed plan, and Titorelli might upset it. No, then of course there's no point going there. It certainly takes a great effort of will to accept advice from such a fellow. Well, just as you like. Here's my letter of recommendation and here's the address.'

Feeling disappointed, K. took the letter and put it in his pocket. Even in the most favourable circumstance any advantage the recommendation could bring him was incomparably less than the damage which lay in the fact that the manufacturer knew about his case and that the painter was spreading news of it. He could hardly bring himself to utter a few words of thanks to the manufacturer, who was on his way to the door. 'I shall go,' he said as he was taking leave of the manufacturer by the door, 'or, as I'm very busy at the moment, I'll write to him to ask him to come to see me in the office sometime.' 'Of course I knew,' said the manufacturer, 'that you would find the best solution. But I did think you would prefer to avoid inviting people like this Titorelli to the bank to talk about the case. And it's not always a good idea to let people like that get their hands on letters. But I'm sure you've thought everything over and know what you ought to do.' K. nodded and accompanied the manufacturer through the outer office. But despite his calm appearance he was shaken by what he had thought of doing. Actually he had only said he would write to Titorelli in order to show the manufacturer he valued his recommendation and would at once consider how best to arrange a meeting with

Titorelli, but if he had come to think Titorelli's help could be useful he would in fact not have hesitated to write to him. But it was only the manufacturer's remark which had alerted him to the dangers which might flow from this. Could he really place such little trust in his common sense? If it was possible for him to write an explicit letter inviting a dubious person to the bank, to ask him for hints about his case when they were separated from the deputy manager only by a door, was it not possible and even highly probable he was overlooking other dangers too or running straight into them? He did not always have someone standing at his side to give him warning. And now, just when he should be applying all his energies, this was the moment he had to be plagued by doubts like this about his alertness, doubts he had not experienced before. Were the difficulties he was experiencing in carrying out his office work going to start in connection with his case too? Now at any rate he could no longer conceive how it had been possible for him to think of writing to Titorelli and inviting him to the bank.

He was still shaking his head over this when the clerk came and drew his attention to three gentlemen sitting on a bench in the outside office. They had been waiting a long time to see him. They had got to their feet as the clerk was speaking to K., and each wanted to use this favourable opportunity to gain access to K. before the others.

As the bank had been so inconsiderate as to let them waste their time here in the waiting-room, they for their part would not show consideration either. 'Herr K.,' one of them was already saying. But K. had already asked the clerk to bring him his winter overcoat, and as he put it on with the clerk's help he said to all three: 'Forgive me, gentlemen, but unfortunately I have no time to see you at the moment. I do apologize most sincerely, but I have an urgent business matter to settle and I have to go away immediately. You yourselves have seen how long I've been held up now. Would you be kind enough to come tomorrow or whenever it suits you? Or could we perhaps discuss your business over the phone? Or would you like to tell me now in brief what it's about, and I can then send you a detailed reply in writing. The best thing would be of course for you to come later.' These proposals of K.'s produced such astonishment among the gentlemen, who now appeared to have waited entirely in vain, that they just looked at each other without a word. 'So we are agreed?' asked K. as he turned towards his clerk who was bringing him his hat as well. Through the open door of K.'s room one could see that the snow outside was falling much more heavily. So K. turned his coat collar up and buttoned it tightly round his neck.

Just at that moment the deputy manager stepped out of the next room, looked with a smile at K.

in his winter overcoat negotiating with the gentlemen, and asked: 'You are going now, Herr K.?' 'Yes,' said K. and straightened himself up, 'I have to go out on business.' But the deputy manager had already turned to the gentlemen. 'And these gentlemen?' he asked. 'I believe you've been waiting quite some time.' 'We've agreed what to do,' K. said. But the gentlemen could no longer contain themselves, they clustered round K. and declared they would not have spent hours waiting if their business were not important and needed to be discussed at once in detail and in private. The deputy manager listened to them for a time, also looked at K., who was holding his hat in his hand and flicking dust off it here and there, and then he said: 'Gentlemen, there's a very simple solution. If you can make do with me, I'll gladly take over the negotiations instead of my colleague. Your affairs must of course be discussed immediately. We are businessmen like you, we know how valuable time is to businessmen. Will you come in here?' And he opened the door which led to his own outer office.

How skilful the deputy manager was at appropriating to himself everything K. was now forced to give up! But was K. not giving up more than was absolutely necessary? While he was running with vague and, he must confess, very slight hopes to an unknown painter his reputation was suffering irreparable damage here. It would probably be much better to take his winter overcoat off again and try to win back at least the two gentlemen who must be having to wait again next door. K. would perhaps have made this attempt if he had not at this moment caught sight of the deputy manager looking for something in the bookcase in K.'s own room as if this bookcase were his own. As K. came to the door in some agitation he cried: 'Ah, you haven't gone yet.' He turned towards K. a face whose mass of taut wrinkles seemed to suggest strength rather than age and immediately resumed his search. 'I am looking for the copy of an agreement,' he said, 'which the firm's representative says should be lodged with you. Won't you help me find it?' K. took a step forward, but the deputy manager said: 'Thank you, I've found it.' And went back to his room with a big packet of documents which contained not only the copy of the agreement but many other things as well.

'Just now I'm no match for him,' K. said to himself, 'but once my personal difficulties have been disposed of, he'll be the first to feel it, and painfully too.' Somewhat pacified by this thought, K. instructed the clerk, who had been holding the door to the corridor open for him for a considerable time, to tell the manager when he got the chance that he had gone out on business, then he left the bank, feeling almost happy because he could now devote himself more completely to his own affair.

He drove at once in search of the painter, who

lived in a suburb at the opposite end of town to the one where the court offices were situated. It was an even poorer district, the houses gloomier, the alleys choked with dirt which circulated slowly on the melting snow. In the building where the painter lived only one side of the big entrance gate was open, but in the others a hole had been broken low down in the wall and from this, just as K. approached, a repulsive yellow liquid shot out in a steaming mess, and a rat fled before it into the nearby canal. At the foot of the steps a small child was lying belly down on the ground and crying, but it could hardly be heard for the deafening noise coming from a plumber's workshop on the other side of the entrance passage. The workshop door was open and three men were standing in a semi-circle round a piece of work they were hammering. A large sheet of tin plate hanging on the wall cast a pale glow between two of the men and illuminated their faces and aprons. K. merely threw a cursory glance at all this; he wanted to get everything over as quickly as possible and go straight back to the bank after sounding out the painter with a few words. Were he to have only the slightest success here, it would have a beneficial effect on the work he still had to do at the bank today. On the third floor he had to slacken his pace, he was utterly out of breath, the steps as well as the storeys were remarkably high, and the painter was said to live right at the top in an attic room. The air was very oppressive too; there was no stairwell, the narrow flight of steps was enclosed between walls, in which there were only a few tiny windows right at the top. Just as K. had stopped for a moment some little girls ran out of an apartment and hurried up the stairs, laughing. K. followed them slowly and caught up with one of the girls who had stumbled and fallen behind the others and he asked her, as they were going up side by side: 'Does a painter called Titorelli live here?' The girl, hardly thirteen years old and a bit of a hunchback, nudged him with her elbow and looked up at him with her head on one side. Neither youth nor physical deformity had saved her from utter depravity. She did not even smile but looked at K. gravely with a sharp challenging gaze. K. pretended he had not noticed her behaviour and asked: 'Do you know the painter Titorelli?' She nodded and asked in her turn: 'What do you want with him?' This seemed to K. a good opportunity to find out something quickly about Titorelli. 'I want him to paint me,' he said. 'To paint you?' she asked, opening her mouth wide, and she gave K. a gentle slap as if he had said something exceedingly surprising or exceedingly stupid, then she hitched up her very short skirt with both hands and ran as fast as she could after the other girls, whose shrieks were already fading away up above. But at the next turning in the stairway K. caught up with all the girls again. They had obviously been told by the hunchback about K.'s intention and were waiting for him. They were standing pressed against the wall on either side of the stairs so that K. might pass easily between them and were smoothing their aprons down with their hands. Their faces and the way they had lined up like this suggested a mixture of childishness and degeneracy. The girls were laughing as they closed ranks behind K., and at their head was the hunchback, who now took the lead. She was the one K. had to thank for finding the right way. He was going to go straight up, but she showed him that to get to Titorelli he must take a side-turning. The stairs leading to him were particularly narrow, very long, had no turning, were open to view from one end to the other, and ended at the top right by Titorelli's door. In contrast to the rest of the stairway this door was comparatively well illuminated because of a small fanlight set over it at an angle, and it was made of untreated boards on which the name Titorelli had been painted in broad red brushstrokes. K. with his retinue had hardly reached the middle of this flight of stairs when the door above was opened a little, obviously in response to the clatter of all these feet, and a man who seemed to be dressed only in a nightgown appeared in the doorway. 'Oh!' he cried as he saw the approaching mob, and he disappeared. The hunchback clapped her hands with joy and the other girls pressed behind K. to drive him on more quickly.

But before they had reached the top the painter threw the door wide open and with a deep bow invited K. to enter. The girls, however, were turned away; he would let none of them in, no matter how much they pleaded, and no matter how hard they tried to force their way in against his will if they could not get his permission. Only the hunchback managed to slip through under his outstretched arm, but the painter rushed after her, seized her by the skirt, whirled her round once, then put her down outside the door by the other girls who had not dared cross the threshold while the painter had abandoned his post. K. did not know how to judge these events; it really looked as if everything were happening in a state of friendly agreement. The girls outside the door craned their necks, one behind the other, and were shouting various remarks to the painter which were evidently meant to be jocular but were incomprehensible to K., and even the painter was laughing as the hunchback he was holding almost flew through the air. Then he closed the door, bowed again to K., shook his hand and said by way of introduction: 'Titorelli, artist.' K. pointed to the door, behind which the girls were whispering, and said: 'You seem to be very popular here.' 'Ah, those rascals!' said the painter, and he tried without success to button up his nightgown at the neck. Also, his feet were bare, and all he had on otherwise was a pair of loose yellowish linen trousers held up by a belt whose long end was swinging freely to and fro. 'These rascals are really a burden to me,' he continued; he stopped fumbling with his nightgown (the top button had just come off), brought a chair and insisted that K. sit down. 'I painted one of them once – she's not even with them today – and ever since then they've all been badgering me. When I'm here they only come in when I give permission, but if I'm away any time there's at least one of them here. They've had a key to my door made, and they lend this to each other. You can hardly imagine what a nuisance that is. For instance, I might come home with a lady I want to paint, I open the door with my key and there's the hunchback by the table painting her lips red with my brushes and all the little brothers and sisters she's supposed to be looking after are rushing around and making a complete mess of the room. Or I come home late at night, as in fact I did only yesterday – that's why I must ask you please to forgive my condition and the disorder in the room – yes, I come home late at night and I'm just getting into bed when somebody pinches my leg, I look under the bed and have to drag out one of those creatures. Why they all press round me like this I don't know, you yourself must have seen just now that I don't exactly try to lure them to me. Of course they disturb me in my work too. If I didn't get this studio rent-free I would have left it long ago.' Just then a small voice called from behind the door, tenderly, fretfully: 'Titorelli, can we come in now?' 'No,' answered the painter. 'Not even if I come by myself?' was the next question. 'No, not even you,' said the painter and he went to the door and locked it.

In the meantime K. had been looking round the room; he himself would never have thought anyone could call this miserable little place a studio. You could hardly take more than two long steps either way. Everything – floor, walls and ceiling – was made of wood with narrow cracks visible between the boards. The bed against the opposite wall was piled high with bedding of various colours. In the middle of the room a picture rested on an easel, covered by a shirt whose sleeves dangled down to the floor. Behind K. was a window through which all that could be seen in the fog was the snow-covered roof of the next house.

The turning of the key in the lock reminded K. he had intended to depart quickly. So he took the manufacturer's letter from his pocket, gave it to the painter, and said: 'I heard of you through this gentleman whom you know and have come here at his suggestion.' The painter skimmed through the letter and tossed it on the bed. If the manufacturer had not spoken most explicitly about Titorelli as someone he knew, as an impoverished man dependent on his donations, it would have been easy to believe that Titorelli did not know the manufacturer or at least could not remember him. And in addition to this, the painter now added: 'Have you come to buy pictures or to have your portrait painted?' K. looked at the painter in astonishment. What was there in the letter? K.

had taken it for granted that in the letter the manufacturer informed the painter K. was coming for no other purpose than to make inquiries about his case. He had rushed here far too hastily and without adequate thought! But now he had to give the painter some kind of answer and said, looking at the picture on the easel: 'You are at work on a picture now?' 'Yes,' said the painter and he threw the shirt which hung over the easel on the bed, where he had thrown the letter. 'It's a portrait. Good bit of work but not quite finished yet.' This was a fortunate chance for K.; it presented him with an opportunity to speak about the court, for it was obviously a portrait of a judge. It was also strikingly similar to the picture in the advocate's study. This was clearly a different judge, a stout man with a bushy black beard which spread far up his cheeks on both sides; also, the other picture was in oils, this was sketched lightly and indistinctly in pastel colours. But everything else was similar; here too the judge was in the act of rising in a menacing way from his chair, whose arms he was gripping. 'That's a judge of course,' K. had almost blurted out, but he restrained himself for a moment and went up to the picture as if he wanted to study the details. He was not able to make out a large figure in the middle behind the back of the chair and asked the painter about it. 'That still needs a bit of work,' answered the painter, and he took a pastel from a side-table and sketched with it round the edges of the figure, but

K. found it no clearer. 'It's Justice,' said the painter at last. 'Ah, now I recognize it,' said K., 'here's the bandage over the eyes and these are the scales. But aren't these wings on the ankles and isn't the figure running?' 'Yes,' said the painter, 'I was commissioned to paint it like that. Actually it is Justice and the goddess of Victory in one.' 'That's hardly a good combination,' said K. with a smile. 'Justice has to be motionless or the scales will waver and there's no possibility of a correct judgement.' 'I'm only following the instructions of the person who commissioned me,' said the painter. 'Yes, of course,' said K., who had not wished to cause offence with his remark. 'You have painted the figure exactly as it's really situated on the chair?' 'No,' said the painter, 'I've seen neither the figure nor the chair, all that's invention, I was simply told what I had to paint.' 'What?' asked K., deliberately pretending not to understand the painter. 'But it is a judge and he is sitting on a judge's chair.' 'Yes,' said the painter, 'but it's not a senior judge and he has never sat on an official chair like that.' 'And yet has himself painted in such a solemn posture? He's sitting there like the president of a court.' 'Yes, the gentlemen are vain,' said the painter, 'but they have permission from above to be painted like that. Each one is told exactly how he may have himself painted. But unfortunately the details of the robes and the chair can't be properly assessed from this picture, pastel colours are not suitable for this kind of representation.' 'Yes,' said K., 'it's surprising it's done in pastels.' 'The judge wanted it like that,' said the painter. 'It's meant for a lady.' The sight of the picture seemed to have stimulated a desire to work; he rolled up his sleeves and selected some pastels, and K. watched as under the moving tips of the pastels a reddish shadow took shape by the judge's head and tapered off in rays towards the edge of the picture. Gradually this play of shadow surrounded the head like an embellishment or a high mark of distinction. But around the figure of Justice everything stayed bright, apart from a slight tinting; in this brightness the figure seemed to be positively thrusting forward, it was scarcely reminiscent of the goddess of Justice any more, nor of the goddess of Victory either; now it looked exactly like the goddess of the Hunt. The painter's activity absorbed K.'s attention more than he had intended, but in the end he reproached himself for having been there so long without doing anything directly about his own concerns. 'What's the name of this judge?' he asked. 'I'm not allowed to tell,' answered the painter who was bending low over the picture and blatantly neglecting the guest he had received at first with such consideration. K. ascribed this to a mood and was angry about it because it was making him lose time. 'You must be some kind of agent of the court?' he asked. The painter immediately put the pastels to one side, straightened up, rubbed his hands together and looked at K. with a smile. 'There's nothing like the truth,' he said. 'You want to find out something about the court, that's what it says in that letter of recommendation, and you talked about my pictures just to win me over. But I'm not offended, you could hardly know that's not my way of doing things. Oh, please!' he said sharply to cut him off as K. tried to make an objection. And then continued: 'You are quite right, by the way, in what you said. I am an agent of the court.' He paused as if to give K. time to digest this information. Now the girls could be heard again outside the door. They must be jostling round the keyhole, perhaps it was possible to see into the room through the cracks too. K. did not offer any kind of apology because he had no wish to create a distraction for the painter, neither did he want the painter to feel too superior and in this way make himself inaccessible, as it were, so he asked: 'Is that a publicly recognized position?' 'No,' said the painter curtly as if that left him nothing more to say. But K. did not want to let him fall silent, and he said: 'Well, unrecognized positions like that are often more influential than recognized ones.' 'That's how it is with me,' said the painter, furrowing his brow and nodding. 'I had a talk yesterday with the manufacturer about your case. He asked me if I wouldn't like to help you; I answered: "The man is welcome to come to see me," and now I'm glad to see you here so soon. You seem to be deeply affected by the case, and of course I'm not surprised about that. Wouldn't

you perhaps like to take your coat off?' Although
K. intended staying only a short time this invitation of the painter's was very welcome all the same.
The air in the room had gradually come to seem
oppressive; he had already looked in bewilderment
several times at a little iron stove in the corner
which was clearly not lit; the stuffiness in the room
was inexplicable. As he took his overcoat off and
unbuttoned his jacket too, the painter said apologetically: 'I must have warmth. It's very snug in
here, don't you think? The room is very well situated in this respect.' K. made no reply; it was not
really the warmth which made him feel uncomfortable, it was the stifling atmosphere which made
it almost impossible to breathe; the room could
not have been aired for a long time. This discomfort was intensified for K. when the painter asked
him to sit on the bed while he himself sat down
on the only chair in the room, in front of the easel.
And also the painter seemed to misunderstand
why K. was sitting on the edge of the bed; he
begged K. to make himself comfortable and, when
K. hesitated, he went over and pushed him deep
into the bedding and pillows. Then he returned
to his chair and finally put the first material question, and this made K. forget everything else. 'Are
you innocent?' he asked. 'Yes,' K. said. To answer
this question was a source of absolute joy to him,
especially as the answer was given to a private
person and so without incurring responsibility. Up
to this time nobody had questioned him so

candidly. To make the most of this joy he added: 'I am completely innocent.' 'I see,' said the painter, who bowed his head and seemed to be thinking. Suddenly he lifted his head again and said: 'If you are innocent, then the matter is very simple.' K.'s eyes clouded over; this man who gave himself out to be an agent of the court was talking like an ignorant child. 'My innocence doesn't simplify the matter,' K. said. In spite of everything he had to smile, then he shook his head slowly. 'What matters are the many subtleties in which the court gets lost. But in the end it produces great guilt from some point where originally there was nothing at all.' 'Yes, yes,' said the painter as if K. were disturbing his train of thought to no purpose. 'But you are definitely innocent?' 'But yes,' K. said. 'That's the main thing,' said the painter. He was not to be influenced by argument, but in spite of his firmness it was not clear if he was speaking like this out of conviction or because of indifference. K. wanted to find out which it was, so he said: 'You obviously know the court much better than I; what I know about it is not much more than what I've heard from various people. But all of them agree that unfounded charges are never preferred and that once the court has made an accusation it is firmly convinced of the accused person's guilt and only with great difficulty can it be persuaded to change its opinion.' 'With great difficulty?' asked the painter, throwing a hand into the air. 'The court can never be persuaded to change its opinion. If I paint all the judges in a row on a canvas, and you argue your defence before this canvas, you'll have more success than you would have before the actual court.' 'Yes,' said K. to himself, and he forgot he had meant only to sound out the painter.

Once again a girl outside the door began to ask: 'Titorelli, won't he be going away soon?' 'Shut up!' shouted the painter in the direction of the door. 'Can't you see I'm in conference with the gentleman?' But the girl was not satisfied with this answer, and she asked: 'You're going to paint him?' And as the painter made no answer she added: 'Please don't paint him, such an ugly fellow.' This was followed by a jumble of voices yelling agreement. The painter leaped to the door, opened it a mere crack – the girls' hands clasped in supplication could be seen – and said: 'If you're not quiet I'll throw you all down the stairs. Sit here on the steps and be quiet.' It seemed they did not immediately do as they were told, for he had to shout: 'Down on the steps!' After that it was quiet.

'Excuse me,' said the painter as he returned to where K. was sitting. K. had hardly turned towards the door; he had left it to the painter to decide if and how he would take him under his protection. Even now he scarcely moved as the painter leaned down and whispered in his ear so as not to be heard outside: 'These girls too belong to the court.' 'What?' asked K., jerking his head to one side and staring at the painter. But the latter sat down again in his chair and said, half jokingly and half by way of explanation: 'Everything belongs to the court.' 'I wasn't aware of that till now,' K. said curtly. The painter's general observation removed the disquieting element from his reference to the girls. All the same, K. looked for some time at the door, behind which the girls were now sitting quietly on the steps. One of them had pushed a straw through a crack between the boards and was moving it slowly up and down.

'You don't seem to have an overall picture of the court yet,' said the painter; he had spread his legs far apart and was tapping his feet on the floor. 'But since you are innocent you won't need it either. I'll get you off by myself.' 'How do you propose to do that?' K. asked. 'When you yourself said just now the court is completely impervious to proof.' 'Impervious only to proof presented before the court,' said the painter, raising his forefinger as if K. had failed to notice a fine distinction. 'But its attitude is different with efforts made in this respect away from the public court, in the consulting rooms, in the corridors or, for example, here too in this studio.' What the painter was saying did not seem so incredible to K. now, it seemed to be in close agreement with what K. had also heard from others. Indeed, it was even a great source of hope. If the judges could really be so easily swayed through personal connections, as the advocate had maintained, then the relationship of the painter to these vain judges was particularly important and at any rate should not be underestimated. The painter would fit very well into the circle of helpers K. was gradually assembling round himself. At the bank his talent for organization had once been legendary; in the present situation, thrown as he was on his own resources, there was a good opportunity to test this talent to the utmost. The painter observed the effect his declaration had had on K. and he said, with a certain unease: 'Doesn't it strike you that I talk almost like a lawyer? It's being constantly with the gentlemen from the court that has affected me like this. I gain a lot from the association of course, but I lose much of my artistic impulse.' 'How did you first get into contact with the judges?' K. asked; he wanted to win the painter's trust before taking him into his service. 'That was very simple,' said the painter. 'I inherited this connection. My father before me was painter to the court. It's a post always handed down by inheritance. New people can't be employed. You see, there are so many complicated and above all secret regulations about how the different grades of officials are to be painted that they just can't be known outside certain families. For example, there in the drawer I've got my father's notes, which I never show to anybody. But only the person familiar with these is qualified to paint judges. And even if I were to lose them, I would still retain in my head so many rules inaccessible to others that no one could dispute my position. After all, every judge wants to be painted just like the great old judges were painted, and I'm the only one who can do that.' 'I envy you,' said K., thinking of his own position at the bank. 'So your position is unassailable?' 'Yes, unassailable,' said the painter, proudly shrugging his shoulders. 'That's why I can occasionally venture to help some poor man with a case pending against him.' 'And how do you do that?' asked K. as if it were not he the painter had just referred to as a poor man. But the painter would not be sidetracked, and he said: 'In your case, for example, as you are completely innocent I shall go about it like this.' The repeated mention of his innocence was becoming tiresome to K. because it sometimes seemed to him that by his observations the painter was making a successful outcome of the case a precondition for his help, which in these circumstances would simply coincide with the result. But in spite of these doubts K. kept himself under control and did not interrupt the painter. He did not want to give up the painter's help, he was resolved about that; this help did not seem to him any more dubious than the advocate's. In fact, K. very much preferred it, because it was offered more frankly and more ingenuously.

The painter had drawn his chair nearer the bed and continued in a subdued voice: 'I've forgotten to ask you what kind of acquittal you want. There are three possibilities: actual acquittal, apparent acquittal, and prolongation. Actual acquittal is of course best, only I don't have the slightest influence on this kind of verdict. I don't believe there is any person at all who could have an influence on actual acquittal. Here, in all probability, only the innocence of the defendant is decisive. As you are innocent it would be possible to depend just on your innocence. In that event you don't need me or any other help.'

This orderly explanation amazed K. to begin with, but then he said, just as quietly as the painter: 'I think you're contradicting yourself.' 'In what way?' asked the painter patiently and he leaned back with a smile. This smile made K. feel he was now trying to uncover contradictions in the legal process itself, not in the painter's words. All the same, he did not retreat but said: 'You said earlier the court is inaccessible to proof, later you limited that to the court in open session, and now you even say an innocent man has no need of help when he faces the court. There's a contradiction there, for a start. Also you said earlier that the judges can be influenced personally, but now you deny that actual acquittal, as you call it, can ever be achieved through personal influence. That's a second contradiction.' 'These contradictions are easily explained,' said the painter. 'We are talking of two different things here – of what is stated in the law and of what I personally have found out. You should not confuse these two. In the law, which incidentally I haven't read, it states on the one hand of course that an innocent man will be acquitted, but on the other hand it is not stated there that the judges can be influenced. Now, I have myself, however, experienced just the opposite. I have never come across an actual acquittal, but I know of many instances where the judges were influenced. Of course it's possible that in all the cases known to me the party was not innocent. But isn't that improbable? In so many cases not one innocent party? Even as a child I used to listen closely to my father when he talked at home about cases, and the judges who came to his studio used to talk about the court; in our circles nobody talks about anything else; as soon as it was possible for me to attend court myself, I made use of the opportunity; I've listened to countless proceedings when they were at a critical stage and kept up with them as long as they were visible and – I must confess – I've never been present at a single actual acquittal.' 'So not one single acquittal,' said K. as if addressing himself and his hopes. 'But that confirms the opinion I already have of this court. It serves no purpose from this aspect either. The whole court could be replaced by one executioner.' 'You mustn't generalize,' said the painter, unhappy with this. 'I was talking only about what I myself have experienced.' 'But that's surely enough,' said K., 'or have you heard of acquittals in earlier times?' 'Such acquittals,' said the painter, 'are indeed said to have occurred. But it's very hard to ascertain the facts. The final decisions of the court are never published, they are not even accessible to the judges, and as a consequence old legal cases are preserved only as legends. These contain (even the majority of them) actual acquittals which can be believed but not proved. All the same, they should not be entirely overlooked, they must contain a certain element of truth, and in addition they are very beautiful. I myself have painted pictures based on such legends.' 'Mere legends don't alter my opinion,' K. said. 'I suppose you can't appeal to such legends if you're before the court?' The painter laughed. 'No, you can't do that,' he said. 'Then there's no point in talking about it,' said K.; for the time being he proposed to fall in with the painter's opinions even if he thought them improbable and they contradicted other accounts. He had no time now to test everything the painter said for truth, or even to refute it; the most he could hope for was to persuade the painter to help him in some way, even if this help were not decisive. So he said: 'Let's put this actual acquittal to one side then; but you mentioned two other possibilities.' 'Apparent acquittal and prolongation. Those are the only ones possible,' said the painter. 'But wouldn't you like to take your jacket off before we talk about these? It must be hot for you here.' 'Yes,' said K., who up to now had paid no attention to anything but the painter's words; now that he was reminded of the heat, sweat broke out violently on his forehead. 'It's almost unbearable.' The painter nodded as if he understood K.'s discomfort very well. 'Couldn't we open the window?' K. asked. 'No,' said the painter, 'it's a pane of fixed glass, it can't be opened.' Now K. realized he had been hoping all the time that either the painter or he himself would suddenly go to the window and fling it open. He was prepared to inhale even the fog through his open mouth. The feeling of being completely cut off from fresh air in this place made him dizzy. He lightly patted the quilt at his side. 'That's uncomfortable and unhealthy, don't you think?' 'Oh no,' said the painter in defence of his window. 'Because it can't be opened, the warmth is kept in better although it's only a single pane of glass than if it had been double-glazed. If I want to ventilate the place, which is not very necessary as air comes in everywhere through the gaps between the boards, I can open one of my doors or even both.' K., a little relieved by this explanation, looked round in search of the second door. The painter noticed this and said: 'It's behind you, I had to put the bed against it.' Now K. saw the little door in the wall for the first time. 'Of course this place is far too small for a studio,' said the painter as if he wanted to forestall K.'s criticism. 'I had to arrange things as best I could. That bed in front of the door is of course in a very bad position. To give you an example: the judge I'm painting just now always comes in through that door by the bed; I've given him a key to the door too so that he can wait for me in the studio if I'm not at home. But he usually comes early in the morning when I'm still asleep. Of course I'm dragged out of even the deepest sleep when the door is opened here next to the bed. You'd lose all your esteem for the judges if you could hear the curses this one gets from me when he climbs over my bed in the early morning. I could of course take the key away from him, but that would only make matters worse. All the doors here could be burst open with the slightest effort.' All the time the painter was talking, K. was considering whether to take his jacket off; finally he realized that if he did not do so he would not be able to stay there any longer, so he took the jacket off but draped it over his knee so that he could put it on at once when the discussion was over. He had hardly taken the jacket off when one of the girls shouted: 'He has taken his jacket off,' and they could all be heard scrambling to the cracks to see this spectacle. 'The girls think I'm going to paint you,' said the painter, 'and that's why you've started undressing.' 'I see,' K. said, not much amused because he hardly felt better than before, although he was now sitting in shirtsleeves. Almost sullenly, he asked: 'What did you call the other two possibilities?' He had already forgotten the phrases. 'Apparent acquittal and prolongation,' said the painter. 'It's up to you which you choose. With my help both are attainable, naturally not without some effort, the difference in this respect being that apparent acquittal requires concentrated but temporary effort, prolongation a much less intense but lasting one. First then, apparent acquittal. If this is what you want, I write a certification of your innocence on a sheet of paper. The text for such a certification was bequeathed to me by my father and can't be challenged. With this certification I go round all the judges I know. I begin, for instance, by laying this certification before the judge I am now painting when he comes for a sitting this evening. I lay the certification before him, explain that you are innocent, and I myself stand surety for your innocence. That's not just a superficial surety, it's really binding.' The painter's eyes seemed to be reproaching K. for wanting to burden him with such a surety. 'That would be very kind,' K. said. 'And the judge would believe you and yet not grant me actual acquittal?' 'As I said just now,' answered the painter. 'But of course it's not absolutely certain every judge will believe me; some judge might, for example, require me to take you to him myself. Then you'd have to come with me. Mind you, if that happens the thing is half won, especially as I'd give you exact instructions beforehand how to conduct yourself before the judge in question. More problematic are the judges who – and this will happen – turn me down right at the outset. We'll have to do without these, though of course I'll make several attempts; but there's no harm in doing this because judges as individuals are not decisive factors here. When I have a satisfactory number of judges' signatures on this certification, I take the certification to the judge in charge of your case. Possibly I've already got his signature and, if that is so, then everything moves a bit quicker than it would normally do. In the main, there aren't many obstacles after that, and for the defendant it's the time of supreme confidence. It's remarkable but true: people are more confident during this time than after the acquittal. No particular effort is required after this. In the certification the judge possesses the surety of a number of judges; he can acquit you with an easy mind, and after going through certain formalities this is what he will doubtless do, to please me and others he knows. And you walk out of the court and are free.' 'So then I'm free,' said K. hesitantly. 'Yes,' said the painter, 'but only ostensibly free or, to put it more accurately, temporarily free. You see, the lowest judges, who include the ones I know, have no authority to pronounce final acquittal; this authority is vested only in the highest court, which is inaccessible to you, to me, and to everybody. How things look up there we don't know and, I should add, we don't want to know. So our judges don't have final authority to absolve a person from an accusation, but they do have authority to disengage him from a charge. That means, if you are acquitted in this way you are for the time being detached from the charge, but it still hovers over you and can be instantly reactivated as soon as the order comes from above. As

I stand in such close relation to the court, I can also tell you how the difference between actual and apparent acquittal is formally expressed in regulations issued to the court offices. With actual acquittal the documents in the case are to be completely discarded, they disappear altogether from the records, not only the charge but also the proceedings and even the acquittal are destroyed. It's different with apparent acquittal. No further change is made to the file, except that the certification of innocence, the acquittal and the reasons for acquittal are added. But it remains active in the case; as the ceaseless routine of the court offices requires, it is forwarded to the higher courts, returns to the lower courts, and thus oscillates between the two regions with greater or lesser swings and longer or shorter pauses. These routes can't be calculated. Seen from outside, it can sometimes appear as if everything has been long cast into oblivion, the file lost, and that acquittal is complete. No knowledgeable person believes this. No file is ever lost, the court never forgets. One day, quite unexpectedly, some judge looks more attentively at the file, recognizes that the charge in this case is still active, and orders immediate arrest. I've assumed here that there's a long interval between the apparent acquittal and the second arrest; that's possible and I know of such cases, but it's just as possible that the man who has just been acquitted goes home from the court and finds officers already there with a warrant for his arrest. Then of course his freedom is over.' 'And the proceedings start again?' asked K. almost incredulously. 'Of course,' said the painter, 'the proceedings start again, but once more there's the possibility, just as there was earlier, of getting an apparent acquittal. You just have to gather all your strength together and never give in.' The painter perhaps made this last observation because of the impression made on him by K., who was looking a little dejected. 'But,' said K., as if he wanted to forestall any revelations the painter might make, 'but isn't getting a second acquittal more difficult than getting the first?' 'In this respect,' said the painter, 'one can't say anything definite. You probably mean the judges are prejudiced against the accused because of the second arrest? That is not so. While pronouncing the acquittal the judges have foreseen this arrest. So this circumstance has hardly any effect. But it's likely that for countless other reasons the mood of the judges as well as their legal assessment of the case can have changed and efforts for a second acquittal must be tailored to the altered circumstances and in general be just as energetic as before the first acquittal.' 'But this second acquittal is again not final,' said K. with a dismissive turn of his head. 'Of course not,' said the painter, 'the second acquittal is followed by the third arrest, the third acquittal by the fourth arrest, and so on. That's already contained in the concept of apparent acquittal.' K. was silent. 'It's obvious you don't think there's any advantage in apparent acquittal,' said the painter. 'Perhaps prolongation will suit you better. Shall I explain the nature of prolongation to you?' K. nodded. The painter had leaned back comfortably in his chair, his nightgown gaped open, he had one hand inside and was stroking his chest and sides. 'Prolongation,' said the painter; and he stared in front of him for a while as if looking for a really accurate explanation. 'Prolongation means the proceedings are kept permanently in their first stages. To achieve this the accused and his helper, but particularly his helper, must keep in uninterrupted personal contact with the court. As I said before, for this you don't have to expend so much energy as for an apparent acquittal, but you have to be a lot more attentive. You mustn't let the case out of your sight, you have to go to the relevant judge at regular intervals and on special occasions too and try by every means to keep him well disposed. If you don't know this judge personally, then you have to have influence exerted through judges you do know but not let this keep you from direct discussions. If you neglect nothing in this respect you can presume fairly definitely that the case will not progress beyond its first stage. The proceedings don't come to a stop, but the defendant is almost as safeguarded against a conviction as he would be if he were free. In comparison with apparent acquittal, prolongation has the advantage that the defendant's future is less uncertain; he is shielded from the shock of sudden arrests and needn't fear he'll have to undertake, perhaps just when his other circumstances are least propitious, the strain and agitation associated with trying to get an apparent acquittal. Mind you, prolongation has certain disadvantages for the defendant which should not be underestimated. I'm not thinking of the fact that it means the defendant is never free; he's not free in a real sense after apparent acquittal either. There is another disadvantage. The case can't stand still, at least not without adequate reason. So from outside something must be seen to be going on. From time to time various decrees must be issued, the defendant must be interrogated, examining sessions held, etc. The case has to be kept constantly moving in the small area to which it has been artificially restricted. Naturally this can have certain unpleasant consequences for the defendant, but you mustn't imagine these are particularly annoying. It's all a show; the interrogations for instance are very brief; if sometimes you haven't the time to go or don't feel like going you can ask to be excused; with some judges you can settle arrangements with them for a long time in advance, by mutual agreement; all it amounts to is that, as you are a defendant, you report to your judge now and again.' During these last words K. had been putting his jacket over his arm and he stood up. Immediately there was a shout from outside the door. 'He's standing up.' 'You're going already?' asked the painter, who had also got to his feet. 'It must be the air in here that's driving you away. I'm very sorry. I've still got quite a lot to tell you. I had to condense things a lot. But I hope I made myself understood.' 'Oh yes,' said K., who had a headache from the strain of forcing himself to listen. In spite of this confirmation the painter said everything again in summary form as if he wanted to give K. some consolation to take home with him: 'What both methods have in common is that they prevent conviction of the defendant.' 'But they also prevent actual acquittal,' K. said quietly as if he felt ashamed for having realized this. 'You have grasped the kernel of the matter,' said the painter quickly. K. placed his hand on his overcoat but could not even make up his mind whether to put it on. What he would have liked best would be to grab all his things and run out with them into the fresh air. Even the girls could not get him to put his coat on with their premature cries that he was doing this. The painter wanted somehow to find out what K.'s opinion was, so he said: 'You've probably not yet made up your mind about my suggestions. I approve. I would in fact have advised you against an immediate decision. The distinction between advantages and disadvantages is extremely fine. Everything should be weighed carefully. But one shouldn't lose too much time either.' 'I'll come again soon,' K. said, and with sudden resolution he put his jacket on, threw the overcoat across his shoulder and hurried to the door, behind which the girls were beginning to shriek. K. believed he could see the shrieking girls through the door. 'But you must keep your word,' said the painter, who had not followed him, 'or I'll have to come to the bank to ask for you myself.' 'Do unlock the door,' said K., and he tugged at the handle which, as he could tell, was being held firmly on the outside by the girls. 'Do you want to be pestered by those girls?' asked the painter. 'You'd better go out this way.' And he pointed to the door behind the bed. K. agreed and hurried back towards the bed. But instead of opening the door the painter crawled under the bed and asked from underneath: 'Just a moment – wouldn't you like to see another picture, one I could sell to you?' K. did not wish to be impolite, the painter had really shown himself very obliging about his problems, had promised to help him further and, because K. had forgotten about it, there had so far been no mention of payment for this help, so K. could not refuse him now. He let him show the picture even though he was quivering with impatience to get away from the studio. The painter pulled a stack of unframed pictures from under the bed, so thick with dust that when the painter tried to blow it off the top picture it swirled round K. for some time in a choking cloud. '*A Moorland Scene*,' said the painter, and handed K. the picture. It showed two spindly trees standing some distance apart in sombre green grass. In the background there was a multi-coloured sunset. 'Nice,' K. said. 'I'll buy it.' K.

had spoken curtly without thinking, so he was relieved when the painter, instead of being offended, picked up another picture from the floor. 'Here's a companion piece to that picture,' said the painter. It might have been meant as a companion piece, but there was not the slightest perceptible difference between this and the first picture. Here were the trees, here the grass, and there the sunset. But K. was not concerned about this. 'They are nice landscapes,' he said. 'I'll buy both and hang them in my office.' 'The subject seems to appeal to you,' said the painter and produced a third picture, 'so it's a good thing I have another picture like those here.' But it was not just like them, it was the absolutely identical same old moorland scene. The painter was making good use of this chance to sell old pictures. 'I'll take this one too,' K. said. 'How much are the three pictures?' 'We'll talk about that next time,' said the painter. 'You're in a hurry now, and we are staying in touch after all. I'm really pleased you like the pictures. I'll give you all the pictures I have under here too. They are all moorland scenes; I've painted so many moorland scenes. Some people don't like pictures like this, they think they're too bleak, but others, and you're one of them, love just this bleakness.' But K. did not feel like listening to the professional experiences of this beggar-painter now. 'Pack all the pictures together,' he cried, cutting across the painter's words. 'My clerk will come for them tomorrow.' 'That's not necessary,' said the painter. 'I hope I can get hold of a porter who'll bring them with you now.' And at last he leaned over the bed to unlock the door. 'Don't be afraid of stepping on the bed,' said the painter. 'Everybody who comes in this way does that.' Even without his invitation K. would not have hesitated, he had in fact already put one foot in the middle of the quilt, when he looked out through the open door and drew his foot back. 'What's this?' he asked the painter. 'What are you surprised at?' asked the other, surprised in his turn. 'Those are court offices. Didn't you know there are court offices here? There are court offices in nearly every attic, why should they be missing just here? Even my studio is part of the court offices, but the court has put it at my disposal.' K. was not so much alarmed at finding court offices here, he was mainly alarmed about himself, at his own ignorance of legal matters. One basic rule for a defendant must be, he thought, to be prepared for anything, never to let himself be taken by surprise, never to be looking unsuspectingly to the right when the judge was standing next to him on the left – and it was just against this basic rule that he was always offending. In front of him stretched a long passage and from it blew a draught of air, in comparison with which the air in the studio was refreshing. Benches ran along either side of the passage just as they did in the waiting-room of the office which had jurisdiction over K.'s case. There appeared to be precise regulations for office arrangements. At this moment not many clients were to be seen. A man was half lying on a bench, his face buried in his arms; he seemed to be asleep; another was standing in the gloom at the end of the passage. K. now climbed over the bed, the painter following with the pictures. Soon they met a court usher – K. was now able to recognize all court ushers by the gilt button worn with ordinary buttons on civilian clothes – and the painter gave him instructions to accompany K. with the pictures. K. staggered rather than walked, holding a handkerchief pressed to his mouth. They had almost reached the way out when the girls came rushing to meet them; he had not been spared even this. They had evidently seen that the second door in the studio had been opened and had run round to get in from this side. 'I can't go any further with you,' cried the painter, laughing as he met the onrush of girls. 'Goodbye! And don't take too long to consider what I've said!' K. did not even look round at him. He was anxious to get rid of the usher, whose gilt button was too prominent for his taste, though probably nobody else noticed it. The usher, in his anxiety to be of service, wanted to sit by the driver but K. got rid of him. It was long past midday when K. arrived at the bank. He would have liked to leave the pictures in the car but was afraid he might need them some time to prove his identity to the painter. So he had them brought to the office and locked them in the bottom drawer of his desk so that for the next few days at least they would be safe from the eyes of the deputy manager.

MERCHANT BLOCK – DISMISSAL
OF THE ADVOCATE

At last K. had really made up his mind to withdraw his case from the advocate. Doubts about whether he was right to do this could not be eradicated altogether, but these were outweighed by his conviction that the step was necessary. Taking this decision had prevented K. from applying his full energy to work on the day he planned to visit the advocate; he was unusually slow at his work, he had to stay late at the office and it was after ten when he eventually reached the advocate's door. Before ringing the bell he considered whether it might not be better to give the advocate his notice by telephone or letter; a personal discussion was bound to be embarrassing. But in the end K. decided he would prefer not to avoid such a discussion; any other form of dismissal would be acknowledged in silence or with a few prim words and, unless Leni could find out something, K. would never know how the advocate had taken the dismissal and what consequences the dismissal might have for K., in the not unimportant opinion of the advocate. But if the advocate were sitting opposite K. and were taken by surprise at the dismissal, then, even if the advocate did not say much, K. could easily learn all he wanted from the advocate's expression and behaviour. He could not exclude the possibility that he would be persuaded it was after all sensible to leave his defence in the advocate's hands and that he would then withdraw his notice of dismissal.

The first ring at the advocate's door produced, as usual, no response. 'Leni could be a bit more lively,' K. thought. But it helped that nobody else intervened, as usually happened, whether it was the man in the dressing-gown or another person beginning to be a nuisance. As K. rang the bell for the second time he looked across at the other door, but this time it too remained closed. At last two eyes appeared at the peep-hole in the advocate's door, but they were not Leni's eyes. The door was unlocked by someone who held it closed for a moment and shouted into the apartment: 'It's him,' and only then opened the door fully. K. had pushed against the door because he heard the key being turned hastily in the lock of the apartment door behind him. So when the door in front of him was finally opened he virtually stormed into the hall and just caught a glimpse of Leni, for whom the warning cry from the door-opener must have been intended, as she ran off in her nightgown down the passage between the rooms. He looked after her for a moment then turned to see who had opened the door. It was a scrawny little man with a beard; he held a candle in his hand. 'You work here?' K. asked. 'No,' answered the man, 'I don't belong to this place. The advocate represents me, I'm here about a legal matter.' 'Without your jacket?' K. asked, and he gestured at the man's deficient clothing. 'Oh, excuse me,' said the man and looked at himself by the light of the candle as if he were observing his own condition for the first time. 'Leni is your mistress?' asked K. abruptly. He had placed his legs slightly apart and his hands, in which he held his hat, were clasped behind his back. Just being in possession of a heavy overcoat made him feel greatly superior to this skinny little chap. 'Oh God,' said the man, raising one hand in front of his face in a shocked gesture of denial. 'No, no, what are you thinking of?' 'You look as if I should believe you,' said K. with a smile. 'All the same – come on.' He waved him on with his hat and let him walk in front. 'What's your name?' asked K. as they were walking. 'Block, I'm a merchant, Block,' said the little man and he turned round as he was introducing himself, but K. did not let him stop. 'Is that your real name?' K. asked. 'Of course,' was the answer, 'why do you doubt it?' 'I thought you could have a reason for hiding your name,' K. said. He was feeling completely at ease, like being in a foreign country and talking to lower-class people, keeping one's own affairs to oneself while conversing placidly about the other person's interests and by this attention giving them a certain importance to oneself, or being able to drop them

214

altogether, just as one likes. K. stopped at the door of the advocate's study, opened it, and called to the merchant who had walked on obediently: 'Not so fast! Bring the light here.' Leni could have hidden here; he got the merchant to throw light into all the corners, but the room was empty. By the picture of the judge K. pulled the merchant back by his braces. 'Do you know this man?' he asked, and he pointed up with his finger. The merchant raised his candle, blinked up and said: 'It is a judge.' 'A high-ranking judge?' K. asked, and he moved to one side to see what impression the picture was making on him. The merchant looked up with admiration. 'It is a high-ranking judge,' he said. 'You don't know much,' K. said. 'Among the lower judges he is the lowest.' 'Now I remember,' said the merchant and he brought the candle down. 'That's what I heard too.' 'But of course,' K. cried. 'I forgot, didn't I? Of course you must have heard it.' 'But why then, why?' asked the merchant as K.'s hands were pushing him towards the door. In the passage outside, K. said: 'But you do know where Leni's hiding?' 'Hiding?' said the merchant. 'No, she's probably in the kitchen making soup for the advocate.' 'Why didn't you tell me that straight away?' K. asked. 'I was going to take you there, but you called me back,' answered the merchant as if he had been confused by these contradictory instructions. 'You must think you're being very clever,' K. said. 'Show me the way then.' K. had never been in the kitchen; it was surprisingly large and well equipped. The cooker alone was three times the size of normal cookers; nothing else could be seen in detail, for now the kitchen was illuminated only by a small lamp hanging by the entrance door. Leni, in a white apron as usual, was at the cooker, dropping eggs into a pan on a spirit flame. 'Good evening, Josef,' she said, glancing sideways. 'Good evening,' said K. as he pointed to an armchair standing to one side as an indication that he wanted the merchant to sit there, and this the latter did. K. himself went close behind Leni, leaned over her shoulder and asked: 'Who is that man?' Leni grasped K. with one hand, stirring the soup with the other, and drew him round towards her and said: 'He's a pitiful creature, a poor merchant, a certain Block. Just look at him.' They both looked behind them. The merchant was sitting on the chair K. had indicated; he had snuffed out the candle, whose light was no longer necessary, and was pressing the wick between his fingers to stop it smoking. 'You were in your nightgown,' said K. and with his hand he turned her head back to the cooker. Leni was silent. 'He is your lover?' K. asked. She was going to pick up the pan, but K. took her by both hands and said: 'Now answer!' She said: 'Come into the study. I'll explain everything.' 'No,' K. said, 'I want you to explain it here.' She clung to him and tried to kiss him, but K. held her off and said: 'I don't want you to kiss me now.' 'Josef,' said Leni with a beseeching yet frank look, 'you are not going to be jealous of Herr Block? Rudi,' she then said, turning to the merchant, 'come and help me. You can see I'm being suspected of something. Stop fiddling with that candle.' Anyone might have thought he had not been paying attention, but he knew exactly what was going on. 'I have no idea why you should be jealous,' he said, not being very quick-witted. 'I don't know either,' said K., smiling as he looked at the merchant. Leni laughed out loud and took advantage of K.'s switch of attention to slip her arm through his, then whispered: 'Let him be. You can see what sort of man he is. I've looked after him a bit because he's a good client of the advocate's, for no other reason. And you? Do you want to speak to the advocate today? He's very ill today but if you like I'll tell him you are here. You'll stay with me tonight, of course. You haven't been here for a long time, even the advocate has been asking about you. Don't neglect your case! I've a lot to tell you too, things I've learned. First of all, take your coat off!' She helped him off with his coat, took his hat, dashed into the hall to hang them up, then ran back to look after the soup. 'Should I announce you first or take him his soup first?' 'Announce me first,' K. said. He was annoyed; his original intention had been to discuss his case in detail with Leni, especially the questionable dismissal he had in mind, but the presence of the merchant made him reluctant to do this. But then he thought his affair really too important to be affected in such a critical way by this petty merchant, so he called back Leni who was already in the passage. 'No, take him his soup first,' he said. 'It'll strengthen him for the interview with me; he'll need it.' 'You are one of the advocate's clients too?' said the merchant quietly from his corner as if he wanted to make sure. But this was not well received. 'What's that to do with you?' said K., and Leni said: 'Be quiet. So I'll take him his soup,' said Leni to K. and she poured the soup into a bowl. 'The only thing to be afraid of then is that he'll fall asleep in no time, he does drop off quickly after eating.' 'What I have to say to him will keep him awake,' K. said. He wanted to make it obvious that he intended to discuss something important with the advocate, he wanted Leni to ask him what it was, and only then would he ask for her advice. But she merely carried out to the letter the instructions she had been given. As she passed him with the bowl she deliberately bumped into him and whispered: 'When he's finished his soup I'll announce you straight away so that I'll get you back as soon as possible.' 'Just go,' said K., 'Just go.' 'Be a bit more friendly,' she said, turning right round again in the doorway with the bowl.

K. looked after her. Now finally it was definite the advocate would be dismissed, and it was probably better there was now no opportunity to discuss it beforehand with Leni; she could hardly have adequate knowledge of the whole affair, would very likely have advised against it and would possibly even have dissuaded K. from giving notice of dismissal this time; he would have continued in doubt and turmoil and after a while would have carried out his intention after all, for this intention was really too compelling. The sooner it was done, the less damage would be caused. But perhaps the merchant might have something to say on the subject.

K. turned round, and as soon as the merchant noticed this he started to get up. 'Stay where you are,' K. said, and he pulled up a chair to sit by him. 'Are you an old client of the advocate?' K. asked. 'Yes,' said the merchant, 'a very old client.' 'How many years has he represented you?' K. asked. 'I'm not sure how you mean that,' said the merchant. 'In legal matters connected with my business – I'm a corn dealer – the advocate has acted for me ever since I took over the business, it must be about twenty years. In my personal law case, which is probably what you are referring to, he has represented me from the beginning, more than five years now. Yes, quite a bit more than five years,' he added, taking out an old wallet. 'I've written everything down here. If you like, I can give you exact dates. It's hard to remember everything. My case must have lasted much longer; it started just after my wife's death, and that's more than five and a half years ago.' K. moved nearer to him. 'So the advocate takes on ordinary legal cases too?' he asked. K. found this conjunction of the courts and normal jurisprudence uncommonly comforting. 'Of course,' said the merchant, then he whispered to K.: 'They even say he's better at the ordinary cases than the others.' He seemed to regret having said this; he put a hand on K.'s shoulder and said: 'I do beg of you – don't betray me.' K. slapped him on the thigh to reassure him. 'No, I don't betray people.' 'He's very vindictive, you see,' said the merchant. 'He surely won't do anything against such a faithful client,' K. said. 'Oh, but he will,' said the merchant. 'When he's worked up he doesn't make any distinctions and as it happens I'm not really faithful to him.' 'In what way?' K. asked. 'Can I trust you?' asked the merchant doubtfully. 'I think you can,' K. said. 'Well,' said the merchant, 'I'll tell you about it, partly, but you must tell me a secret too, so that we support each other against the advocate.' 'You're very careful,' said K., 'but I'll tell you a secret which will reassure you completely. So how are you unfaithful to the advocate?' 'Besides him,' said the merchant hesitantly as if confessing to something dishonourable, 'besides him I have other advocates too.' 'But that's not so terrible,' said K., a little disappointed. 'It is here,' said the merchant who had been breathing heavily since his confession but seemed now to gain confidence from K.'s remark. 'It's not permitted. And least of all is it permitted to take back-street lawyers in addition to a so-called advocate. And that's just what I've done, I have five back-street lawyers apart from him.' 'Five!' cried K., astonished by the number. 'Five lawyers apart from this one?' The merchant nodded. 'I'm actually negotiating with a sixth.' 'But what do you want so many lawyers for?' K. asked. 'I need them all,' said the merchant. 'Won't you explain that to me?' K. asked. 'Willingly,' said the merchant. 'The main thing is that I don't want to lose my case, that goes without saying. So I can't leave out anything that might help me; even when there doesn't seem much prospect of benefit from a particular action I just can't reject it out of hand. So I've spent everything I've got on this case. I've taken all the money out of my business, for instance. At one time my business offices took up a whole floor, now I make do with a small back room where I work with a trainee. This decline is due not merely to removal of money but even more to the diversion of my energies. If you want to pursue your case you can't really do much else.' 'So you put in some work at the court yourself?' K. asked. 'That's just what I'd like to hear more about.' 'I can only tell you very little about that,' said the merchant. 'I tried it at first, but I soon stopped. It's too exhausting and doesn't show much result. To work there myself and take part in negotiations proved quite impossible, at least for me. Merely sitting and waiting about in that place is a great strain. You yourself know how stuffy the atmosphere is in the offices.' 'How do you know I've been there?' K. asked. 'I happened to be in the waiting-room as you walked through.' 'What a coincidence!' cried K., carried away and quite forgetting how ridiculous the merchant had seemed earlier. 'So you saw me! You were in the waiting-room as I walked through. Yes, I walked through there once.' 'It's not such a great coincidence,' said the merchant, 'I'm there nearly every day.' 'I'll probably have to go there often now, as well,' said K., 'but I don't suppose I'll be received as respect-fully as I was that time. Everybody stood up. They must have thought I was a judge.' 'No,' said the merchant, 'we were paying our respects to the court usher. We knew you are a defendant. News like that travels fast.' 'So you knew that,' K. said. 'Then my behaviour must have seemed arrogant to you. Didn't anybody pass remarks about that?' 'No,' said the merchant, 'on the contrary. But that's a lot of foolishness.' 'What's foolishness?' K. asked. 'Why ask?' said the merchant peevishly. 'You don't seem to know the people there yet and you'll perhaps take it all wrong. You must remember that in this business many things are constantly coming up for discussion which are beyond the range of the intellect; people are just too tired and distracted to cope with a lot of things and so take refuge in superstition. I'm talking about the others, but I myself am no better. One of the superstitions, for instance, is that, according to many people, the outcome of a case can be seen in the accused man's face and particularly in the line of his lips. And these people said that, judging by your lips, you are sure to be convicted, and soon. I repeat, it's a ridiculous superstition and in most instances it's utterly refuted by the facts, but when people live together in that place it's hard to distance yourself from such opinions. Now just think what a strong effect this superstition can have. You spoke to one man there, didn't you? He could hardly answer you. Of course there are many reasons why he should be confused in that place, but one of them was the sight of your lips. He said later he believed he had seen the mark of his own condemnation too on your lips.' 'My lips?' asked K., taking out a pocket mirror and examining himself. 'I can't see anything peculiar about my lips, can you?' 'Neither can I,' said the merchant, 'not at all.' 'How superstitious those people are,' K. cried. 'Didn't I tell you?' asked the merchant. 'Do they have a lot to do with each other and exchange opinions?' K. said. 'So far I've kept myself to myself.' 'In general they don't have much to do with each other,' said the merchant. 'That would not be possible, there are so many of them. They have few interests in common. When belief in a common interest bobs up sometimes in a group, it's soon shown to be an error. Nothing can be done in combination against the court. Each case is investigated individually, this court is most painstaking. So you can't do anything in combination, but an individual occasionally achieves something in secret; only when it has been achieved do the others hear about it; nobody knows how it has happened. So there's no community as such; people do come together now and then in the waiting-rooms, but there's little discussion. The superstitious beliefs date from time immemorial and seem to propagate themselves.' 'I saw the people there in the waiting-room,' K. said. 'Their waiting seemed pointless to me.' 'The waiting is not pointless,' said the merchant, 'the only thing that's pointless is independent intervention, I told you just now that besides this one I have five other lawyers. You might believe – I myself believed this at first – that I could delegate the matter entirely to them now. But that would be wrong. I'm less able to delegate it to them than when I had only one. You probably don't understand that?' 'No,' said K. and, to slow the pace of the merchant's rush of words, he put his hand reassuringly on his hand. 'I would only ask you to speak a little more slowly, these things are all of great importance to me and I can't follow you properly.' 'I'm glad you reminded me of that,' said the merchant. 'You are of course a newcomer, a mere boy. Your case is six months old, isn't it? Yes, I've heard of it. Such a fledgling of a case! But I've already thought these things through countless times, to me they are the most familiar things in the world.' 'You must be glad your case has made such good progress?' asked K. who did not want to ask directly how the merchant's affairs stood. But he got no clear answer. 'Yes, I've been trundling on with my case for five years,' said the merchant, and he bowed his head, 'that's no mean achievement.' Then he was silent for a while. K. listened for Leni's return. On the one hand he did not want her to come back because he still had many questions to ask and had no wish to be caught by Leni in confidential discussion with the merchant, but on the other hand he was annoyed that although he was there she was staying so long with the advocate, much longer than was necessary just to give him his soup. 'I have a clear recollection of the time,' the merchant began again, and K. was immediately attentive, 'when my case had been going on about as long as yours has now. At that time I had only this one advocate but was not very satisfied with him.' 'Now I'm going to hear everything,' thought K., and he nodded his head vigorously as if this could encourage the merchant to tell everything worth knowing. 'My case,' continued the merchant, 'was making no progress. Hearings did take place; I attended all of them, collected material, deposited all my business accounts with the court (I found out later this wasn't even necessary), I kept running to my advocate, he filed various pleas . . .' 'Various pleas?' K. asked. 'Yes, definitely,' said the merchant. 'This is very important for me,' K. said. 'He's still working on the first plea in my case. He has done nothing so far. I now see he is neglecting me shamefully.' 'There may be various good reasons why the plea isn't finished yet,' said the merchant. 'In any case it became clear with my later pleas that they were utterly worthless. Through the kindness of a court official I was able to read one of them myself. It was certainly scholarly but really without substance. First of all a lot of Latin, which I don't understand, then page after page of general appeals to the court, then flattering references to certain individual officials, not named of course but easily identified by those in the know, then tributes from the advocate to himself, and here he grovelled before the court like a dog, and finally scrutinies of ancient legal cases supposedly similar to mine. These scrutinies were in fact, as far as I could understand them, done very carefully. What I'm saying is not meant as a judgement on the advocate, and the plea I read was only one among many, yet I couldn't see any progress in my case at that time. That's what I want to talk about now.' 'What sort of progress did you hope to see?' K. asked. 'That's a reasonable question,' said the merchant with a smile. 'In a case like this you can seldom see progress. But I didn't know that then. I'm a merchant and in those days I was much more of a merchant than I am now, I wanted to see tangible progress, the whole thing ought to be working towards a conclusion or at least advancing in regular stages. Instead of that there were only interrogations, mostly on the same lines; I had the responses ready like a litany. Several times a week agents of the court came to my place of business, to my house or wherever they could find me; that was of course a nuisance (today it's better in this respect at least, a phone call is much less disturbing); rumours about my case began to spread among my business associates and in particular among my relatives; so a lot of damage was being caused, but there was not the slightest indication that even

226

the first court hearing would take place soon. So I went to my advocate and complained. He gave long explanations of course but firmly declined to act in the way I wanted, said nobody could influence the court about a date for the hearing; to press for it in a plea, as I wanted, was simply unheard of and would destroy him and me. So I thought: what this advocate doesn't want to do or can't do, another will and can. I looked around for other advocates. To come to the point – not one of them has asked for or managed to fix a date for the main hearing; it's truly impossible, with one reservation which I'll talk about in a minute; so my advocate hadn't deceived me about this, but otherwise I had no reason to regret having turned to other lawyers. You may already have heard a lot from Dr Huld about back-street lawyers, he's probably told you they are contemptible, and in fact that's what they are. But whenever he speaks of them and makes a comparison between them and himself and his colleagues he always makes a little mistake, and I'll just draw your attention to this in passing. When he's doing this he always differentiates the advocates of his circle as "the great advocates". That's not correct. Of course anybody can call himself "great" if he likes, but in this matter legal custom is definitive. According to this there are, apart from back-street lawyers, only small and great advocates. This advocate and his colleagues are, however, only small advocates, but the great advocates, of whom

227

I've heard but never seen, rank incomparably higher above the small advocates than these do above the despised back-street lawyers.' 'The great advocates?' K. asked. 'Who are they then?' How do you get in touch with them?' 'So you haven't heard of them before,' said the merchant. 'There's hardly a defendant who doesn't dream of them for a considerable time after hearing about them. But better not let yourself be misled into doing that. Who the great advocates are I don't know, and it's probable nobody can make contact with them. I know of no case where it can be said with certainty they had intervened. They do defend a certain number of people, but you can't get them to act for you simply because you want them to, they will defend only those they wish to defend. Whatever case they take up must, however, have progressed beyond the lower court. On the whole it's better not to think of them because you'll find conferences with other advocates and their advice and services so nauseating and useless (that's been my experience) that what you would like to do most of all would be to give it all up, take to your bed at home and ignore everything. But that of course would be utterly stupid; even in bed you wouldn't have peace for long.' 'So you didn't think of consulting the great advocates at that time?' K. asked. 'Not for long,' said the merchant, and he smiled again. 'Unfortunately you can't forget about them completely, especially at night. But at that time I was looking for quick results, so I went to the back-street lawyers.'

'How very confidential!' cried Leni who had returned with the bowl and was standing in the doorway. They were actually sitting very close to each other; at the slightest movement they could have banged their heads together; the merchant who, apart from being small in stature, was also crouching had compelled K. to bend down low as well in order to hear everything. 'We won't be a moment,' cried K. to Leni to ward her off, and his hand, still covering the merchant's hand, twitched impatiently. 'He wanted me to tell him about my case,' said the merchant to Leni. 'So tell him, tell him,' she said. She addressed the merchant in a loving but condescending way. This did not please K., who now realized the man had a certain standing after all, at least he had had experiences and was well able to communicate them. Leni was probably misjudging him. He looked on irritably as Leni took the candle the merchant had been holding all this time, wiped his hand with her apron, then knelt down to scrape off some grease which had dripped on his trousers from the candle. 'You were going to tell me about the back-street lawyers,' K. said, and without further remark he pushed Leni's hand away. 'What are you doing?' Leni asked, giving K. a little slap and going on with her work. 'Yes, the back-street lawyers,' said the merchant, and he passed his hand over his forehead as if thinking. K. tried to prompt him by saying: 'You wanted

quick results, so you went to back-street lawyers.'
'Quite right,' said the merchant, but he did not
go on. 'Perhaps he doesn't want to talk about it
in front of Leni,' thought K. and he checked his
impatience to hear more about it now and did not
pursue the matter.

'Have you told him I am here?' he asked Leni.
'Of course,' she said. 'He's waiting for you. Leave
Block alone. You can talk to him later, he's staying
here.' K. still hesitated. 'You're staying here?' he
asked the merchant. He wanted a direct answer
from him; he did not like hearing Leni speak of
the merchant as if he were not present; he was
full of suppressed indignation against Leni today.
But again the only response came from Leni: 'He
often sleeps here.' 'Sleeps here?' cried K., who had
thought the merchant would wait for him only
until he had quickly disposed of the interview with
the advocate, when they could go off together and
have a detailed discussion undisturbed. 'Yes,' said
Leni, 'not everybody is treated like you and can
see the advocate just when they like, Josef. You
don't seem at all surprised that in spite of his
illness the advocate is seeing you at eleven o'clock
at night. You take what your friends are doing for
you a bit too much for granted. Of course your
friends, or I at least, do it with pleasure. I don't
ask for thanks and the only thanks I need is that
you'll be fond of me.' 'Fond of you?' K. thought,
and only now did he realize: 'But yes, I am fond
of her.' Then, putting this to one side, he said: 'He

230

is seeing me because I am his client. If I needed outside help just to see him, I'd be begging and thanking simultaneously and all the time.' 'What a mood he's in today, don't you think?' Leni asked the merchant. 'Now I'm the one who's not here,' thought K., very nearly angered even by the merchant when he copied Leni's discourtesy and said: 'The advocate has other reasons for seeing him too. His case happens to be more interesting than mine. And it's only in its beginnings too, so not yet very muddled, and the advocate can take pleasure in it. That will change later.' 'Yes, yes,' said Leni, who was laughing as she looked at the merchant. 'How he chatters! But . . .' here she turned to K. '. . . you shouldn't believe anything he says. He's so sweet, so talkative. Perhaps that's why the advocate can't stand him. He only sees him when he feels like it. I've tried hard to change that, but it's impossible. Just think – I sometimes announce Block, but he'll only receive him on the third day after that. But if Block isn't here when he's called, then everything's down the drain and he has to be announced all over again. That's why I let Block sleep here; it's happened before now that he's rung for him in the night. So Block is now ready even in the night. Of course it can happen too that when the advocate sees Block is here he sometimes cancels his instruction to let him in.' K. looked questioningly at the merchant, who nodded and said, as frankly as when he had spoken to K. earlier (perhaps shame was confusing

231

him): 'Yes, later on you get very dependent on your advocate.' 'He's only pretending to complain,' said Leni. 'He likes sleeping here very much, he's often told me so.' She went to a little door and pushed it open. 'Would you like to see his bedroom?' she asked. K. went across and from the threshold looked into a windowless chamber which had a low ceiling and was almost totally filled by a narrow bed. Anyone trying to get into this bed would have to climb in over the bedposts. In the wall at the head there was a recess in which a candle, inkpot and pen were neatly arranged, together with a bundle of papers, probably legal documents. 'You sleep in the maid's room?' asked K., turning back to the merchant. 'Leni lets me have it,' answered the merchant. 'It's very convenient.' K. stared at him for a long time. His first impression of the merchant had perhaps been right after all; the man had had many experiences because his case had been going on for a long time, but he had paid dearly for these experiences. Suddenly K. could not stand the sight of the merchant any longer. 'Put him to bed!' he cried to Leni, who did not seem to know what he meant. But he wanted to go to the advocate and by dismissing him get rid not only of the advocate but of Leni and the merchant too. But before he reached the door the merchant spoke to him quietly: 'Sir!' K. turned, visibly angered. 'You've forgotten your promise,' said the merchant, who was stretching up to K. from where he was sitting and seemed to be appealing to him. 'You were going to tell me a secret.' 'That's true,' K. said, and he glanced at Leni, who was watching him attentively, 'so listen. But it's hardly a secret any more. I'm going to the advocate now to dismiss him.' 'He's dismissing him!' cried the merchant, who jumped out of his chair and ran round the kitchen with arms held high. And again and again he shouted: 'He's dismissing the advocate!' Leni rushed at K., but the merchant got in her way so she gave him a thump with her fist. She was still holding her fists up as she ran after K., but he had a considerable start over her. He was already in the advocate's room when Leni overtook him. He had almost closed the door, but Leni put a foot in the crack and grabbed his arm and tried to pull him back. But he twisted her wrist so sharply that she moaned and released him. She would not dare force her way in, but K. turned the key in the lock.

'I've been waiting for you a long time,' said the advocate from the bed; he placed a document he had been reading by candlelight down on the bedside table, put on a pair of glasses and gave K. a severe look. Instead of making excuses K. said: 'I won't be here for long.' The advocate ignored K.'s remark, as it was not an apology, and said: 'I won't let you in at this late hour again.' 'That suits me,' K. said. The advocate looked at him inquiringly. 'Sit down,' he said. 'Only because you ask me,' said K., who drew a chair up to the bedside table and sat down. 'It seemed to me you locked the door,' said the advocate. 'Yes,' K. said, 'because of Leni.' He was not in the mood to spare anybody. But the advocate asked: 'Has she been impertinent again?' 'Impertinent?' K. asked. 'Yes,' said the advocate, who laughed when he said this, was overtaken by a fit of coughing and, when he had got over it, began to laugh again. 'You must have noticed how impertinent she is?' he asked, and he patted K. on the hand he had unwittingly placed on the bedside table and which he now quickly withdrew. 'You don't think that matters much,' said the advocate. 'All the better, or I would have had to apologize to you. Leni has one idiosyncrasy I've long forgiven her and wouldn't mention now if you hadn't just locked the door. This idiosyncrasy – you are the person least in need of an explanation, but you are looking at me in such alarm and that's why I'm telling you – this idiosyncrasy is that she finds nearly all accused men handsome. She is attracted to them all, loves them all, and seems to be loved by them too. To amuse me she sometimes tells me about these affairs, when I let her. I am not as amazed about all this as you seem to be. When you've got the proper eye for it, accused men do often appear handsome. This is a remarkable, you might even call it scientific, phenomenon. Of course, there's no clear and exactly definable change in their appearance because of the accusation. After all, it's not like in other legal cases; most of these men continue their normal way of life and if they have a good advocate to look after them they're not much impeded by the proceedings. Yet those with experience in these matters can pick out the accused men, every single one of them, in the largest mass of people. How do they do this, you may ask. My answer will not satisfy you. The accused men are simply the most handsome. It can't be guilt which makes them handsome because – at least in my opinion as an advocate – not all are guilty; neither can it be future punishment which makes them handsome in advance, for not all are punished; so it can only be an attribute of the proceedings instituted against them. Of course, among the handsome ones a few are especially conspicuous. But all are handsome, even Block, that miserable worm.'

When the advocate had finished, K. was completely in command of himself. At the last words he had nodded conspicuously, confirming in his mind his previous opinion that the advocate was always trying to distract him, and was doing so now, through making general statements which had nothing to do with the case, hoping to divert his attention from the central question of what he had actually done in K.'s business. The advocate must have noticed that this time K. was putting up more resistance than usual, for he kept silent to give K. a chance to speak, then, since K. said nothing, he asked: 'Did you come to me today with any special intention?' 'Yes,' K. said, and he partly screened the candle with his hand so as to see the advocate better, 'I wanted to tell you that as from today I withdraw my representation from you.' 'Have I understood you correctly?' asked the advocate, half rising from the bed and propping one hand against the pillow. 'I assume you have,' said K., upright and tense as if on watch. 'Well, let's discuss this plan, shall we?' said the advocate after a pause. 'It's not just a plan any more,' K. said. 'That may be,' said the advocate, 'but we mustn't be too hasty.' He used the word 'we' as if he had no intention of letting K. break away and wanted to remain his adviser even if he could not be his representative. 'Nothing of this is hasty,' said K. as he stood up slowly and moved behind his chair, 'it has been well considered, and perhaps for too long. My decision is final.' 'Then just let me say a few words,' said the advocate, who pushed the quilt to one side and sat on the edge of the bed. His bare legs covered with white hairs were trembling with cold. He asked K. to pass him a blanket from the sofa. K. fetched the blanket and said: 'You are risking a chill like that, and there's no need for it.' 'The reason for it is important enough,' said the advocate as he enveloped his upper body in the quilt and wrapped the blanket round his legs. 'Your uncle is my friend and in the course of time I've grown fond of you too. I tell you that frankly; I've no need to be ashamed of it.' The old man's affecting words were by no means welcome to K., for they compelled him to give a fuller explanation, something he would have preferred to avoid; they confused him too, as he frankly admitted to himself, though they would never make him go back on his decision. 'Thank you for your friendly attitude,' he said. 'I also acknowledge that you've looked after my affairs as well as you could in the way that seemed most advantageous to me. But recently I've become convinced this is not enough. You are so much my senior, you have so much more experience that I shall of course never try to convert you to my point of view. If I've sometimes tried to do this without thinking, then please forgive me, but the matter is, as you yourself said, important enough, and I'm convinced the case must be pursued far more vigorously than it has been up to now.' 'I understand you,' said the advocate. 'You are impatient.' 'I am not impatient,' said K., a bit irritated and not so careful now in his choice of words. 'You may have noticed that on my first visit, when I came to you with my uncle, I didn't take the case very seriously; when I was not, so to speak, forcibly reminded of it I forgot all about it. But my uncle insisted I become your client; I did that to please him. And then you'd think I'd be even less aware of the case than before; the whole idea of taking on an advocate is to transfer some of the burden of the proceedings from oneself. But the opposite happened. I'd never previously had such worries about my case as I've had since you took over my representation. When I stood alone I did nothing in my affair and was hardly aware of it, but now I had a representative and everything was put in train for something to happen; all the time, and more and more expectantly, I awaited your intervention, but it never came. I did get from you certain information about the court which I would probably not have had from anyone else. But that's not enough, now that the case, going on entirely in secret, is coming closer and closer to me personally.' K. had pushed his chair away and was standing erect with hands in his jacket pockets. 'From a certain moment,' said the advocate softly and calmly, 'nothing really new happens in one's practice. So many clients have come to see me just like you, at just the same stage in the proceedings, and have said just the same things.' 'Then all these similar clients,' said K. 'have been just as right as I. That doesn't prove me wrong.' 'I wasn't trying to prove you wrong,' said the advocate, 'but I wanted to add that I expected better judgement from you than from other people, especially as I've given you more insight into the judicial system and my activities than I usually give clients. What I see now is that in spite of everything you don't have enough confidence in me. You don't make things easy for me.' How the advocate was humbling himself before K.! Without any regard for professional dignity, which must be at its most sensitive in an area like this. And why was he doing that? To judge by appearances he was a very busy advocate and a wealthy man; any reflection on his merit or the loss of a client could hardly mean much to him. He was in poor health too and should have known he would have work taken away from him. And yet he clung to K. so tenaciously. Why? Was it out of personal sympathy for his uncle or did he really think K.'s case was so extraordinary and perhaps hoped to distinguish himself in it either for K.'s benefit or – and this possibility could never be excluded – on behalf of his friends in the court? Nothing could be read in his face, however carefully K. scanned it. He almost seemed to have put on a deliberately blank expression as he waited to see what effect his words would have. But he was obviously interpreting K.'s silence grossly in his own favour when he went on: 'You will have noticed I have extensive chambers but no assistants. It was different in the old days. There was a time when several young lawyers worked for me; now I'm on my own. This has been brought about partly by a change in my practice caused by restricting myself more and more to cases of your type, but partly also because of the deeper knowledge I've gained through working on these cases. I found I couldn't delegate work to anyone or I'd be in breach of my obligations to clients and to the business I'd undertaken. But my decision to do all the work personally had inevitable consequences. I had to reject most applications for my services and accepted only those that seemed intriguing – there are plenty of wretched creatures, even in this neighbourhood, who are glad to fight for any scrap I throw away. Overwork affected my health too. But all the same I don't regret my decision. Perhaps I should have rejected even more commissions; my dedication to the cases I did accept proved absolutely vital and justified by results. I once read in an article a very fine definition of the difference between acting for a client in normal law cases and acting in a case like yours. It went like this: The first advocate leads his client by a thread to the judgement, but the other takes his client on his shoulders from the beginning and carries him to the judgement and, without setting him down, carries him beyond. And that's how it is. But it wasn't quite right when I said I never regret taking up this great work. When it is so utterly misunderstood, as it is by you, then I do almost have regrets.' Rather than convincing K., these words only made him impatient. He thought he could detect in the advocate's tone of voice just what he could expect if he gave way now – promises of later success would begin again, references to progress with the plea, to the improved temper of the law officers, but also to the immense difficulties confronting the work; in short, everything so sickeningly familiar would be produced again to fool K. once more with vague hopes and to torment him with vague fears. All this must be stopped once and for all, so he said: 'What do you propose to do for me if I retain you?' The advocate even ignored the insult inherent in this question, and he answered: 'Take what I have already done for you even further.' 'I knew it,' K. said. 'Anything else I say would be superfluous.' 'I'll make one more effort,' said the advocate, as if what was agitating K. were not happening to K. but to himself. 'I suspect you have been misled into underestimating my services as your legal adviser and also into your present behaviour because, in spite of being an accused man, you have been treated too well or, to express it more accurately, treated with negligence, with what seems like negligence. There's a reason for this. It's often better to be in chains than to be free. But I'd like to show you how other accused men are treated; you might learn from this. What I'll do is send for Block, so unlock the door and sit down here by the bedside table.' 'Very well,' said K., who did what the advocate asked; he was always ready to learn. But to cover all eventualities he asked: 'But you have taken note that I am withdrawing my case from you?' 'Yes,' said the advocate, 'but you may retract that today.' He lay down in bed again, pulled the quilt up to his chin and turned to the wall. Then he rang.

Almost instantaneously Leni appeared. She glanced round quickly to ascertain what had happened; the sight of K. sitting calmly by the advocate's bed seemed to reassure her. She smiled and nodded to K., who stared at her. 'Fetch Block,' said the advocate. But instead of going for him she merely went to the door and shouted: 'Block! The advocate wants you!' Then she slipped behind K.'s chair, probably because the advocate had his face to the wall and could see nothing. From now on she annoyed him by leaning over the back of his chair or running her hands gently and warily through his hair and over his cheeks. In the end K. tried to stop her by gripping one of her hands, which she surrendered to him after a slight struggle.

Block had come at once in answer to the call but stood outside the door and seemed to be wondering if he should come in. He raised his eyebrows and held his head to one side as if listening whether the command to come to the advocate would be repeated. K. could have encouraged him to come in, but he had promised himself he would make a complete break not only with the advocate but with everything and everybody in this place, so he remained motionless. Leni too was silent. Block noticed that at least nobody was driving him away and he entered on tiptoe, his face tense, his hands clenched behind his back. He had left the door open in case he had to retreat. He paid no attention to K. but looked only at the mound of quilt under which the advocate was not even visible as he had moved right up to the wall. Then his voice was heard. 'Block here?' he asked. This question affected Block, who had already moved some way closer, like an actual blow in the chest, then in the back; he staggered, stopped in a crouching position, and said: 'At your service.' 'What do you want?' asked the advocate. 'You've come at a bad time.' 'Wasn't I called for?' asked Block, who seemed to be directing the question more to himself than to the advocate; he held his hands up defensively and was ready to run off. 'You were called for,' said the advocate, 'but all the same you've come at a bad time.' And after a pause he added: 'You always come at a bad time.' From the moment the advocate began to speak, Block no longer looked towards the bed but stared into a corner and merely listened as if the sight of the speaker would be too dazzling for him to endure. But listening was difficult too, for the advocate was speaking close to the wall, quietly and rapidly. 'Do you want me to go away?' asked Block. 'Now that you're here,' said the advocate. 'Stay!' Anybody would have thought that instead of granting Block's wish the advocate had threatened to have him thrashed, for now he really began to tremble. 'Yesterday,' said the advocate, 'I paid a visit to my friend the third judge and I gradually turned the conversation round to you. Do you want to know what he said?' 'Oh, please,' said Block. As the advocate did not immediately answer, Block repeated his request and stooped as if going to kneel. At this K. turned on him. 'What are you doing?' he cried. As Leni had tried to stop him shouting he seized her other hand too. He held her, but not with a loving pressure, and she moaned several times and tried to free her hands. But it was Block who was punished for K.'s outburst, for the advocate asked him: 'Who is your advocate?' 'You are,' said Block. 'And apart from me?' asked the advocate. 'Nobody apart from you,' said Block. 'Then don't consult other people,' said the advocate. Block felt the force of this, looked at K. angrily and shook his head at him vigorously. Translated into words, these gestures would have been foul insults. And this was the man K. had wanted to discuss his own affairs with, in such a friendly way! 'I won't trouble you any more,' said K., leaning back in his chair. 'Kneel or crawl on all fours, do what you like, it won't bother me.' But Block still had some feelings of self-respect, for he advanced on K., threatening him with his fists, and shouted as loudly as he dared in such proximity to the advocate: 'You can't talk to me like that, it's not right. Why are you insulting me? And here in the presence of the Herr Advocate too, where both of us, you as well as I, are tolerated only out of compassion? You are no better than I am, you too are a defendant, you have a case pending against you. If in spite of everything you are still a gentleman, then I'm a gentleman too, if not a better one. But if you think you are privileged just because you are allowed to sit here and listen while I crawl on all fours, as you put it, then I'll remind you of the old legal maxim: For a man under suspicion movement is better than rest, for the man who is at rest can always, without knowing it, be on the scales being weighed together with his sins.' K. said nothing, he merely stared with unwavering eyes at this befuddled man. What a change had come over him in this last hour alone! Was it his case which agitated him like this and made him unable to distinguish friend from foe? Could he not see the advocate was humiliating him intentionally with no other purpose than to parade his power before

K. and by this means subjugate K. too, if possible? But if Block was not capable of recognizing this, or if he stood in such fear of the advocate that even recognizing it would not help him, how was it he was cunning enough or bold enough to deceive the advocate and keep him in ignorance of the fact that he was employing other lawyers too? And how did he dare attack K., who could give away his secret in an instant? But he dared even more: he brought his complaints about K. to the advocate in his bed. 'Herr Advocate,' he said, 'you heard how this man spoke to me. The duration of his case can be counted in hours, and he's trying to give instruction to me, a man whose case has been going on for five years. He even abuses me. Knows nothing and abuses me – I who have paid special attention, as far as my feeble powers allow, to the requirements of decency, duty and legal tradition.' 'Don't concern yourself about anybody,' said the advocate. 'Just do what you think is right.' 'Certainly,' said Block as if to encourage himself, and with a hasty glance to one side he dropped to his knees right by the bed. 'I am kneeling, my Advocate,' he said. But the advocate kept silent. Cautiously Block stroked the quilt with his hand. In the silence which now reigned Leni freed her hands from K.'s grasp, saying: 'You're hurting me. Let me go. I'm going to Block.' She went across and sat on the edge of the bed. Her arrival delighted Block; he immediately begged her with lively but mute gestures to intercede for

245

him with the advocate. He was obviously very eager to hear what the advocate had to say, but perhaps only so that he could make use of it through his other lawyers. Leni evidently knew exactly how to get round the advocate; she pointed to the advocate's hand and pouted her lips in a kiss. Block immediately kissed the hand and did it again twice at Leni's prompting. But the advocate was still silent. Then Leni bent over the advocate, showing the lovely lines of her body as she stretched, and with her face close to his she stroked his long white hair. This now produced an answer. 'I hesitate to tell him,' he said, and he could be seen shaking his head, perhaps to enjoy the pressure of Leni's hand all the better. Block was listening with his head bowed as if by listening he was transgressing against a commandment. 'Why do you hesitate?' asked Leni. K. had the impression he was hearing a well-rehearsed dialogue, often repeated in the past and often to be repeated in the future; only for Block could it never lose its novelty. Instead of answering, the advocate asked: 'How has he behaved today?' Before answering, Leni looked down at Block and watched for a moment as he raised his hands to her and rubbed them together in supplication. In the end she nodded gravely and turned to the advocate and said: 'He has been quiet and industrious.' An elderly merchant, a man with a long white beard, was begging a young girl for a favourable testimonial! Even if he had reservations, nothing could justify him in the eyes of a fellow man. He almost degraded the onlooker. K. did not understand how the advocate could have thought of winning him over by putting on an exhibition like this. If he had not alienated K. earlier, this performance would have done it for him. K. had fortunately not been exposed long enough to the advocate's methods, but their end result was now clear: the client forgot in the end about the outside world and merely hoped to drag himself along this illusory path to the end of his case. The client was no longer a client, he was the advocate's dog. If the advocate had ordered him to creep into his kennel under the bed and bark from there, he would have done it willingly. As if K. had been commissioned to take careful note of everything said here and to report on it to a higher authority and file an account, he listened critically and objectively. 'What has he been doing all day?' asked the advocate. 'So that he wouldn't, disturb me in my work,' said Leni, 'I locked him in the maid's room, where of course he usually is. Now and again I looked through the hatch to check what he was doing. Each time I looked he was kneeling on the bed, he had the documents you've lent him spread out on the window-sill and was reading them. That made a good impression on me because that window opens into an air shaft and there's hardly any light. That Block was reading in spite of that showed me how obedient he is.' 'I'm glad to hear this,' said the advocate, 'but did he understand what he was reading?' During these words Block was constantly moving his lips, evidently formulating the answers he hoped Leni would give. 'I can't of course tell you that definitely,' said Leni, 'but I could see he was really concentrating. He was reading the same page all day, and as he read he was following the words with his finger. Every time I looked in he was sighing as if he was finding this reading hard work. The documents you've lent him are probably difficult to understand.' 'Yes,' said the advocate, 'they certainly are. And I don't believe he understands anything of them. They're only to give him an idea of how difficult the battle I'm waging on his behalf really is. And for whom am I fighting this difficult battle? For – just mentioning the name is really too ludicrous – for Block. He'll have to learn what that means too. Did he continue his studies without a break?' 'Almost without a break,' said Leni, 'only once he did ask me for a drink of water. I gave him a glass through the hatch. I let him out at eight and gave him something to eat.' Block shot a sideways look at K. as if what was being said here was greatly to his credit and must surely make an impression on K. too. He now seemed much more hopeful, was more relaxed and shuffled about on his knees. So it was all the more noticeable how he froze at the advocate's next words. 'You praise him,' said the advocate, 'but that only makes it hard for me to tell him. You see, the judge hasn't pronounced favourably either about Block himself or his case.' 'Not favourably?' asked Leni. 'How can that be possible?' Block was looking at her with a tense expression as if he thought her capable even now of giving a favourable turn to the words uttered long ago by the judge. 'Not favourably,' said the advocate. 'He was in fact irritated when I started to talk about Block. "Don't talk about Block," he said. "He is my client," I said. "You are being imposed upon," he said. "I don't regard his cause as lost," I said. "You are being imposed upon," he repeated. "I don't think so," I said. "Block works hard at the proceedings and is always in close contact with his affair. He almost lives at my place just to keep up with things. You don't come across zeal like that every day. Of course he's personally unpleasant, has disgusting manners and is dirty, but in everything connected with his case he is faultless." I said faultless; I exaggerated on purpose. To this he said: "Block is just cunning. He has accumulated a lot of experience and knows how to prolong the proceedings. But his ignorance is even greater than his cunning. I wonder what he would say if he heard his case has not begun yet, that the bell which signals the beginning of a case has not even been rung yet." Quiet, Block,' said the advocate, for Block was beginning to rise on shaky knees and obviously wanted to beg for an explanation. This was the first time the advocate had addressed Block directly. His weary eyes stared partly into space and partly at Block, who slowly sank to his knees again under the influence of this gaze. 'That declaration by the judge has no significance at all for you,' said the advocate. 'Don't panic at every word. If you do that again, I won't tell you any more. I can't begin a sentence without having you staring at me as if you expected to hear your final judgement. You should be ashamed of yourself, behaving like this in front of my client! And you're shaking the confidence he has in me. What do you want? You're still alive, you're still under my protection. What senseless anxiety! You've read somewhere that in some cases the final judgement may come unexpectedly, from any source and at any time. With many reservations that is indeed true, but it's just as true that your excessive anxiety disgusts me and that I see in this a lack of necessary confidence. What then have I said? I've reported what a judge told me. You will know that various opinions pile up round every case like an impenetrable thicket. This judge, for instance, believes the case begins at a particular time, but I believe it begins at a different time. A difference of opinion, that's all. At a certain point in the proceedings custom dictates that a signal should be given with a bell. According to this judge the proceedings begin with this signal. I can't tell you now all the arguments against this belief. You wouldn't understand them anyway, so it's enough for you to know there are lots of arguments against it.' In his distress Block was running his fingers through a fleecy rug by the bed. His terror at the judge's words made him forget for the moment his subservience to the advocate; he was thinking only of himself and was turning the judge's words round in his mind. 'Block,' said Leni in a warning voice, and she jerked him up a little by his coat collar. 'Leave that rug alone and listen to the advocate.'

IN THE CATHEDRAL

K. had been given the assignment of showing the local artistic monuments to one of the bank's important business associates, an Italian making his first visit to the town. At any other time he would have regarded this as an honour, but now he accepted it with reluctance and only because he had to do all he could to uphold his position in the bank. Every hour spent away from the office grieved him. It was true he could not make such good use of his time at the office as he used to, for he passed many an hour doing the bare minimum necessary to make it appear he was working, but this meant his worries were all the greater when he was not at the office. He imagined then that the deputy manager, who was of course always on the watch, was entering his office from time to time, was sitting at his desk, rummaging through his papers, receiving clients who had been K.'s friends for years and luring them away, perhaps even finding mistakes, for K. now seemed to be threatened by mistakes from every direction and could no longer avoid making them. So if he was asked at any time to go out on a business trip or even a short journey – such assignments had by chance become increasingly common lately – then, although these might seem a mark of distinction, there was always the suspicion that they wanted to get him out of the office for a while to check his work or, at the very least, that they felt they could easily do without him in the office. He could have declined most of these assignments without difficulty, but he did not dare do this because, if his fears had even the slightest foundation, declining an assignment would be an avowal of his anxiety. For this reason he accepted such assignments with apparent equanimity and even kept silent about a serious chill when he was due to make a strenuous business trip lasting two days, for fear he would be forbidden to go because of the rainy autumnal weather prevailing just then. When he returned from this trip with a raging headache he learned he had been appointed to accompany the Italian businessman on the following day. The temptation to refuse just this one time was very great; what had been planned for him here was not work directly connected with bank business; the fulfilment of this social duty towards their business associate was in itself doubtless important enough, but not for K., who knew very well he could only maintain his position through success at work and that, if he did not achieve this, any unexpected success he had at beguiling the Italian would be of no value at all; he did not wish to be pushed out of the sphere of work even for one day, for his fear that he would not be allowed back was too great, a fear he well knew was exaggerated but a fear which was stifling him all the same. This time in fact it was almost impossible to think up an acceptable excuse; K.'s knowledge of Italian was not very great but sufficient; but the decisive factor was that K. had acquired in earlier days some knowledge of art history and this had become known throughout the bank in considerably exaggerated form because K. had been for a period – and this only for business reasons – a member of the Society for the Conservation of Municipal Monuments. It was rumoured that the Italian was an art connoisseur, so K. was a natural choice to be his companion.

It was a very wet and stormy morning when K., who was really annoyed at the prospect before him, arrived very early at the office (it was seven o'clock) to get through some work at least before the visitor took him away from it all. He was very tired, for he had spent half the night studying an Italian grammar to prepare himself a little. Lately he had got into the habit of spending far too much time sitting at the window and this now attracted him more than his desk, but he resisted the temptation and sat down to work. Unfortunately, just at this moment the clerk came in and said that the manager had sent him to see if K. had arrived; if he had, would he be so kind as to step over to reception as the gentleman from Italy was already there. 'I'll come now,' K. said. He put a small dictionary in his pocket, tucked an album of municipal sights he had prepared for the visitor under his arm, and made his way through the deputy manager's office to the manager's room. He was glad he had come to work so early and was able to be at their disposal so soon; they could not really have expected this. The deputy manager's office looked of course as empty as if it had been dead of night; probably the clerk had been sent to call him to reception as well but had not found him there. When K. walked into reception the two gentlemen rose to their feet from deep armchairs. The manager smiled amiably; he was obviously very pleased K. had come. He made the introduction and the Italian shook K.'s hand vigorously and with a laugh referred to someone as an early riser; K. did not understand exactly whom he meant, it was also an unusual word whose meaning K. guessed only after a while. He replied with a few trite phrases which the Italian received with another laugh while nervously fingering his steel-grey bushy moustache. This moustache was evidently scented; K. felt tempted to go up close and smell. After they had all sat down and entered on a brief introductory conversation, K. noticed with some disquiet that he understood the Italian only fragmentarily. When he spoke quite calmly he could understand nearly everything, but those were exceptional moments; more often the words simply poured out of his mouth and he kept shaking his head as if this delighted him. When he was talking like this he regularly fell into some dialect which seemed to have no relationship to the Italian K. knew but which the manager not only understood but also spoke, and this was something K. should have anticipated, for the Italian came from the south of Italy and the manager too had lived there for some years. At any rate, K. saw that there was little likelihood he could communicate with the Italian, for the latter's French too was barely comprehensible, and the moustache concealed the lip movements which might have helped K. understand. K. began to feel there was trouble in store. For the time being he gave up trying to understand the Italian – this was a pointless exercise as long as the manager was there, for he understood him so easily – and confined himself to watching morosely as the man sat easily and comfortably in his deep chair and tugged occasionally at his short and elegantly tailored jacket, and at one point tried to illustrate with flying arms and flexible wrist movements something K. could not comprehend, though he leaned forward so as not to lose sight of the hands. In the end K., who had been merely following the to and fro of the conversation mechanically with his eyes, felt his earlier weariness creeping over him and he was alarmed to realize, fortunately just in time, that he was about to get up in a fit of abstraction and turn and go out. At last the Italian looked at his watch and jumped to his feet. After he had taken leave of the manager he pressed towards K. and came so close that K. had to push his chair back before he could move. The manager, who must have seen from K.'s eyes what difficulty he was in with regard to this Italian, joined in the conversation and indeed so cleverly and tactfully that while it seemed he was only giving bits of advice he was in reality letting K. know briefly the sense of everything the Italian was saying as the latter indefatigably interrupted his words. K. learned from him that the Italian had some other items of business to settle now, that he would unfortunately have only a limited time available, that he had no wish to rush round all the sights in great haste, so he had decided – only of course if K. agreed, the final decision was his – to restrict himself to viewing the cathedral, but this in detail. He was exceptionally pleased to be able to do this in the company of such a learned and affable man – by this he meant K., who was concentrating on shutting out the Italian's words and taking in quickly what the manager was saying – and he asked him to be at the cathedral in two hours' time, say at ten o'clock, if this was convenient. He himself hoped definitely to be there at that time. K. made an appropriate response, the Italian shook hands with the manager, then with K., then again with the manager and, accompanied by both, he made his way to the door, half turning towards them without any interruption in what he was saying. K. stayed for a while with the manager, who looked particularly poorly today. He thought he owed K. an apology and said – they were standing in confidential proximity to each other – that he had intended at first to go with the Italian himself but then had decided to send K. instead; he gave no exact reason for this. If he did not understand the Italian to begin with, he must not let this disconcert him, he would come to understand very quickly and, even if there was a lot he did not understand, that was not so unfortunate because as far as the Italian was concerned it was not so important that he should be understood. In any case, K.'s Italian was surprisingly good and he was sure to cope with the assignment very well. With that he and K. parted. He used the rest of the available time writing out from the dictionary unusual words he might need for his tour of the cathedral. This was extremely tiresome work; clerks brought the post, officials came with various inquiries and stayed by the door when they saw K. was busy but would not go away until K. had heard them out; the deputy manager did not miss this chance to disturb K., came in several times, took the dictionary from his hand and riffled through the pages obviously without any purpose; when the door was opened clients bobbed up in the semi-darkness of the outer office and bowed hesitantly, wanting to draw attention to themselves without, however, being sure they could be seen – all this revolved round K. as its focal point while he himself listed the words he needed, then looked them up in the dictionary, then wrote them out, then practised their pronunciation and finally tried to learn them off by heart. But the excellent memory he used to have seemed to have deserted him; sometimes he fell into such a rage with the Italian who was causing him all this effort that he buried the dictionary under a pile of papers, firmly resolved to do no more preparation, but then he realized he could not after all just parade up and down in front of the cathedral's art treasures without saying a word to the Italian, and he pulled the dictionary out again with an even greater burst of rage.

At exactly half-past nine, just as he was about to leave, there was a phone call. Leni wished him good morning and asked how he was. K. thanked her hastily and said he could not possibly talk now, he had to go to the cathedral. 'To the cathedral?' asked Leni. 'But yes, to the cathedral.' 'But why the cathedral?' asked Leni. K. tried to give her a quick explanation, but hardly had he started than Leni suddenly said: 'They are hounding you.' Pity he had neither asked for nor expected was something K. could not endure; he curtly said goodbye, but as he replaced the receiver he said, half to himself and half to the distant girl whose voice he could no longer hear: 'Yes, they are hounding me.'

But it was getting late and he already ran the risk of not arriving on time. He travelled by car; at the last moment he remembered the album he had not been able to hand over earlier and so took it with him now. He held it on his knees and drummed on it nervously during the whole journey. The rain had eased off, but the morning was damp, cool and dark; it would not be possible to see much inside the cathedral, and in all likelihood K.'s chill would get considerably worse through prolonged standing on cold flagstones.

The square in front of the cathedral was deserted. K. recalled that even as a child he had noticed how nearly all the blinds in the houses round this constricted square were permanently down. In today's weather this was more understandable than usual. The cathedral too seemed empty; of course nobody would think of coming here now. K. walked quickly through both side-aisles and came across only an old woman wrapped in a warm shawl who was on her knees before a picture of the Virgin, on which she had her eyes fixed. Then he saw in the distance a limping verger disappear through a door in the wall. K. had arrived exactly on time; just as he walked in the clock had struck eleven, but the Italian was not there. K. returned to the main entrance, stood there irresolutely for a while, then walked round the outside of the cathedral in the rain in case the Italian might perhaps be waiting at a side-entrance. He was nowhere to be seen. Could the manager have made a mistake about the time? How was it possible to understand that man properly? At any rate, whatever the situation might be, K. would have to wait at least half an hour for him. As he was tired he thought he would sit down; he went back into the cathedral, came across a little scrap of what looked like carpet on a step and moved this with his foot in front of a nearby pew, then wrapped himself up more closely in his overcoat, pushed the collar up, and sat down. To pass the time he opened the album and looked through the pages for a while but soon had to stop because it was getting so dark that when he looked up he could hardly make out any separate detail in the aisle near him.

In the distance a large triangle of candle flames flickered on the high altar. K. could not have said with certainty whether he had seen them earlier on. Perhaps they had just been lit. Vergers are stealthy by profession and are scarcely noticed. When K. happened to turn round he saw not far behind him a tall thick candle also alight, this time fixed to a pillar. However beautiful it looked, it was quite inadequate to illuminate the altarpieces which mostly hung in the gloom of the side-chapels; it only made the darkness more intense. By not coming, the Italian had proved himself sensible as well as discourteous, for nothing could have been seen, they would have had to be satisfied with examining a few pictures inch by inch under the light of K.'s electric torch. To see what might be expected in these conditions K. went to a little side-chapel near by, ascended a few steps to a low marble balustrade and leaned over to shine his torch on the altarpiece. The eternal light in front of it flickered disturbingly. The first thing K. saw, and partly guessed at, was a tall knight in armour portrayed at the extreme edge of the picture. He was leaning on a sword he had thrust into the bare earth in front of him – only a few isolated blades of grass were visible. He seemed to be paying close attention to some event going on before him. It was amazing that he stood like that and did not go nearer. Perhaps he was obliged to stand guard. K., who had not seen any pictures for some time, looked at the knight for a considerable period although he had to blink constantly because he could not stand the green light from the lamp. When he shifted his light to see the rest of the picture he found it was a conventional treatment of Christ's burial, a modern painting. He put the torch in his pocket and returned to his seat.

It was probably unnecessary to wait for the Italian now, but it must be pouring outside and it was not as cold here as K. had expected, so he decided to stay for the time being. Near by was the great pulpit and on the top of its small round canopy two plain golden crucifixes were semi-recumbent and arranged so that their tips crossed. The outer surface of the balustrade and the connecting portion to the supporting pillar were ornamented with realistic foliage to which little angels were clinging, some in movement, some at rest. K. went up to the pulpit and examined it from all sides. The treatment of the stone was extremely precise. The shadow between the foliage and the stone behind looked as if it had been captured and held prisoner. K. put his hand into one of these gaps and felt the stone carefully; until now he had not known of this pulpit's existence. Then he happened to notice a verger standing behind the next row of pews; he wore a black gown which hung in loose folds, held a snuff-box in his left hand, and was watching him. 'What does the man want?' K. wondered. 'Do I seem suspicious to him? Does he expect a tip?' But when the verger saw that K. had noticed him, he pointed with his right hand – he still held a pinch of snuff between two fingers – in a vague direction. His behaviour was almost incomprehensible. K. waited for a while, but the verger kept pointing his hand at something, and he reinforced this with nods of his head. 'What does he want?' asked K. quietly, not daring to raise his voice here, then he took out his purse and pushed through the next row of pews to get to the man. But the verger immediately made a dismissive gesture with his hand, shrugged his shoulders, and limped away. When K. as a child was pretending to ride a horse, he had jogged along with a gait just like this hurried limp. 'What a childish old man,' thought K., 'he has just enough sense left to perform this verger work. See how he stops when I stop, how he watches to see if I'm still coming.' With a smile K. followed the old man along the whole length of the side-aisle as far as the high altar; the old man continued to point at something, but K. deliberately refused to turn round; this pointing had no other purpose than to deter him from following the old man. Eventually he stopped following him; he did not want to worry him too much nor did he want to scare this apparition away entirely, for the Italian might yet arrive.

As he entered the nave to look for the place where he had been sitting and had left the album he noticed a small ancillary pulpit attached to a pillar almost next to the choir-stalls, a simple structure made of smooth grey stone. It was so small that from a distance it looked like an empty recess intended for a statue. A preacher could scarcely take one full stride back from the balustrade. And the stone vaulting above the pulpit began unusually low down and curved up without ornamentation; a man of average height would not be able to stand upright, he would have to lean forward over the balustrade all the time. It seemed designed to be a form of torture for preachers. It was hard to understand what this pulpit was for when they had the other, so large, so splendidly ornamented.

This small pulpit would certainly not have been

noticed by K. but for the lighted lamp above it, the usual indication that a sermon was about to be preached. Was a sermon to be delivered now? In this empty church? K. looked down at the flight of steps attached to the pillar and leading to the pulpit, so narrow it seemed more like a mere decorative touch on the pillar than a stairway for people. But at the foot of the steps – K. smiled in amazement – there really was a priest with his hand on the rail, ready to go up, looking at him. Then the priest nodded his head slightly, and this prompted K. to cross himself and bow, something he should have done before. The priest gave himself a little swing to gain momentum and quickly climbed up the steps. Was a sermon really going to begin? Was the verger not so idiotic after all but had merely wanted to herd K. in the direction of the preacher – something very necessary in this empty church? But of course there was also an old woman somewhere before a picture of the Virgin; she should have been there too. And if there was going to be a sermon, why was it not being introduced by an organ prelude? But the organ was silent, visible only as a faint gleam high up in the darkness.

K. wondered if he should not go away as quickly as possible; if he did not do that now there was little prospect that he could leave during the sermon, he would have to stay as long as it lasted; he was losing so much office time; there was no obligation to wait any longer for the Italian. He looked at his watch, it was eleven. But was a sermon really going to be delivered? Could K. by himself be regarded as a congregation? What if he were a stranger who had come there only to look at the church? And of course that is what he was. It was senseless to think a sermon was to be preached now, at eleven o'clock on a weekday in the most horrible weather. The priest – he was certainly a priest, a young man with a smooth dark face – must be going up just to extinguish the lamp which had been lit by mistake.

But this was not so. The priest examined the lamp instead, turned it up a bit, then turned slowly towards the balustrade and gripped the squared edge in front with both hands. He stood like this for some time and looked round without moving his head. K. had retreated a considerable distance and was leaning on his elbow against the front row of pews. Dimly he could see somewhere, without being able to tell exactly where, the hunched back of the verger crouching peacefully as if conscious of a task accomplished. What silence in the cathedral now! But K. would have to break it; he had no intention of staying here. If it was the priest's duty to preach at a specified time without regard to circumstances, he could do so. It could be managed without K.'s support, just as K's presence would certainly not heighten the effect. So K. slowly put himself in motion, sidled along the pew on tiptoe, came to the centre aisle and walked along this without hindrance, disturbed only by the ringing of his cautious steps on the stone floor and by the echo sounding faintly but continuously in regular multiple progression round the vaulted roof. K. felt a little exposed as he walked alone between the empty pews, perhaps observed by the priest; and the size of the church seemed to him to border on the very limits of what was humanly endurable. When he reached the place where he had been sitting he did not stop but snatched at the album he had left there and picked it up. He had almost left the pew area and was approaching the open space between this and the entrance doors when he heard the priest's voice for the first time. A powerful, practised voice. How it pierced the expectant cathedral! But it was not directed at a congregation. It was unambiguous and there was no escape; he was calling: 'Josef K.!'

K. stopped abruptly and stared at the floor. For the time being he was still free, he could walk on and make his way from there through one of the three small dark wooden doors not far in front. That would show he had not understood, or that he had indeed understood but was taking no notice. But if he turned round he was caught, for then he was admitting he understood very well, that he was really the person called for, and that he would comply. If the priest had called out again,

K. would certainly have walked on but, as everything remained quiet all the time he waited, he turned his head slightly to see what the priest was doing now. He was standing motionless in the pulpit as before, but it was obvious he had noticed the movement of K.'s head. It would have been like a puerile game of hide-and-seek if K. had not turned round completely now. He did so, and the priest beckoned him nearer with his finger. Since everything was now in the open he ran with long flowing strides towards the pulpit, doing this out of curiosity and also because he wanted to cut the business short. He stopped by the first row of pews, but the distance still seemed too great for the priest, who stretched out his hand and pointed with a sharply bent finger to a spot right in front of the pulpit. K. followed this instruction too. From this spot he had to bend his head far back to keep the priest in view. 'You are Josef K.?' said the priest and he raised one hand from the balustrade in an indeterminate gesture. 'Yes,' said K., thinking how frankly he used to give his name at one time and what a burden it had become recently; now his name was known to people he was meeting for the first time; how pleasant it was to introduce himself first and only then be known. 'You are accused,' said the priest in a particularly low voice. 'Yes,' K. said, 'I have been told about that.' 'Then you are the one I am seeking,' said the priest. 'I am the prison chaplain.' 'I see,' K. said. 'I had you summoned to this place,' said the priest, 'to have a talk with you.' 'I didn't know that,' K. said. 'I came here to show an Italian round the cathedral.' 'Never mind that, it's not important,' said the priest. 'What is that in your hand? Is it a prayer book?' 'No,' K. replied. 'It's an album of municipal attractions.' 'Put it away,' said the priest. K. threw it away so violently that it flew open and slid some way across the floor on crumpled pages. 'Are you aware that your case is going badly?' asked the priest. 'That's how it looks to me too,' K. said. 'I've taken all the trouble I can, but so far without any result. Of course, my plea hasn't been filed yet.' 'What do you think the end will be?' asked the priest. 'I used to think it would end well,' K. said, 'but now I feel doubtful about it sometimes. I don't know how it will end. Do you know?' 'No,' said the priest, 'but I fear it will end badly. You are considered guilty. Your case will perhaps never get beyond a lower court. But for now at least your guilt is considered a proven fact.' 'But I am not guilty,' K. said. 'It's a mistake. How can a human being ever be guilty? We are all human beings here after all, each the same as the other.' 'That is right,' said the priest, 'but everyone who is guilty always talks like that.' 'Are you prejudiced against me too?' K. asked. 'I am not prejudiced against you,' said the priest. 'I thank you,' K. said. 'But all the others involved in the case are prejudiced against me. And they pass this prejudice on to those not involved. My position is getting more and more difficult.' 'You misunderstand the facts,' said the priest. 'Judgement does not come suddenly; the proceedings gradually merge into the judgement.' 'So it's like that,' said K. and he bowed his head. 'What will you do next?' asked the priest. 'I shall look for help,' said K. and he raised his head to see how the priest would take this. 'There are still some possibilities I haven't used up yet.' 'You look for too much outside help,' said the priest disapprovingly, 'and especially from women. Don't you see it is not true help?' 'Sometimes, often even, I could agree with you,' said K., 'but not always. Women have great power. If I could persuade some of the women I know to work together to help me, I would be bound to succeed. Especially before this court, which is composed almost exclusively of lechers. Just let the examining magistrate see a woman in the distance and he'll dive over his table and the defendant to get there in time to catch her.' The priest was bending his head down to the balustrade; only now did the roof of the pulpit seem to press on him. What sort of weather could there be outside? It was not just a dreary day any more, it was the depth of night. No gleam of stained glass from the great windows broke the wall of darkness. And this was the moment when the verger began to extinguish the candles on the high altar one by one. 'Are you angry with me?' K. asked. 'You perhaps don't know the kind of court you are serving.' He received no answer. 'I'm speaking only about my own experience,' K. said.

There was still no movement up above. 'I didn't mean to insult you,' K. said. At this the priest screamed down at K.: 'Can't you see two inches in front of your nose?' It was screamed in anger, but at the same time it was like a scream from someone who sees a man falling and, because he is himself frightened, cries out involuntarily and without restraint.

Now both were silent for a long time. It was certain the priest could not see K. clearly in the darkness down below, but K. saw the priest plainly by the light of the small lamp. Why did the priest not come down? He had not preached a sermon, only told K. some things more likely to do him harm than good if he took account of them. But K. had no doubts about the priest's good intentions; it was not impossible that if he were to come down he would make common cause with him, it was not impossible that he might receive from him some decisive and acceptable advice which could for instance show him, not how influence could be exerted on the case, but how to break out of the case or circumvent it and how to live outside the case. This possibility must exist; K. had often thought about it lately. But if the priest knew of such a possibility he would perhaps disclose it if asked, although he belonged to the court and although, when K. had attacked the court, he had suppressed his gentle nature and even screamed at him.

'Won't you come down?' K. asked. 'There's no

sermon to preach. Come down to me.' 'I can come now,' said the priest; perhaps he was sorry he had screamed. While taking the lamp off the hook he said: 'I had to speak to you from a distance first. Otherwise I am too easily influenced and forget my duty.'

K. waited for him at the foot of the steps. The priest stretched out his hand to him while still on the steps. 'Have you a little time for me?' K. asked. 'As much time as you like,' said the priest, giving K. the little lamp to carry. Even in close proximity he did not lose the solemnity which seemed to surround his figure. 'You are very kind to me,' K. said. They walked up and down close to each other in the darkness of the side-aisle. 'You are an exception among all those who belong to the court. I have more trust in you than in any of them, and I know so many. With you I can speak openly.' 'Don't be deceived,' said the priest. 'In what should I be deceived?' K. asked. 'You are deceiving yourself about the court,' said the priest. 'In the introductory writings to the law, that deception is presented in this way: Before the law stands a door-keeper. A man from the country comes to this door-keeper and asks for entry into the law. But the door-keeper says he cannot grant him entry now. The man considers and then asks if that means he will be allowed to enter later. "It is possible," says the door-keeper, "but not now." Since the door to the law stands open, as it always does, and the door-keeper steps to one side, the man bends to look through the door at the interior. When the door-keeper notices this, he laughs and says: "If you are so tempted, just try to enter in spite of my prohibition. But take note: I am powerful. And I am only the lowest door-keeper. But from room to room stand door-keepers each more powerful than the last. The mere aspect of the third is more than even I can endure." Such difficulties had not been expected by the man from the country; the law is supposed to be accessible to everyone and at all times, he thinks, but as he now looks more closely at the door-keeper in his coat of fur, at his great pointed nose and his long and straggly black Tartar beard, he decides it would be better to wait until he gets permission to enter. The door-keeper gives him a stool and lets him sit to one side of the door. There he sits for days and years. He makes many attempts to be allowed in and wearies the door-keeper with his entreaties. The door-keeper occasionally subjects him to brief interrogation, asks about his home and many other things, but these are the kind of apathetic questions great lords ask, and in the end he tells him each time that he cannot allow him to enter yet. The man, who has equipped himself well for his journey, gives everything he has, no matter how valuable, to bribe the door-keeper. The latter indeed accepts everything, but, as he does, he says: "I accept this only so that you may not think you have neglected anything." During these many years the man keeps watch on the door-keeper almost without a pause. He forgets the other door-keepers, and this first door-keeper seems to him the only obstacle to his entry into the law. He curses this unfortunate chance, loudly in the first years and later, as he grows old, he merely mumbles to himself. He becomes infantile, and as in the many years spent watching the door-keeper he has come to know even the fleas in his fur collar, he begs the fleas themselves to come to his aid and persuade the door-keeper to change his mind. Finally his sight grows weak and he does not know if it is really getting darker round him or if his eyes are deceiving him. But he does manage to distinguish in the dark a radiance which breaks out imperishably from the door to the law. He does not live much longer. Before his death everything he has experienced during this time converges in his mind into the one question he has not yet put to the door-keeper. He beckons him, as he can no longer raise his stiffening body. The door-keeper has to bend down low to him, for the difference in size between them has changed, very much to the disadvantage of the man from the country. "What else do you still want to know?" asks the door-keeper. "You are insatiable." "But everybody strives for the law," says the man. "How is it that in all these years nobody except myself has asked for admittance?" The door-keeper realizes the man has reached the end of his life and, to penetrate his imperfect hearing, he roars at him:

"Nobody else could gain admittance here, this entrance was meant only for you. I shall now go and close it."'

'So the door-keeper deceived the man,' said K. at once, very much taken by the story. 'Don't be too hasty,' said the priest, 'don't take somebody else's opinion without testing it. I have told you the story in the words of the document. There is nothing there about deception.' 'But it's clear,' said K., 'and your first interpretation was quite right. The door-keeper gave the message of salvation only when it could no longer help the man.' 'He was not asked before then,' said the priest. 'Consider too, he was only a door-keeper and as such he fulfilled his duty.' 'Why do you believe he fulfilled his duty?' K. asked. 'He did not fulfil it. His duty was perhaps to keep all strangers away, but this man, for whom the entrance was intended, he should have admitted.' 'You have insufficient respect for the written record and you are altering the narrative,' said the priest. 'The narrative contains two important statements from the door-keeper about admission into the law, one at the beginning, one at the end. The first is that he "cannot grant him entry now" and the other "this entrance was meant only for you". If there were a contradiction between these statements, then you would be right, and the door-keeper would have deceived the man. But there is no contradiction. On the contrary; the first statement leads to the second. It might almost be said the door-keeper exceeded his duty when he presented the man with the prospect of possible admittance in the future. At that time his sole duty seems to have been to turn the man away. And in fact many interpreters of the script express surprise that the door-keeper goes so far as to make this suggestion, for he seems punctilious and strictly performs the duties of his office. Over many years he does not leave his post and closes the door only at the very end; he is very conscious of the importance of his office, for he says: "I am powerful"; he has deep respect for his superiors, for he says: "I am only the lowest door-keeper"; with regard to fulfilling his duties he is not to be moved or angered, for it is said of the man from the country that he "wearies the doorkeeper with his entreaties"; he is not talkative, for during all these years he asks only what are called "apathetic questions"; he is not corrupt, for when he takes a present he says he accepts it "only so that you may not think you have neglected anything"; finally, his external appearance also suggests a pedantic character – his great pointed nose and the long and straggly black Tartar beard. Can there be a more dutiful door-keeper? But the door-keeper has other characteristics which are very auspicious for anyone craving admittance and also help to explain why he could exceed his duty by presenting the prospect of possible admittance in the future. You see, it cannot be denied he is a little naïve and consequently a little conceited. Even if his utterances about his power and the power of the other door-keepers and their aspect which even he cannot endure – I say even if all these utterances may be correct in themselves, yet the way he makes them shows his understanding has been dulled by naïvety and presumption. The commentators say on this point: Correct understanding of a matter and misunderstanding of the same matter do not exclude each other entirely. But in any event it must be assumed that this naïvety and presumption, however faintly expressed, must weaken the safeguarding of the entrance; they are blemishes in the door-keeper's character. In addition, the door-keeper seems to be friendly by nature; he is by no means always an official kind of person. Right at the beginning he plays a joke on the man by inviting him to enter in spite of the express and strictly enforced prohibition, then does not send him away but, as the narrative says, gives him a stool and lets him sit to one side of the door. His patience in enduring the man's entreaties through all these years, those brief interrogations, his acceptance of presents, his civility in letting the man beside him curse aloud the unfortunate chance which has placed the door-keeper there – all this leads us to conclude he feels compassion. Not every door-keeper would have behaved like that. And finally he bends down low to the man when he beckons, to give him the opportunity to ask his last question. Only a trace of impatience – the door-keeper knows of course everything is at an end – finds expression in the

277

words: "You are insatiable." Some people take this line of interpretation even further and hold that the words "you are insatiable" express a kind of friendly admiration, not, however, free of condescension. At any rate, the figure of the door-keeper is thus interpreted in a way that differs from your opinion.' 'You know the story better than I, and have known it longer,' K. said. They were silent for a while. Then K. said: 'So you think the man was not deceived?' 'Don't misunderstand me,' said the priest. 'I am only telling you the opinions which exist. You must not pay too much attention to opinions. The written word is unalterable, and opinions are often only an expression of despair. In this case there is even an opinion that it is the door-keeper who is deceived.' 'That is a farfetched opinion,' K. said. 'What's the argument for that?' 'The argument,' answered the priest, 'originates in the door-keeper's naïvety. They say he does not know the interior of the law but only the path he has to patrol in front of the entrance. The ideas he has about the interior are held to be childish and it is assumed he himself is afraid of what he tries to make fearful for the man. Indeed, he fears it more than the man, for the latter is determined to enter even when he has heard of the terrible door-keepers of the interior, but the door-keeper on the other hand has no wish to enter, at least nothing is said about this. Others do say he must already have been in the interior, for he was after all taken into the service of the law sometime, and that could have happened only in the interior. To this one might answer that he could have been appointed door-keeper by a shout from the interior and is unlikely to have been deep in the interior because he cannot after all endure the aspect of the third door-keeper. And in addition it is not reported that during all these years he has ever related anything about the interior, apart from his remark about the door-keepers. He could have been forbidden to do this, but he said nothing about any prohibition either. From all this it has been concluded he knows nothing about the appearance and significance of the interior and is deceived about it. He is said to be deceived about the man from the country too, for he is subordinate to this man and does not know it. That he treats the man as subordinate to himself can be seen from much that you probably still remember. That he is in fact subordinate to the man can be deduced just as clearly, according to this argument. In the first place, a free man is superior to the bondsman. Now the man from the country is really free, he can go where he likes, it is only entry into the law which is denied him, and this only by one individual, the door-keeper. When he sits down on the stool to one side of the door and remains there his whole life long, this happens voluntarily, the narrative tells of no compulsion. The door-keeper on the other hand is tied to his post by his office, he may not go elsewhere and, to judge by appearances, neither may he go into the interior, even if he wanted to. Also, it is true he is in the service of the law, but he serves only for this entrance, so only for the man for whom alone this entrance is destined. He is thus subordinate to the man for this reason as well. It must be assumed he has performed mere hollow service over many years, as long as it takes to grow to manhood, for it is said a man came, that is, somebody grown to manhood; so the door-keeper had to wait a long time before achieving his purpose, and indeed he had to wait just as long as the other wished, for after all the man came of his own free will. And the end of his service too is determined by the end of the man's life, so he remains subordinate to him to the end. And again and again it is emphasized that the door-keeper seems to know nothing of all this. But this is not considered anything remarkable, for according to this argument the door-keeper suffers under an even greater illusion; this concerns his service. At the end he speaks of the entrance and says: "I shall now go and close it," but at the beginning it is written that the door to the law stands open, as it always does; but if it always stands open – always, that is, independent of the life-span of the man for whom it is destined – then not even the door-keeper can close it. Opinions differ about whether, by announcing he is now going to close the door, the door-keeper is merely giving an answer or whether he wants to stress his devotion to duty or wants to make the man feel regret and sorrow at the very last moment. But many are united in the opinion that he will not be able to close the door. They even believe that, at least towards the end, he is subordinate to the man in knowledge too, for the latter sees the radiance which breaks out from the entrance to the law, while the door-keeper must because of his duty be standing with his back to the entrance and says nothing to indicate he has noticed any change.' 'That is well argued,' said K., who had been repeating several passages from the priest's explanation in a low voice. 'It is well argued, and now I too believe the door-keeper is deceived. But that does not mean I have changed my earlier opinion, for the two opinions coincide in some respects. Whether the door-keeper sees clearly or is deceived is not crucial. What I said was, the man from the country is deceived. If the door-keeper sees clearly, one might doubt the truth of that statement, but if the door-keeper is deceived, then this deception must necessarily be transferred to the man. In that case, the door-keeper is indeed not a cheat, but so naive that he should be dismissed from his job immediately. After all, you must consider that the deception practised on the door-keeper does him no harm but does infinite harm to the man.' 'Here you meet a counterargument,' said the priest. 'Some people say the story gives no one the right to pass judgement on the door-keeper. However he may appear to us, he is after all a servant of the law, so belongs to the law, and so is detached from human judgement. In that case we may not believe either that the door-keeper is subordinate to the man. To be tied by his duty to the entrance to the law means incomparably more than living free in the world. The man only makes his way to the law, the door-keeper is already there. The law has appointed him to its service; to doubt his worthiness is to doubt the law.' 'I don't agree with that opinion,' said K., shaking his head, 'for if you accept it you must believe everything the door-keeper says is true. But that this is not possible, you yourself have shown in detail.' 'No,' said the priest, 'one does not have to believe everything is true, one only has to believe it is necessary.' 'Depressing thought,' K. said. 'It makes the lie fundamental to world order.'

K. said this in conclusion, but it was not his final verdict. He was too tired to follow all the deductions that could be drawn from the story; they led him into unaccustomed trains of thought, removed from reality and more suitable for academic discussion among court officials. The simple story had become perplexing, he wanted to be rid of it; and the priest, showing great delicacy of feeling, let him do this, receiving K.'s remark without a word, although it certainly did not coincide with his own opinion.

They walked on for a time in silence. K. kept close to the priest without being able to get his bearings in the dark. The lamp in his hand had

gone out long ago. Once the silver sheen of a
saint's figure gleamed right in front of him then
instantly spilled off into the darkness again. So as
not to be completely dependent on the priest, K.
asked him: 'Aren't we near the main doors now?'
'No,' said the priest, 'we are some way from them.
Do you want to go now?' Although K. had not
been thinking of this just then, he immediately
said: 'Yes, of course I must go. I have a responsible
position in the bank, they will be waiting for me;
I only came here to show a foreign business friend
round the cathedral.' 'Very well,' said the priest,
and he gave K. his hand, 'then go.' 'But I can't
find my own way in this darkness,' K. said. 'Go
left to the wall,' said the priest, 'then follow the
wall without leaving it, and you will find a door
to the outside.' The priest had taken a few steps
away when K. called in a loud voice: 'Please wait.'
'I am waiting,' said the priest. 'Is there nothing
more you want of me?' K. asked. 'No,' said the
priest. 'You were so kind to me earlier,' K. said,
'and explained everything to me, and now you
dismiss me as if I meant nothing to you.' 'But
you do have to go,' said the priest. 'But yes,' K.
said. 'You must understand why.' 'You must first
understand who I am,' said the priest. 'You are
the prison chaplain,' K. said as he approached the
priest; his immediate return to the bank was not
as necessary as he had claimed, he could easily
stay here longer. 'That means I belong to the

court,' said the priest, 'so why should I want anything of you? The court asks nothing of you. It receives you when you come and it releases you when you go.'

END

On the evening before K.'s thirty-first birthday – it was about nine o'clock, when there is a lull in the streets – two gentlemen came to his apartment. In frock-coats, pale and fat, with top hats, apparently the non-collapsible kind. After a short exchange of formalities by the front door to decide which should enter first, they repeated the exchange with greater elaboration at K.'s door. Without having been informed about the visit, K., dressed like them in black, was sitting in a chair by the door, slowly pulling on a pair of tight new gloves, in the attitude of a man expecting guests. He stood up at once and looked at the gentlemen with curiosity. 'So you are for me?' he asked. The gentlemen nodded, each pointing to the other with the top hat held in his hand. K. admitted to himself he had expected different visitors. He went to the window and looked out once more at the dark street. Nearly all the windows on the other side of the street too were still dark; in many the blinds were down. In a lighted window of the tenement two small children were playing behind a window guard, not able to move but reaching out to each other with tiny hands. 'They send clapped-out old actors for me,' said K. to himself and he turned round to see if his first impression was right. 'They want to get rid of me cheaply.' K. turned to them suddenly and asked: 'At what theatre are you playing?' 'Theatre?' inquired one gentleman of the other, the corners of his mouth twitching. The other gestured like a mute struggling with an unmanageable animal. 'They haven't been coached to answer questions,' K. said to himself, and he went for his hat.

On the stairs the gentlemen tried to slip their arms through K.'s, but K. said: 'Not till we get to the street; I'm not ill.' But right at the door they took him by the arms in a way K. had never experienced before. Their shoulders were close behind his, they did not bend their arms but twined them round the length of K.'s outstretched arms, and down below they held K.'s hands in a regimented and rehearsed grip which was irresistible. K. walked stiffly between them; all three now formed such a unity that if one were destroyed all would be destroyed. It was the kind of unity which hardly anything but inanimate matter can form.

Under street-lamps K. tried several times, in spite of the difficulty caused by the close proximity of his companions, to get a better view of them than had been possible in the twilight of his room. Perhaps they are tenors, he thought, seeing their gross double chins. He was revolted by the cleanliness of their faces. He had a vision of a cleansing hand busy at eye corners, rubbing the upper lip, scraping out the folds of the chin.

When K. thought of this, he stopped, so the others stopped too. They were at the edge of an open square ornamented with flower-beds, and not a person in sight. 'Why did they send just you!' he shouted rather than asked. The gentlemen seemed to be lost for an answer; with their free arms dangling they waited like sick-nurses when the invalid has to have a rest. 'I'm not going any further,' K. said tentatively. The gentlemen had no need to answer; they responded by not loosening their grip at all and trying to lift K. away from the spot, but K. resisted. 'I shall not need much strength after this, I'll use it all now,' he thought. He was reminded of flies wrenching their legs off in the struggle to free themselves from fly-paper. 'These gentlemen will have hard work.'

Then Fräulein Bürstner appeared in front of them, coming up a short flight of steps into the square from a lower alley. It was not really certain this was she, but the resemblance was strong. But K. was not at all concerned about whether it was Fräulein Bürstner or not, he merely knew at once that resistance was futile. There was nothing heroic in resisting, in making difficulties for the gentlemen now, in putting up a defence at this point in an effort to enjoy a final glimmer of life. He set off again, and some part of the pleasure this gave the gentlemen seeped through to him. They allowed him to decide the direction now, and he followed the course the Fräulein was taking in front of them, not because he wanted to overtake her, not because he wanted to keep her in sight as long as possible, but only because he wanted to keep in mind the reproach she signified for him. 'The only thing I can do now,' he said to himself – and the fixed rhythm of his footsteps and the steps of the other three confirmed his thoughts – 'the only thing I can do now is preserve my logical understanding to the end. I always wanted to grab at life, and not with the best of intentions either. That was not right; and am I to show now that not even these proceedings lasting a whole year could teach me anything? Am I to depart as an utterly stupid man? Are they going to say when I have gone that I wanted to end the case at the beginning and that now, at the end, I want it to begin again? I don't want people to say that. I'm thankful they've given me these stupid inarticulate companions for this journey and that they've left it to me to say what has to be said to myself.'

In the meantime the Fräulein had turned off into a side-street, but K. could do without her now, and he yielded himself completely to his companions. All three passed in perfect agreement over a bridge in the moonlight; the gentlemen willingly followed the slightest movement made by K. – when he turned towards the parapet they also turned in that direction, making a solid front. The water glittered and quivered in the moonlight and parted round a small island where masses of foliage from trees and shrubs had been crushed and piled up. Beneath them but now out of sight there were gravel paths with comfortable benches on which K. had stretched and relaxed during many a summer. 'Oh, I didn't mean to stop,' he said to his companions; their willing compliance made him feel ashamed. One of them seemed to give the other a mild reproach behind K.'s back about this misunderstanding, then they went on.

They passed through several steep alleyways where occasionally they saw policemen standing about or walking, sometimes in the distance, sometimes very close at hand. One, who had a bushy moustache and was fingering the hilt of his sabre, seemed to step deliberately towards this not exactly innocent-looking group. The gentlemen stopped short, the policeman seemed about to open his mouth, and K. exerted his strength to drag the gentlemen forward. He turned round several times as a precaution to see if the policeman was following; but when they had a corner between them and the policeman, K. began to run and the gentlemen had to run too despite severe shortness of breath.

So they came quickly out of the town, which in this direction merged into fields almost without transition. A small quarry, dreary and deserted, was situated near an urban-looking house. Here the gentlemen came to a stop, perhaps because this place had been their goal from the beginning, perhaps because they were too exhausted to run any further. They now released K., who waited in silence. They took their top hats off and used their handkerchiefs to wipe the sweat off their brows as they looked round the quarry. The moonlight covered everything with the natural serenity possessed by no other light.

After an exchange of some courtesies with regard to which of them should carry out the next part of their task – the gentlemen seemed to have been given their commission without specific individual assignments – one of them went to K. and took off his jacket and waistcoat and finally his shirt. K. shivered involuntarily, which made the gentleman give him a gentle reassuring slap on the back. Then he laid the things together carefully like articles which would still be needed, if not in the immediate future. So as not to leave K. exposed without movement to the rather cold night air, he took him by the arm and walked him up and down a bit while the other gentleman was examining the quarry for a suitable spot. When he had found one he waved, and the other gentleman conducted K. there. It was near the rock face; a detached boulder lay on the ground. The gentlemen sat K. down, put him to lean against the boulder and rested his head on it. In spite of all their efforts and K.'s willing cooperation, his posture remained forced and improbable. The one gentleman therefore requested the other to leave the disposal of K. to him for a moment, but even this did not improve matters. In the end they left K. lying in a position which was not even the best of those already tried. Then the one gentleman opened his frock-coat, and from a sheath hanging on a belt round his waistcoat he took a long thin double-edged butcher's knife and held it up in the light to test the sharpness of the edges. The repulsive courtesies began once more; one handed the knife over K. to the other, who then passed it back above K.'s head. At this moment K. was perfectly aware it was supposed to be his duty to seize the knife as it hovered from hand to hand above him and drive it into himself. But he did not do this; instead, he turned his neck, which was still free, and looked about him. He was not able to prove his own worth completely, he was not able to relieve the authorities of all work; responsibility for this ultimate defect lay with whoever had denied him the remainder of the requisite strength. His eyes fell on the top storey of the house at the edge of the quarry. The casement window flew open like a light flashing on; a human figure, faint and insubstantial at that distance and height, forced itself far out and stretched its arms out even further. Who was it? A friend? A good man? One who sympathized? One who wanted to help? Was it one person? Was it everybody? Was there still help? Were there objections which had been forgotten? Certainly there were. Logic is of course unshakeable, but it cannot hold out against a man who wants to live. Where was the judge he had never seen? Where was the high court he had never reached? He raised his hands and spread his fingers wide.

But the hands of the one gentleman were at K.'s throat while the other drove the knife into his heart and turned it there twice. With his failing sight K. could still see the gentlemen right in front of his face, cheek pressed against cheek, as they observed the decisive moment. 'Like a dog!' he said. It was as if the shame would outlive him.